Sandy Curtis lives on Queensla
short stories have appeared in Au
magazines and she is the author
Black Ice, *Deadly Tide* and *Until De* address
is www.sandycurtis.com and her email address is
novels@sandycurtis.com

Also by Sandy Curtis

DANCE WITH THE DEVIL
BLACK ICE
DEADLY TIDE
UNTIL DEATH

Dangerous Deception

SANDY CURTIS

Pan Macmillan Australia

First published 2005 in Macmillan by Pan Macmillan Australia Pty Limited
St Martins Tower, 31 Market Street, Sydney

National Library of Australia
cataloguing-in-publication data:

Curtis, Sandy.
Dangerous deception.

ISBN 1 4050 3652 4.

I. Title.

A823.4

The characters and events in this book are fictitious and any resemblance to real persons, living or dead, is purely coincidental.

Typeset in 13/16 pt Bembo by Post Pre-press Group
Printed in Australia by McPherson's Printing Group

Papers used by Pan Macmillan Australia Pty Limited are natural, recyclable products made from wood grown in sustainable forests. The manufacturing processes conform to the environmental regulations of the country of origin.

ACKNOWLEDGMENTS

When I pack a finished manuscript into an envelope and drop it into the mailbox, I sigh with relief and promise myself that I won't even *think* about writing for weeks, perhaps months. But within a few days, some character starts knocking on my brain, demanding my attention. I can tell him or her to go away, that I'm having a break, but it's no use. They become very insistent that I have to write *their* story, that this is *the* scene that will set the tone of the book. So I usually give in and plonk down in front of the computer and let them have their way.

I was halfway through writing *Black Ice* when Chayse Jarrett did this to me – insisting I had to write the prologue for *Deadly Tide*, that it would explain to the readers his mindset, as well as sowing the seeds for revelations at the end of the story. It was difficult to ignore him, and when I acquiesced and wrote the prologue, I had to admit he was right – it was exactly how the story needed to begin.

As well as getting my characters right, I feel an obligation to my readers to do my best to present facts they can rely on. So I always feel very, very grateful to those people who go out of their way to help me with my research.

My thanks go to:

Macky Edmundson and Shelby Elliott at Queensland Institute of Medical Research. Macky was a font of information, and I'm indebted to him. Sally Pittman for scientific research and background info on Melbourne research institutes set-ups.

Trish Parsons, General Manager of Carnarvon Gorge Wilderness Lodge for her friendship and allowing me to use the Lodge as a location; Peter Keegan and Ranger in Charge Bernice Sigley, for information on Carnarvon Gorge National Park; Ranger Mark O'Brien and David Mainwaring for their experiences with feral pigs – I'll never look at a pork chop in quite the same way again.

Phil Hystek of The Paragliding Centre of South East Queensland for sharing his knowledge and experience. Greg and Wendy and Duncan McKenzie – thank you for showing me your dairy farm.

David Russell for gun info. Darryl Dorron and Damien Simpson for Navy details. Christene Spearman and Marie Campbell for help with Melbourne locations. Elizabeth Wilde, Black Widow Investigations, and Melanie Bruty for many things secretive. Dr Wendy Halloran for medical advice, and Pip Anderson for forensic information.

To Ina Venn and Marsh Long, thanks for tramping around taking photos of the Bird Hide at Middle Lake, Kerang, I'm sure you had a lot of fun, and thanks to Charlie Gilbert for details of the surrounding swamp. Rob O'Brien, Department of Primary Industries, Kerang for information on flora in the Ibis Rookery.

To the wonderful people at Pan Macmillan, it's a privilege and a delight to work with you all. Your kindness smooths the bumps on this sometimes rocky road of writing.

To my husband and family, and Diane Esmond and the Cafe Writers, your support, as always, is invaluable and very much appreciated.

PROLOGUE

The glare of headlights in the drizzling rain distracted Professor John Raymond as he pulled out into the traffic. A delivery van screeched to a halt, narrowly avoiding impact with the rear of the professor's small sedan.

Normally he would have berated himself for such a lack of concentration while driving, especially in hazardous conditions. But this was no normal night. What should have been the culmination of many years hard work had turned into a disaster even greater than that he had experienced fifteen years ago. And he had made it happen.

Now he hoped that what he had set in motion could be stopped. His one chance to salvage his reputation depended on it. He patted the tiny computer pen drive in his pocket. The scientific world would have to believe this. And he'd made sure that the irrefutable proof was now safe.

With that thought, he tried to subdue the demon in his gut. The detached, analytical part of his mind could visualise the acid chewing into his stomach lining, the pressure in his veins pounding faster with each beat of his heart. He'd known the risk he'd been running for the past few years, hadn't needed his doctor to tell him, but it was impossible for him to ease off. He was already past normal retirement age. No, he didn't have enough time left to take it easy.

The rain lessened as he turned left into South Road, one of the main streets in Melbourne's North Hampton. The traffic, while heavier, was also faster, and he accelerated to keep pace.

The first symptom was so mild he didn't notice it. A slight tremor and weakness in his left hand. A moment later he realised he was having trouble holding on to the steering wheel. His right hand was also losing its gripping power. He willed his hands to work, but it was as though his body was refusing to obey the instructions.

Realisation dawned.

'Noooo . . .' the word oozed from his slackening mouth.

His hands fell from the steering wheel and he slumped forwards, horribly aware he'd forgotten to secure his seat belt.

With disbelieving eyes he watched as his car veered into the path of an oncoming truck.

He heard the sound of impact like an explosion, felt a brief searing pain, then nothing.

As the professor's body flew from the mangled wreck and rolled across the road, the pen drive fell from his coat pocket and slid into the gutter.

CHAPTER ONE

It wafted on the night air.

A sound so soft she could have imagined it, but so out of place in the leafy suburban Melbourne street, it made Breeanna Montgomery's neck stiffen with tension.

She realised, then, that the security light on her front patio had not lit her vehicle's approach as it normally did. No insects buzzed in the crisp spring air. No breeze ruffled the shrubs in her small front yard. The stillness suddenly seemed oppressive. Her stomach clenched. Perhaps her instincts about the professor *had* been accurate. She hadn't wanted to believe him, didn't need that kind of suspicion in her life. But the worry now spiralling up to her throat and restricting her breathing couldn't be suppressed. Too many odd things had happened. Things she'd been trying to ignore so she wouldn't have to confront that part of her that she'd always managed to conceal.

Shaking her head against her fears, Breeanna took a deep

breath, rolled up the car window, and opened the door. Her footsteps echoed softly between the overgrown bordering hedge and the house as she walked swiftly up the path and across the concrete patio to the front door.

Clouds covered the sliver of moon and she used her fingertips to sort through the key ring. It jangled as she inserted the correct key into the slot. Familiar though the noise was, it grated on her already tight nerves. She stepped into the living room and reached for the light switch. As her fingers connected and light flooded the room, a rustling noise made her turn.

A black-clad figure rushed through the front doorway and grabbed her around the throat, slamming her back against the wall.

Cold metal jabbed into her cheek, and she realised the sound she had heard as she'd sat in her car was that of a gun being cocked.

A sawn-off pump-action shotgun.

Keeping a cool head had helped Breeanna extricate herself from some dicey situations in the past, but a wild glitter in the eyes revealed in the man's ski-mask caused almost paralysing fear to shiver up her spine.

He was high on something. Something that jerked his body and twitched the arm that held the shotgun. His black denim jacket smelled of stale sweat, nicotine and too many joints.

'Where is it?' Staccato, high-pitched, the words spat at her.

Speed freak. A very dangerous speed freak. Breeanna fought to stay calm, but heard the tremble in her voice. 'Where is what?'

'The book. You know. He told you.'

'Who told me?'

The barrel pressed harder. 'The professor. Now, hand it over. Or I'll pull the trigger.' A sharp giggle escaped his thin lips.

Breeanna's heart thumped hard and fast. Whatever he was after, she didn't have it. But with the state he was in, he probably wouldn't believe her. *And he would possibly carry out his threat.*

'I'll give it to you,' she lied. 'It's in my bag.' She half lifted her shoulder bag with her left hand, the right tightening on her key ring. 'But I feel so dizzy, so . . .' She let her voice fade, eyelids quivering almost closed, slumping her body so that her weight rested against the hand clamped around her throat.

'Shit!' The gunman released his grip and reached for the bag, the gun easing away from Breeanna's cheek. She kicked up, crunching her knee into his groin, and punched the keys into his face.

He screamed in pain, folding forwards, clutching at his crotch with one hand, the other still holding the shotgun.

Breeanna ran.

The short distance to her car seemed impossibly long, the remote control too slow in unlocking the doors. Terror pounded through her veins as she scrambled into the driver's seat and locked the door.

A shriek of rage tore through the night. Her attacker hobbled off the patio, shotgun aimed at her car window.

Breeanna turned the key in the ignition. The engine purred.

A shot sounded.

She expected the glass to shatter, to feel pain as pellets tore into her flesh, but instead saw the intruder's face explode before he toppled backwards.

Shocked beyond movement, Breeanna sat, staring at the body.

A man, gun held two-fisted in front of him, stepped out from the hedge and walked past her car. When he reached the body he bent over, slipped his gun into a holster under his suit coat, and efficiently frisked the corpse. He straightened, and walked back to the car. He tried to open the driver's door then, realising it was locked, knocked on the window.

The sound shook Breeanna out of her daze. She slid the window down. The engine hummed quietly, a normal sound in a far from normal night.

'You're safe now, Miss.' The words were innocuous, the tone neutral, but Breeanna sensed something in the man that . . . Unease gnawed into her stomach. She made no move to open the door. The man bent towards the window. With the light coming through the front doorway behind him, his features were in shadow, but the glow of the dash lights revealed deep-set eyes above a straight nose and wide lips pulled thin as though trying to hide his impatience. An irrelevant thought struck Breeanna that in his younger days he must have been quite good looking.

He held out his hand, open palmed. 'You can give it to me now.'

It.

The man lying dead on her front path wanted *it*. Was prepared to kill her for *it*. Whatever *it* was. She forced herself to remember. A book. From the professor, he'd said. She didn't have it, didn't know what it was supposed to be. But one man was dead, and the professor was lying in a hospital bed so terrified that it was a wonder he hadn't had another stroke.

'I'll take care of it. See it gets to the right people.' Impatience now tinged his voice. Breeanna felt waves of greed and excitement emanating from him. Like a dog that has the scent of blood and wants to kill again, she thought, and realised his hand was moving closer to his gun.

'Right,' she breathed, surprised she sounded so calm. Pretending to reach for her bag, which she'd flung onto the passenger seat, she slipped the automatic gear into reverse and pushed hard on the accelerator.

Tyres screeching, the car shot backwards up the short driveway, throwing the man off balance, then slammed out into the street. Breeanna hit the brakes, pulled the gearstick into Drive, and scorched rubber on the bitumen as she sped away.

'Get this mess cleaned up. Quickly,' Vaughn Waring growled as he kicked the body lying in front of Breeanna's patio. Shooting the idiot who would have killed the Montgomery woman had been necessary, but going up to her afterwards in an attempt to win her trust had been a risk. A risk that hadn't paid off. Not only had she been scared off, she might have seen enough of his face to recognise him again. At the moment, that gave her an advantage he preferred her not to have.

'I'll get the car.' A man had emerged from behind the hedge and joined Vaughn, who turned and strode quickly up the driveway. Vaughn's frustration hissed out through clenched teeth. At least that was one thing he could count on – Mark Talbert was as efficient as he was quiet. Good qualities in a subordinate who needed to carry out orders without questioning.

Quickly, Vaughn walked into the house, took out his handkerchief, and used it to switch off the light and pull the door closed behind him as he went back outside.

Only the reversing lights indicated the presence of the dark car moving smoothly into the driveway. The boot popped open. Mark Talbert emerged from the driver's seat, spread a blanket across the floor of the boot, then lifted the body from the path and placed it on the blanket.

Vaughn unwound a hose from a tap at the corner of the house and sprayed the path. Fresh blood would dilute quickly and soak into the soil beneath the hedge. And from what he'd witnessed, it was doubtful there would be anyone inquiring as to the whereabouts of the dead man. Well, certainly not inquiring with the police, he thought. He rewound the hose, and got into the passenger seat.

As the car moved quietly out of the driveway, Vaughn scanned the neighbouring houses. In a street of high dividing fences, thick shrubbery and established trees, it was feasible to assume his gunshot could have been mistaken for a car backfiring, but it was wiser to be cautious. Not all neighbours kept to themselves. He was relieved to see no curtain pulled aside, no person coming out into their front yard to investigate.

Vaughn took out his mobile phone. If Breeanna Montgomery thought she had eluded him, he smiled grimly, she was very much mistaken.

Five minutes later, Breeanna parked in front of an all-night cafe and sat, hands shaking on the steering wheel, trying to calm the pounding in her chest and the thoughts spinning furiously in her mind.

Whatever Professor Raymond was supposed to have given

her was evidently worth killing for. She cursed herself for not taking him more seriously. His fear had been real, that was obvious, but until tonight she'd tried to believe it was the fear of a man who'd escaped possible death and now had to face a life as a quadriplegic. His implication of her family troubled her greatly, but she had had no reason to confront them. Until tonight. Until it had become obvious that the professor's fears were based on reality.

She could go to the police, but if Paige was involved . . . Breeanna sighed. While they weren't as close as she would have liked, Paige was still her half-sister, and Breeanna loved her. The instinct to protect her sibling was too strong to ignore. If only she knew how to contact her father. She was sure he could work out what had driven Professor Raymond to make such an accusation. The professor had accused her uncle, James Montgomery, as well, but as Breeanna knew, the two men barely tolerated one another so that wasn't surprising.

The events of the past five days flashed through her mind, and she cursed herself for choosing to ignore the feeling of unease she'd harboured since the professor's accident. Perhaps if she'd had the courage to acknowledge her instincts, she would have been able to prevent what had happened tonight.

A young couple emerged from the cafe, and the aroma of their takeaway food reminded Breeanna she hadn't eaten since breakfast. The last few days she'd worked through her lunch break, trying to cover the professor's work as well as her own. But at the moment food wasn't a high priority. She knew the man who'd killed her attacker would be looking for her, and she guessed he would kill again in order to possess what the professor had supposedly given her. Which meant she couldn't take refuge with her friends, as that would endanger them. She'd considered and discarded the idea he was a police officer; everything about him had indicated the opposite.

So where could she hide while she tried to make contact with her father? She thought of a book she'd read several years before about a woman on the run who was taught by an ex-prostitute how to hide so she couldn't be found by the men chasing her. Money. She would need as much cash as she could get her hands on. Several buildings up, lights illuminated an automatic teller machine.

Quickly exiting her car, Breeanna strode to the ATM and withdrew her daily limit. She looked at the crisp notes in her hand. One thousand dollars. Not enough, but it would have to do for now. She walked back to the cafe. Though her stomach was churning, she knew she needed to eat.

The shop was warm, and smelled of cooking oil and chips and sizzling steak. Breeanna placed and paid for her order, then sat at a corner table. As the minutes ticked by she tried to formulate a plan, but her thoughts kept being distracted by the memory of the intruder's face as it exploded.

A reflection of moving red and blue on the window caught her eye. A police car was slowing down outside the shop. It paused briefly behind her car. She stared at it for a few seconds before realising that the officer in the passenger seat was speaking into a radio handset as he looked at her number plate. Normally, Breeanna would think herself paranoid getting alarmed because a cop was giving her car the once-over, but tonight her skin crawled with apprehension.

She watched the car drive slowly forwards, watched it turn right at the next intersection and disappear. Relaxing was out of the question. She was going with her instincts now, and they told her the police hadn't gone away. They were waiting.

Waiting out of sight. And she had a terrible suspicion she knew who they were waiting for.

The cafe attendant called out to her as she ran for the door. She grabbed the proffered white paper bag and was in her car within seconds. Leaving the headlights off, she turned back the way she had come, away from the police car. Two intersections later she turned right and headed north as quickly as the speed limit would allow.

'She must have seen the bloody cop car.' Vaughn's irritation was barely controlled as Mark returned to their vehicle and related what the cafe attendant had observed.

'Why didn't she go straight to the police?' Mark mused, replacing in his jacket pocket the photo of Breeanna he had shown the attendant. 'Wouldn't that be your first reaction if you'd been attacked?'

'Perhaps she's like us. Perhaps she wants it for herself, doesn't want the word to get out. If it's as valuable as we've been told, then it would be tempting.'

'Maybe she doesn't know who to trust.'

Vaughn lit up a cigarette as he looked at the younger man. What was he getting at?

'You'd just killed someone in front of her,' Mark explained. 'How was she to know she could trust you? Perhaps I should approach her next time.'

Average in looks and height, Talbert had a kind face most people instinctively trusted. There was sense in what he was saying, but Vaughn was reluctant to let him be involved any more than was necessary. When Vaughn had received the details on this case, it had seemed like the opportunity he'd been waiting for. The chance to make some *real* money.

Although well paid for his services, he hungered for more. And if what he suspected were true, an even more precious prize could be at stake. At fifty-nine, Vaughn was beginning to feel the limitations age was placing on his body, and knew his days in the field were numbered. And the generous pay-out that would be made to him could never buy what he wanted. He exhaled smoke out the window and reached for the laptop at his feet. Police were covering the homes of the Montgomery woman's friends, but perhaps there was something he had overlooked. The screen glowed into life, and he quickly scanned the relevant files.

Nothing. Nothing he hadn't already covered. She hadn't gone to her sister or her uncle, so she was either still running or was hiding somewhere. He tempered his urge to swear. Giving in to frustration wouldn't help. He couldn't risk making a mistake. There was too much to lose.

The red light on Breeanna's fuel gauge began to glow. Although it meant she could travel another sixty or so kilometres, she preferred to fill up now in case the man who'd shot her attacker caught up with her.

Aware of the higher police presence on the major freeways, she had driven through suburban streets, her gaze flicking constantly to her rear-view mirror. In the past ten minutes she had decided to drive north for a few hours and book in at a caravan park while she worked out what to do next. She'd managed to eat her burger while driving, and now the thought of a cup of coffee was tantalising. The shock of what she'd witnessed had worn off, and a shot of caffeine might help to keep her alert as she drove. A service station with a cafe attached seemed like a good option.

A couple of times in the previous five minutes she'd had the feeling she was being followed, but the only car consistently behind her appeared to be driven by someone whose attention was focused more on weaving from lane to lane than keeping up with Breeanna's white Laser.

Another ten minutes passed before Breeanna spotted a service station with the longed-for cafe. A group of teenagers spilled out through the doors, laughing and shouting. Breeanna pulled in and parked in front of the bowser. She took her bag and locked the car, keeping a watchful eye on approaching traffic. By the time she'd finished filling the tank other vehicles were waiting, so she drove her car to a parking space against the boundary fence.

She paid the attendant, walked through to the cafe and ordered coffee. A young couple walked up to the counter, and Breeanna stepped away, backing up against a stand of bread and groceries. A horn blew and she glanced outside to where the teenagers were making impolite gestures at a car speeding along the street.

Movement near her Laser caught her eye. A man, solidly built and average in height, was moving from her driver's side door and around the back of her car. Apprehension snaked up Breeanna's spine as he stopped at the front passenger door. Two seconds later he walked back up the row of parked cars as though he were heading towards the service station. At the last car he walked around to the passenger side, placed his forearm on the roof, and leaned down slightly to speak to the passenger. As he did so, his suit coat lifted and revealed a shadow, dark against the white of his shirt. A shadow that could, without any imagination, assume the shape of a shoulder holster.

The attendant called her number. With shaking hands she

grabbed her coffee and retreated behind the grocery stand, sipping on the steaming liquid, and watched again.

The man was now walking towards the service station, his determined pace matching his expression.

Breeanna shrank back, heart pounding. He wasn't the man who'd shot her attacker, but his movements were suspicious. Too suspicious to disregard. Of all the cars parked out there, why would he be checking hers? No, it wasn't coincidence, and as he got closer to the cafe her trepidation grew.

The urge to run to her car and speed away was strong, but logic told her that she wouldn't get away this time. Whoever had located and followed her must be a professional. The door of the service station section slid open and Breeanna watched him walk up to the cash register operator and hold out a photograph.

Breeanna strode back to the cafe counter, her mind racing. Pushing in front of another customer, she asked the attendant for the location of the ladies' toilet, and he pointed towards a corridor at the end of the room. Still clutching her coffee, she walked briskly past lemon-coloured walls to a closed door with a Ladies sign attached, and noticed the corridor branched to the right, ending in two doors marked Staff Only. She tried one. A storage room. She opened the other. A handbasin and mirror were attached to the wall, and an open door revealed a toilet.

Damn! She was trapped. Then she saw another door at the side of the room. It had a lock which required a key to open it from the outside. Without hesitating she wrenched it open, and found herself behind the building.

She forced down the panic rising in her chest and looked around. A closed roller-doored workshop with 'Mechanic' painted on it stood to her right. Parked in front were a large refrigerated truck and a smaller truck with a high canvas-covered back. As she stood there, frantically considering her options, a stout figure in crumpled pants and flannelette shirt strolled around the service station corner, munching on a spring roll and fries. Breeanna placed her coffee on the ground and pretended to fix the strap on her shoe as she watched him climb into the cabin of the smaller truck and close the door.

After only a slight hesitation, she made up her mind. Before the truck's engine rumbled into life, she raced across and released one of the clips securing the canvas cover at the back. Grateful she'd chosen to wear pants instead of a skirt that morning, she stepped onto the tow bar and hauled herself inside. The truck lurched into reverse and she rolled forwards, banging her arm on a big wooden box. She stifled her cry of pain, and gripped the box for support as the truck moved off.

It was only when the vehicle had been travelling for what seemed like hours, but she knew could only have been about thirty minutes, that she dared to look out through the gap in the canvas.

As she recognised the route the driver had taken, Breeanna realised that fate had chosen her course of action for her.

Mark walked to where Vaughn waited near Breeanna Montgomery's car. When their associate had informed them that Breeanna had purchased fuel and gone into the cafe, they had closed in, hoping to trap her, and Vaughn had sent Mark to check on her while he waited.

'Well?' Impatience edged Vaughn's voice.

'The cafe attendant said she asked for the toilet. He saw

her go in but didn't see her come out. I checked. The toilet was empty and has no exit, but a staff toilet further along has access to the yard and workshop out the back.'

'So we've lost her.'

Mark nodded. 'It looks like it. She's definitely not in the building, and I searched the surrounds.' He watched the other man's reaction with interest. He knew Vaughn lived and breathed his job, but something personal had entered into this case. Something that Vaughn wanted. Badly.

'Get her photo to every cop in the country, but let them know there's to be no media involvement. I'm to be informed the moment she's found, but they're to take no further action except keep her under surveillance. *Discreet* surveillance.'

Mark punched numbers into his mobile phone. It irked him that Vaughn hadn't given him any details about what they were after. A records book that the Montgomery woman was supposed to have – he'd supplied that much – but nothing to indicate what information was in it. But Mark was a patient man. It was one of the reasons he had been chosen for this job.

He hoped there would be no need for his other skills.

CHAPTER TWO

'How could you have used such an imbecile to get the stuff off the Montgomery woman?' Frank Delano thundered, his black eyebrows bristling at the bridge of his fleshy nose.

Darren 'Doggie' Kennett cringed as Frank thumped his desk, the only piece of furniture in his office that looked substantial enough to withstand the force of the overweight bar owner's temper. Frank had bestowed the nickname on Doggie because the man's long face and droopy ears and eyes reminded him of his favourite childhood cartoon character, but he sometimes wondered if Doggie was any more intelligent than the animal he was named after.

'We've always worked together pretty good before.' Doggie's left shoulder rose in a half shrug that made it seem divorced from the rest of his body. 'He'd told me he was clean. Reckoned he hadn't used in months. When he turned up he seemed okay, but after we'd waited a while I could tell he was getting high. I told him to piss off but he was determined to stay 'cause he needed the dough.'

'You shoulda shoved a fifty in his pocket and kicked his arse out of there.'

'It was too late. The car pulled in and he followed her into the house. I was going to go in after him when I saw these two other guys. Creepy, they were. Just seemed to come from nowhere. They must have seen what was happening 'cause they didn't go into the house; they hid in the shadows. I didn't know what to do, so I stayed put.'

Frank hauled his bulky body from the chair, and heard the air suck slowly back through the leather. 'And watched them shoot your mate and let the Montgomery woman get away.'

The words were soft but the tone was steel, and the sweat of fear glistened on Doggie's forehead. He wiped at his face, and wondered if the airconditioning was working. 'I have no idea who those blokes were, Frank, honest. But they didn't get nothing either. They shot through as soon as they'd . . . picked up the body.'

Frank tried to think logically. Disposing of the body and cleaning up the scene certainly didn't fit into the MO of anyone he knew, and from what Doggie had told him of the events, the men involved were professionals. Of some kind. Which led him to the only logical conclusion.

Someone had blabbed.

Someone had wanted to cut him out of the equation.

That someone would pay.

The chair groaned as he sat back down and reached for the phone.

*

Paige Montgomery looked up as Allan Walters walked into the reception area of the Montgomery Medical Research Institute at St Kilda. His unbuttoned lab coat flapped with each lanky stride, and as he bent over Paige's desk his straight brown hair fell onto his glasses.

'Have you heard from Breeanna?' he asked.

Paige frowned. 'Isn't she at work?'

'She hasn't come in this morning, and with the professor away I've had to take over the routine checks on both their experiments as well as trying to do my own work. She's not answering her phone or her mobile. I've tried several times.' His hair flopped again as he shook his head. 'She's usually reliable.' He looked at his watch, and pushed back his glasses as they began to slide down. 'It's nearly twelve. I've got more checks to do.' With an impatient toss of his head he stalked back down the passageway that connected the administration and laboratory buildings.

Paige watched him retreat. He might carry on like a disturbed ibis, but Allan was right. Breeanna *was* normally reliable. If she hadn't phoned in sick, something must be very wrong. The professor's accident a week ago had upset her, but after seeing him in hospital a couple of days later, Breeanna had appeared distracted and . . . *disturbed*. Paige's teeth worried at her bottom lip. She would have to go to Breeanna's house and see if she was all right.

A small waiting area, furnished in maroon tapestry-covered lounge chairs that complemented the cream walls and classic paintings, separated Paige's reception desk from two closed doors on the other side of the cosy room. Paige had suggested to her father that modernising the furniture would make it more impressive, but George Montgomery had smiled gently and said the chairs were still functional and would stay as long as they remained so. Paige knew that any profit made from the laboratories' commercial activities would be ploughed back into the cancer research so dear to her father's heart.

Picking up her handbag, she walked over to the left-hand door and knocked. At her uncle's brief 'Come in', Paige opened the door.

James Montgomery's office contrasted greatly with the conservative, almost old-fashioned appearance of the reception area. An advertisement for chrome and glass, it seemed an appropriate setting for its occupant. James looked up at Paige's entrance, and the grey streaks in his thinning brown hair caught the overhead light. His dark-charcoal suit was tailor-made for his tall, slim figure, but Paige noticed with surprise that it seemed a little crumpled, as though James had not paid his usual meticulous attention to his appearance. He had arrived late this morning, and Paige had barely glimpsed him as he'd hurried into his office.

Quickly she related what Allan Walters had said. 'Could you please answer the phone while I go to check on Breeanna?' she finished.

James stood up. 'I'll go with you,' he said. 'If she is ill I might be of some assistance.' He walked around and placed a comforting hand on Paige's shoulder. 'We'll go in my car.'

As James drove to East Malvern, where Breeanna lived, Paige tried to push aside her concern for her sister and respond to his conversation. She was very fond of her uncle.

Although she knew her father loved her, she'd always been a little in awe of him. Perhaps if she'd seen more of him when she was a child it would have been different, but infrequent holidays with him in Melbourne had reinforced her perception of his emotional remoteness, his preoccupation with his dream of one day finding a cure for the cancer that had killed Morag, Breeanna's mother. And if she admitted it to herself, Paige had also been jealous of his love for his dead wife. As a teenager she'd come close to hating him for the pain he'd caused her mother. In marrying to procure a mother for Breeanna, George Montgomery had only succeeded in creating a wife who felt her love was unreciprocated, and a daughter who felt alienated by his work.

His younger brother, James, on the other hand, was personable, charming, and took the time to talk to Paige as though she were important. For a twenty-six year old who'd grown up in Perth and had seen her father only on brief visits, Paige had found in James the father figure she'd always wanted. So when he'd offered her a job at the Institute two years before, she'd happily accepted.

Now she watched the large residences of East Malvern pass by the Camry's window. James turned down into the back streets and the housing changed, became smaller, less affluent. In a street where tending to gardens seemed a low priority, the car slowed down.

Soon they pulled up in front of a small, lowset brick house that Paige knew had been Breeanna's great-grandparents' home after the First World War. The property had passed down through her mother's family, and several years ago Breeanna had decided to move out of her father's home and live there.

Breeanna's car wasn't in the driveway. In the past Paige had always considered her half-sister a little strange, but the constant contact through work had revealed a warm, caring side to Breeanna that Paige had come to love, and she now felt her worry increase.

'You'd think she'd do something about this yard,' James muttered as they walked up the driveway.

Paige looked around at the blossom on the shrubs and found the profusion of colours appealing. 'They might be a little unkempt, Uncle James, but they're very pretty, and the perfume's lovely.'

James smiled thinly and she realised how tired he looked. The grey streaks had recently appeared in his brown hair, and deeper lines now creased his high forehead. With the worry of running the Institute while his brother was overseas, and the extra burden of the professor's accident, Breeanna's unexplained absence must be adding to his concerns.

The sound of the doorbell echoed through the house as James pressed the button. And waited. Pressed it again. Waited again.

'Do you still have the spare key Breeanna gave you?'

Paige opened her handbag, rummaged through it, and finally drew out a solitary key on a thin ribbon. They opened the door and walked inside, Paige calling out Breeanna's name. Two steps into the living room Paige stopped.

'Oh!' The sound was out before she could stop it. She saw her uncle's frown, and explained. 'Breeanna's normally so neat. I'm . . . surprised.' She gestured to the half-full tea cup, some of its contents obviously slopped over the coffee table, and a slew of crumpled magazines. Minimal furniture gave the small room an impression of spaciousness: low-backed green-cushioned lounge, stereo wall unit and high bookcase tucked into the far corner.

'Come on,' said James. 'She could be in bed.'

Paige was equally shocked by the state of the bedroom. Rumpled sheets on the queen-size bed, clothing heaped on a white cane chair in the corner and half fallen to the floor, shoes scattered as though kicked off and left. Worry ate into her further. She picked up a framed photo that had fallen down on the dresser and looked at it. Black hair that gleamed as though burnished by the sun framed a face neither beautiful nor plain, but arresting in the strength of the jawline and the fullness of the smiling mouth. But it was the eyes that held Paige's attention. Warm and dark, they seemed capable of looking into your soul, and Paige felt the same fascination she always did when she gazed at the photo.

'It's like looking at Breeanna, isn't it?'

James had walked quietly up behind her, and Paige gave a little start. She quickly stood the frame down. 'Yes. But Breeanna's prettier than her mother was. Well,' she shrugged, 'from what I've seen in the photos.'

'Morag was a stunning woman,' James said, as though to contradict her. 'Charismatic, compelling . . .'

He turned away, but she caught the whispered word 'beautiful' and it added further to the mystery she had always felt surrounded her father's first wife.

James glanced back at her. 'I'll search the rest of the house. You see if there's anything here that might give us a clue to where she's gone.'

Paige looked again at the dresser. Breeanna wore minimal make-up and the few articles there confirmed that. Paige opened the top drawer. A jewellery case, personal items, a spare set of house keys, Christmas and birthday cards that must have been special to her. Nothing to give Paige an idea what had happened to her sister. She began to search through the other drawers. Underwear, knit tops, shorts. She pushed the last drawer closed. A muffled knock sounded. Puzzled, she pulled it open again and felt through the silky pants and slips and sports briefs until she touched something solid. She pulled out a black plastic case no bigger than a small box of chocolates. Her fingers moved to open it, then stopped. No, she shouldn't do it. It would be violating Breeanna's privacy. She lowered the case to the drawer as James entered the room.

'What's that?'

'I don't know. It was in the drawer. I was just putting it back.'

Before Paige could replace the case, James took it from her and opened it.

As the contents were revealed, the air rushed from Paige's lungs. She stared as though mesmerised, then shook her head in disbelief.

'Oh, no.' Shock rasped her voice, and her hand flew to her mouth as though to stop the words. 'Not Breeanna.'

CHAPTER THREE

Nine days later

The pain was almost unbearable.

It ate into Rogan McKay's body, twisting him on the sweat-soaked sheets. He tried to rise, to get help, but the agony pinned him down.

Then the pain stopped. And there was only the ache, the soreness where it had been. For a minute it gave him rest, allowed his breathing to return to normal.

Then it came back.

He clenched his teeth with the effort not to scream, to cry out for it to stop. When the next respite came he reached an exhausted hand over the bedside lamp and turned it on.

2.53 a.m.

He'd been so tired, so damn tired when he'd crashed onto

the bed at midnight, that when the pain started dragging him out of a thick, deep sleep he'd thought it was a bad dream. But the intensity of it soon affirmed it was no nightmare to be thrown off with full consciousness.

A harsh cry strangled in his throat as the pain threw him back against the pillow. This time was worse than anything he'd ever felt . . . his muscles tensed against it, the tendons and veins in his neck stretched like singing ropes. The sweat on his forehead poured into his eyes. His brain was painting blackness through his mind, shunning all thought in its efforts to cope with an agony beyond endurance.

Suddenly it was gone.

He slumped down on the bed as the swirling mists in his brain subsided, dragging air into his lungs in great panting gulps. Gingerly he moved his arms, his legs. Finally he swung his body over the side of the bed and stood, weak and unsteady, fighting to make sense of what had happened.

Slowly he became aware of a great emptiness in his soul. A desolation, a sense of loss so profound his gut clenched with the knowledge of it.

Because now he knew. He understood. But his brain refused to believe.

Like a very old man he shuffled out of the bedroom into an adjoining study. He turned on the light, collapsed onto the chair at the desk and willed his reluctant hand to pick up the phone. He punched in a series of numbers. And waited.

Finally it rang out. He tried a different set. An automated voice asked him to leave a message. He spoke several words, then replaced the receiver.

A window on the opposite wall mirrored the despair registering in his eyes. Eyes so brilliantly blue they glittered like icebergs in the warm light. Eyes he feared would never again look back at him.

'Didn't you sleep well last night, son?' Alice McKay asked as Rogan flopped onto a kitchen chair and poured himself a glass of orange juice.

He pushed long strands of sun-bleached hair off his forehead before replying. 'It always takes me some time to adjust when I get off the boat, Mum.'

Alice smiled. 'You've been home two days. I think your socialising with Meryl and your brothers might have more to do with it.'

Rogan saw the flash of pain in his mother's eyes. It was six months since his youngest brother, Ewan, had been murdered, and although Rogan had helped put the killer behind bars, he knew it had given his parents only a small sense of closure. While she hadn't shown obvious preference for him, Ewan had been their mother's favourite. She had tried to bury her grief in the hard work involved in running the family's dairy farm, but Rogan had seen how his brother's death had aged her. Her hair, once the same tawny colour as his, had gone grey, and the extra kilos she'd gained in middle age had fallen away, leaving her face drawn and lined. His father, too, no longer seemed as strong and tireless as Rogan had always thought him.

It had shocked him, this sudden ageing of his parents, and now he realised he couldn't tell them of the dread eating its way into his chest. They had lost one son; he didn't want to tell them they might have lost another. As soon as he'd woken this morning he'd made a few phone calls, but the answers only seemed to confirm what he already suspected.

'Thought I might drive to Melbourne and see Liam,' Rogan remarked, the casualness in his voice not betraying his need to jump into his vehicle and take off immediately. He looked around the spacious farmhouse kitchen with its timber cupboards, cream walls and large wooden table and chairs. It spoke of solidity and security, but Ewan's death had made them all realise that physical security could be an illusion.

'He'd like that.' Alice placed a plate of sausages, eggs and tomatoes in front of her son. Her face grew wistful. 'You two haven't been together since Ewan's funeral.'

'We keep in touch.' Rogan picked at his food with his fork then, seeing his mother's frown, began to eat. He knew she must have come back early from helping his father with the milking so she could cook breakfast for him. Alice and Duncan McKay had raised five sons and two daughters, and no matter what else the family may have lacked in assets, there had never been a shortage of food on the table.

Alice smiled fondly at Rogan. 'The connection's still there, isn't it?' She poured tea into two mugs and sat opposite him at the table. 'Even when you were just toddlers you didn't need to talk: you always acted like you could read each other's minds. And it didn't matter how far apart you were, one always cried if the other got hurt.'

He'd heard his mother talk about this before, but now he felt guilt shaft through him. How could he tell her he feared Liam was more than hurt, that he might be dead? How else could he explain the deep, aching emptiness in his soul?

'I'll leave after breakfast,' he said between mouthfuls.

'So soon?' His mother frowned. 'Your father will be disappointed. He was hoping . . . Never mind.'

'Hoping what, Mum?' Rogan was surprised to see colour rise in his mother's cheeks.

'Well . . .' Alice seemed a little flustered, 'last night he mentioned us going down to the coast for a day or two. He thought you might take over the milking. Meryl said she'd give you a hand.'

'Dad? The Gold Coast? I thought he hated the crowds and the traffic.'

Alice sipped her tea before replying. 'He thought a few days away might be a nice fortieth wedding anniversary present.'

Thick bastard, McKay, Rogan berated himself. His younger sister had reminded him of the occasion, but last night's trauma had wiped it from his mind. 'Sorry, Mum. Can it wait until I get back? The repairs to the boat engine will take at least ten days, and I'll be back before then.'

'Of course, dear. But you'd better go and tell your father now, before he makes any plans.'

Lush green fields sloped gently alongside the road before reaching the edge of the plateau and tumbling into the Numinbah Valley below. They provided rich feed for the dairy cattle on the small farms between Beechmont and Binna Burra on the hinterland behind Queensland's famous Gold Coast.

Rogan left the sprawling old farmhouse with its white-painted weatherboards and brown-framed windows like eyes on a sleepy labrador, and walked to where the mountain began its descent. He looked across to another mountain range rearing its craggy peaks into the blue, then up the valley to where, in the far distance, high-rise buildings dotted the narrow coastal strip and the ocean shimmered in the sunlight.

He breathed in deeply. The air, so crisp and clean, almost sweet in comparison with the salt tang of the ocean, was balm to his troubled spirit. He rammed clenched fists into his jeans pockets. It was always like this when he was at home – this tearing at his guts, this yearning for the limitless expanse of blue-green sea against the almost primal urge to dig himself into the fertile earth and put down roots to connect himself to this land he loved equally well. Happy in each world, but constantly longing for the other, he realised. He had always been a very physical person, expressing his love for his family by deeds rather than words, but sometimes, when he felt almost overwhelmed by the beauty of nature, he longed to be able to create poetry that could express what he felt. He smiled. His old navy mates would have been shocked beyond belief if he'd told them that.

Liam was the words man. His mirror image. The quiet, thoughtful balance to Rogan's extrovert nature. The ache deepened when he thought again of his twin. Sheer exhaustion had granted Rogan some sleep in the remaining hours before dawn, but the emptiness, the desolation, had still been there when he awoke.

He looked across the paddock. Friesian and Illawarra cows were milling about in the holding yard near the milking shed. His father would be almost finished now, and Rogan felt a pang of guilt that he couldn't stay and give his parents the break they so badly needed. He hurried into the wooden shed where stainless-steel vats were slowly being filled through the plastic hoses connected to the milking machines. The cadence of well-maintained machinery echoed in the small room. He took off his sneakers, and pulled on a pair of rubber boots.

As Rogan walked through to the milking bays, Duncan McKay glanced up from attaching teat cups onto a cow's udder, and smiled. The tiredness in his eyes notched Rogan's guilt up further. Cows were still waiting in the remaining three bays, with two standing patiently outside in the yard. Rogan picked up the chain attached to the nearest bay and secured it across the cow's rear to keep her there, then roped the outer rear leg to prevent her kicking. Rain the previous afternoon had muddied the ground, and the smell of warm manure had attracted numerous flies. Rogan brushed them away as he propped himself on a small stool and dipped each teat into a disinfectant mix, cleaned it with paper towelling, then shoved the teat cup on.

He reached over and tipped feed and supplement into a tin near the cow's head to keep the animal calm during the milking process, slipping effortlessly into the routine he'd known since childhood. Soon the last cow was ambling through into the holding yard.

'Thanks for the help, son,' Duncan said as he began to clean the machines to get them ready for sterilising.

Before he could say any more Rogan spoke quickly. 'I'm leaving this morning for Melbourne, Dad. Going to see Liam. When I get back I'll take over for a few days and give you and Mum a break.'

Duncan pushed dark-brown hair streaked with grey from his forehead and stretched the kinks from his back. 'Thanks, son. Your mother needs to get away for a while.'

As he watched the tired slump of his father's shoulders, Rogan prayed that what he had experienced last night would turn out to be just a bad dream.

But the hollow feeling in his heart betrayed that hope.

★

An hour later Rogan drove into Beechmont village. He turned into the yard of a small log cabin and switched off the engine of his fawn four-wheel-drive dual-cab Rodeo. Before he could get out, a young woman with breasts a little large for her slim body opened the front door of the house, walked up to the driver's window and leaned her forearms against the opening.

Rogan could never understand why his sister-in-law had resorted to something as extreme as breast implants in an effort to keep Ewan faithful. Childhood sweethearts, Meryl and Ewan had married as soon as they turned eighteen. The next year Ewan had joined the navy. Self-indulgent to the core, he had only ever been faithful to his goal of acquiring whatever he wanted no matter what the methods. A trait that had led to his murder at the hands of a violent criminal.

An aspiring actress and part-time make-up artist, Meryl had dyed her hair an attractive shade of honey to suit the minor character she was portraying in a movie.

'Didn't expect to see you today, Rogan,' Meryl smiled. 'Thought I'd have to go into work, but there's been a technical hitch and they don't need me until tomorrow.'

Rogan quickly explained about his concern for Liam and that he was on his way to Melbourne. 'It's just a precaution, Meryl, but if something's happened to him, I'd appreciate you being here for Mum and Dad.'

A few minutes later Meryl watched as Rogan continued his drive down the winding mountain road. In the past few days she'd wondered if she'd fallen in love with the wrong brother. Then she smiled. No, Rogan would always be her friend, but she knew that was all there would ever be between them.

She had noticed a change in Rogan after he'd left the navy, and she wondered if anyone would be able to penetrate the emotional wall he appeared to have built around himself. His love for his family and concern for his friends were obvious but, although he had previously had a couple of serious girlfriends, in the past few years no woman had managed to draw him into a relationship of any depth, and she was perplexed as to what had caused this.

In the years since Liam had made his home in Melbourne, Rogan had tried to visit as much as he could. Although their physical appearance made it almost impossible to tell them apart, emotionally the twins complemented one another, and Rogan had never met anyone who made him feel at ease in his own skin like Liam did. Which was why the aching sense of loss he now felt was almost a physical pain.

As the countryside sped past, so did memories of a shared lifetime. Normally inseparable, a twisted ankle had kept Rogan at home when both boys should have been at a school camp together. A camp that had resulted in Liam coming down with rheumatic fever and suffering slight damage to a heart valve. Although not serious enough to curtail Liam's involvement in their teenage escapades, the damage had been sufficient to prevent him joining up with his brother in the Royal Australian Navy.

If the worry in his gut had allowed it, Rogan would have smiled as he remembered Liam's frustration when he was rejected. His normally quiet brother had stomped around the house like a bull denied his favourite cow, then he'd made a last-minute application to study law at university. Several years later, Liam had surprised them all by announcing he had joined a firm of private investigators in Melbourne, and after some time with them had branched out on his own.

For the past twenty hours, as Rogan had driven southwards, he had tried to piece together the fragments of conversation he'd had with Liam that could give him some clue to what may have happened. Normally they phoned each other at least once a week, and Rogan couldn't recall anything in their last few calls that might be suspicious. He frowned. *Except for Liam's off-hand remark about meeting the woman of his dreams.* Liam had refused to elaborate and Rogan had bitten back his curiosity, confident that his twin would blurt it out sooner or later.

When Rogan had tried Liam's home, business and mobile phones over the past day and a half, Liam hadn't answered. And Liam's lawyer mates hadn't been any help either. Not that Rogan blamed them. With the often dangerous work Liam undertook, his friends weren't going to hand out information on the strength of a vague phone inquiry. He would just have to ask them in person.

As he crested a rise on the Hume Highway, Rogan saw the smog that hung like a pall in the distance, and knew he was getting close to his destination. Like most large cities, Melbourne couldn't escape the air pollution that came from factories and constant traffic.

His need for sleep growing with each kilometre travelled, Rogan stopped at a small cafe and bought a coffee. The thought of an ice-cold beer was tempting, but that would have to wait until he reached Liam's apartment. At least he would miss arriving in morning peak hour, but as the traffic into Melbourne was always constant, he just hoped for a smooth run.

By the time he swung into the driveway of Liam's strata

title unit in Chelsea Heights, Rogan doubted he could keep his eyes open another five minutes. Liam's was the back unit of the dual-occupancy set, surrounded by high brick fences on three sides and separated from the front unit by a low hedge. He parked in front of the roller door, and scrabbled in the vehicle ashtray for the spare keys Liam had given him. When the rising garage door revealed Liam's car, Rogan's stomach lurched. He got out of the Rodeo, stretched the kinks from his back, and grabbed his duffle bag from the back seat. He walked into the garage and looked through the windows of Liam's car. The contents of the open glove box were strewn over the front seat, but otherwise the car was empty.

Rogan unlocked the door into the small laundry area, and stepped inside. The cupboard had been ransacked, washing powder and cleaning products spilled across the floor. Rogan dropped his bag and hurried into the kitchen. A similar scene awaited him there.

Stomach knotting, he walked cautiously into the living room.

Whoever had searched the townhouse had been thorough, but not careful. The lounge cushions had been cut open, their filling ripped out. Paintings hung crookedly on walls, the bookcase was bare, its contents scattered across the carpet, every drawer in the wall unit emptied in a heap. Even the dining chairs had been upended onto the table so they could be checked over.

Now more afraid than he could remember ever feeling, Rogan made his way to Liam's bedroom. Apart from the mess he now expected, it was empty. Liam used the second bedroom as an office, and it was here that Rogan saw how thorough the intruders had been. Not a single file remained in the cabinet, equipment had been upended, and the computer tower was missing.

As he reached across for the phone that had been shoved to the back of the desk, he caught sight of something that made his heart pound. At the side of the desk, partially obscured by a sheet of paper, the carpet had been stained by a liquid.

A liquid dark enough to be blood.

CHAPTER FOUR

A camera flash caught Rogan's attention. From his position on one of the lounge chairs, he watched a police forensic officer methodically photograph and examine Liam's office. The woman's deliberate movements seemed agonisingly slow, and his gut clenched with frustration.

'What made you come down to Melbourne to see your brother, Mr McKay?'

Detective-Sergeant Ed Bruin's question focused Rogan's attention back to where the police officer sat on the opposite side of the table. The detective's partner had been called away soon after their arrival, and Bruin appeared to relish being left in charge. Rogan considered the burly policeman thoughtfully. If he gave the true reason, he doubted the detective would believe him. Rogan had grown up thinking there was nothing unusual in the connection he shared with his twin, but at high school he soon realised teenagers who were demonstrably different from the pack would be labelled 'weird'. Or worse.

'I often visit my brother, Sergeant Bruin,' he replied. 'Well, as often as my work allows.'

'And what is your work, Mr McKay?'

'I'm a partner in a fishing and diving charter boat on the Barrier Reef.'

A spark of more-than-professional interest lit the detective's eyes. 'How come you're on holidays? Wouldn't this be a good time of year for you to operate?'

Rogan tried to keep his impatience in check. The stain on the carpet wasn't huge, but that didn't mean Liam wasn't lying somewhere bleeding to death while he sat around discussing optimal charter seasons with a police officer. 'The engine on our boat needed repairs so I decided to catch up with my brother.'

The detective nodded as though this was reasonable, then asked Rogan what he knew about his brother's associates and the type of work he undertook. Although Liam had rarely discussed individual cases, Rogan knew that when he had worked for the firm of private investigators he had often been sent on undercover jobs, particularly in the areas of industrial espionage and missing persons. And when he had branched out on his own, his former employers had sometimes sent similar cases his way.

Rogan explained to the detective that because of Liam's need for secrecy in a lot of the cases he undertook, he operated under the name of Liam Kennedy and used a mobile phone and post office box in that name for his work. He worked from home but would meet clients only at selected locations such as coffee shops. When this wasn't possible, he would hire office space on a pre-paid cash basis for the duration of the interview. As far as associates went, there were only two of Liam's friends who Rogan knew, and they were lawyers Liam had met through his previous work and who he now used for his personal legal matters. Rogan gave Bruin the men's names, and asked how soon he would be interviewing them.

Bruin snapped his notebook closed. 'Very soon, Mr McKay.' He stood up. 'Where will you be staying, so we can keep in touch with you?'

Rogan looked through to Liam's office. The forensic officer was taking a sample of the stain. 'I thought I'd stay here. If my brother comes back I want to be around.'

'I'm sorry, this is a crime scene now. Until forensic have finished here I'm afraid we can't risk you possibly contaminating the scene.'

Before Rogan could protest, the constable who had stood on guard at the front door walked into the room and caught Bruin's eye. 'There's a woman here who says she's a neighbour.'

'Bring her in,' Bruin nodded. 'She might be able to shed some light on what's happened.'

The constable's attempt to escort the woman was thwarted by her scooting under his arm and marching up to Bruin. 'I'm Janey Dearmoth. I live in the front unit. Is Liam all right? Good Lord!' Her hand flew to her chest as she noticed Rogan. 'I should have recognised the vehicle. Liam isn't . . .'

'He's missing, Janey,' Rogan said. He had a great deal of respect for the sparrow-like woman who had taken a motherly interest in Liam when he'd moved into the unit several years ago. A retired schoolteacher, she was an enthusiastic volunteer for several charities, but it was her sense of humour that had endeared her to Liam and Rogan. She'd once told them that 'I might be a miss, but I haven't missed much', and the twinkle in her eyes confirmed it.

'When did you last see him?' Rogan asked.

Janey thought a moment. 'Early last Wednesday morning. Six days ago. He was driving out when I was working in the garden and he stopped to mention that he'd be away, and it could be more than a week before he came back. That's why I was worried when I saw the police car just now. I thought he may have had an accident.'

'So you didn't know he'd returned?' Bruin asserted his role and scribbled in his notebook.

'No.' She looked at Rogan. 'I'm sorry.'

Bruin looked up as the forensic officer approached. 'Bloodstain tell you anything?' he asked.

'It looks reasonably fresh to me, maybe a day or so.'

A day or so. Rogan cursed himself for deciding to drive down. He could have saved almost a day if he'd come by plane. But his need to protect his parents from something he wasn't exactly sure about himself had overridden his normal reaction to feelings he received from Liam. Guilt ate heavily into his chest.

'We might need to talk to you further, Ms Dearmoth,' Bruin said, 'so could I please have your contact details?'

'It's *Miss* Dearmoth,' Janey corrected him, and gave her phone number.

Bruin turned to Rogan. 'Here's my card. Let me know where you'll be staying in case I need to get in touch.'

'He'll be staying with *me*.' Janey's tone brooked no argument, and Rogan smiled. She would have been a tartar in the classroom, but no kid would have felt unprotected while she was around.

Several hours later Ed Bruin flung his coat onto the rack behind his desk and picked up his coffee mug. His progress to the lunch room was stopped by another officer telling him he was wanted in the Inspector's office. With an exasperated curse fuelled by his need for caffeine, Bruin soon presented himself in front of the Inspector's desk.

Short grey hair and thin grey eyebrows added to the pallor of the senior officer's face. But it was the expression there that worried Bruin. The man was obviously pissed off about something. Coffee looked like it could be a long time coming.

'What have you found out in the McKay case?' the Inspector asked.

'Very little. None of the neighbours saw or heard anything, except that a resident's dog barked about two or three o'clock in the morning two nights ago. The forensic report should tell us if that's close to the time McKay was injured. That's if it is his blood on the carpet. And as soon as I've checked through the contacts supplied by McKay's former employers, I'll interview his friends.'

'Forget about that. And when you get the forensic results I want you to put them with your notes and give the file to me.'

'Sir?'

'You heard me. The order's come through from the Local Area Commander. We're to stop investigating the case and hand in all documentation.'

Bruin's puzzlement must have shown on his face because the Inspector spread a dismissive hand on the desk, then relented. 'Apparently it has something to do with national security. We have to keep our noses out of it and let the Feds investigate. And that's not to be divulged to the relatives. Your official line is that we're working on it. The apartment is to be left taped off as a crime scene as well.'

The expletives that sprang to Bruin's mind remained unspoken. He'd only moved up into homicide recently, and this was the first case he'd been allowed to handle on his own. Now it looked even more interesting, and he was being told to forget about it.

He nodded reluctantly, and left the room.

As he paced the small office that was their Melbourne base, Vaughn Waring cursed the vagaries of fate. Placing a surveillance camera in McKay's apartment had seemed a shrewd measure after the private investigator had disappeared last week. That was the second time he had given them the slip, but a check of his vehicle registration had supplied all his details. Unfortunately, the inconsistent comings and goings of the elderly woman who occupied the front unit had made it difficult to access McKay's apartment until the day after they'd lost track of him. But using the camera to alert them to any movement in the apartment had freed him and Mark Talbert from physical surveillance and allowed them to concentrate on their own search for the Montgomery woman.

What Vaughn hadn't counted on was the pair of armed men who'd followed McKay into his apartment when he'd returned. The camera had picked up part of their search, but the hidden microphone had captured McKay's brutal interrogation. Then the camera had shown the pair carrying out McKay's body, bleeding from a wound to the head. The intruders had also taken away a case of CDs, as well as the computer tower.

The rage that had filled Vaughn while he'd watched the tape had been tempered by perverse satisfaction as he imagined their faces on discovering the hard drive was missing from the tower. Apart from his ability to deactivate security systems, Mark Talbert had excellent computer skills, *and* a knack for hiding surveillance cameras so they were almost impossible to detect.

The presence of the intruders was something Vaughn hadn't expected, and he berated himself for thinking he and Talbert were the only ones following the progress of McKay's search for Breeanna Montgomery. But he had assumed that the woman's attacker was a drug addict desperate for a quick dollar, and not someone who'd got wind of what Vaughn was sure she possessed.

And now McKay's damned twin brother had turned up! Not that he appeared to know anything. But his visit was bloody inopportune. *Or was it?* Perhaps he had access to leads that Vaughn knew nothing about. Switching surveillance to him might prove more effective than what they were doing now.

Mark looked up from his computer as Vaughn walked over to him.

'Any luck?' Vaughn asked.

'No.' Mark shook his head. 'I can't crack the password, and the email program and protocol has a PGP encryption scheme. We need a super computer to break the code but usually only the military and intelligence services have those.' He shot Vaughn a sideways look. 'You're cleared with both. Why don't you use them?'

'Not yet. We don't know there's anything on this that's of any use to us. I'd prefer not to have too many people aware of this at the moment.'

Vaughn had already stepped outside the parameters of his authority several times in order to get the information he'd needed. But he didn't want to risk drawing too much attention to this operation. Not just because they were his orders, but because it would make it easier for him to slip through his employer's net once he had procured the professor's records.

Waiting was something that Rogan didn't do well. Unlike his twin, his patience was definitely in short supply, and he knew it. The discipline he'd worked under in the navy had tempered his zeal into a force that usually allowed him to attain the goals he focused on, and having to wait for the police to investigate Liam's disappearance was irritating him badly.

After pacing Janey's unit all morning, he had taken her advice to get his hair cut and visited a local barber. As his sun-streaked locks fell to the floor and Liam's face looked back at him from the mirror, he couldn't stop the anxiety that grabbed him.

A phone call to Sergeant Bruin proved useless, and after lunch Rogan gave in to his body's need for sleep. His years of shipboard living had trained him to sleep deeply for a short time, and when he awoke, his need to be actively involved in finding Liam became too great to resist. An hour later he walked through the doors of an elegant office in Moorabbin and asked the receptionist if he could see either of the lawyers he knew were friends of Liam's. Before he could give his name, she pressed the intercom and told Keith Reynolds that Liam McKay was here to see him.

Rather than correct her, Rogan decided to wait for Keith's reaction. As he went to sit in one of the plush armchairs in the reception area, a door in the adjoining corridor opened, and Keith Reynolds walked out, brown tie loosened at the neck of the lemon shirt straining against his massive arms and chest. Rogan still couldn't get used to the idea of a lawyer who did weightlifting, and Keith's cherubic face and overgrown brown moustache added to the incongruity.

'Liam. Come in, mate.' Keith stepped aside and waited for Rogan to walk into his office, a symphony in varying shades of pale green with aubergine highlights. 'Take a seat. Catch me up on the Montgomery case.'

Puzzled by Keith's seeming lack of interest in Liam's welfare, and wondering if Bruin had contacted the lawyer, Rogan asked, 'Keith, have the police been around to see you today?'

'No. Has there been another development? Have they found Breeanna? I thought the family wanted the police kept out of it?'

'Keith, I'm not Liam. I'm Rogan.'

'Rogan!' Keith's head flicked to the side like a parrot's. 'I always thought I could tell you two apart. Well, I'll be stuffed.' His eyes narrowed. 'Why are you here? Has something happened to Liam? Is that why the police are coming?'

Briefly, Rogan filled him in on what he had discovered at Liam's townhouse. He didn't like the way Keith's frown deepened, particularly when he mentioned the bloodstain.

'Do you have Bruin's phone number?' Keith asked when Rogan had finished.

Rogan handed him the card. Keith punched the numbers into his phone and handed the card back. The conversation that ensued was cryptic, and Rogan felt the tension in the room rising.

'Well, something strange is going on there,' Keith said as he replaced the receiver. 'Bruin was evasive and couldn't give a plausible reason why he hadn't contacted me.'

The fact that Keith was clearly worried didn't ease

Rogan's gut feeling at all. 'When did you last see or talk to Liam?' he asked.

'I actually asked him to take on a missing person case . . .' Keith looked through his diary, 'just under two weeks ago.'

'The Montgomery case you mentioned?'

'Yes, but look, Rogan, it's confidential.'

'My brother's life could be at stake, Keith. I don't give a *shit* about confidential!'

Keith held up a large placating hand. 'I'm going to tell you, but I just need you to appreciate what we're dealing with. The missing woman is Breeanna Montgomery. Her father, George Montgomery, is a very prominent doctor here in Melbourne and runs a well-respected medical research institute. He's currently overseas attending several medical conventions and visiting some of the large medical centres like the Mayo Clinic. When Breeanna's sister, Paige, contacted me, she stipulated that her father wasn't to be alerted as they were hoping to get Breeanna back and into treatment before he returned.'

'Who are *they*? And what does this Breeanna need treatment for?'

'George's younger brother, James, also works at the research institute. Apparently, he advised Paige not to worry her father while he's away but to ask us to recommend a private investigator who could find Breeanna. According to Paige, they found evidence that Breeanna is a drug addict. They think she was stealing drugs from the Institute. The professor in charge there had an accident and won't be returning, so James went through his records to allocate his work to the other researchers. The professor's a secretive old bugger and Breeanna was the only one he'd work closely with. James and Paige think Breeanna got spooked when she thought her theft might be discovered and that's why she disappeared.'

Rogan leaned back in the chair. 'How did you get involved?'

'My father had handled all the legal work for George Montgomery and the Montgomery Medical Research Institute, and I took over his clients after he died. James and Paige said they trusted me to find them an investigator of high calibre.'

'So you thought of Liam.'

'Naturally. Apart from being a friend, Liam is one of the most ethical people I know.' Keith gave a short laugh. 'Which is probably why he got out of law. It's damned hard to defend a client you're sure is guilty, and he wasn't keen on boring work like conveyancing. Liam also has a talent for going undercover and finding out information people would rather keep hidden.'

Patience. That virtue that Rogan found so elusive. Liam had it in spades, all right. Bided his time, waited for the chink in someone's armour to show. Asked the right question at the right moment. Rogan could think of numerous occasions that Liam's patience had secured him the information he needed. But this time it looked as though he'd run out of the luck that PIs need as much as patience.

'Rogan, you should consider that Liam's disappearance may have nothing to do with the Montgomery case,' Keith continued. 'He would have made a few enemies in the years he's been a private investigator.'

'I've thought about that. Can you tell me where I can find this Montgomery Institute? I want to find out what they know about Liam. He would have reported back to them, so they're probably the last people to see him. If Bruin isn't going to do anything . . .'

Keith nodded and reached for pen and paper. 'I'll phone and let them know you're coming. I don't normally give my clients' information out, but I'm sure they'll understand in these circumstances. Besides, you won't get in through the security gates unless they're expecting you.' He wrote quickly, handed the paper to Rogan, then said, 'Don't forget, Rogan, Liam's disappearance might not be related to the Montgomery case.' He picked up his pen again. 'Better give me your mobile number if you have one, just in case anything crops up.'

The first thing Rogan did was buy a new street directory. If he was going to follow Liam's trail he'd probably need a more current version than the old one Liam had handed on.

Although he and Liam had driven through Brighton before, they'd always been on their way to somewhere else and Rogan had never really paid a lot of attention to the buildings, only gaining an impression of size and quality that spoke of wealth in a well-modulated voice rather than a scream. Big, imposing concrete fences, electronically controlled gates, tennis courts, huge trees, vast buildings – white cement, sandstone, different shades of cream and autumn, gardens carefully tended to exude an air of casual grace.

Varied shades of green foliage against the blue sky were in pleasant contrast with the bare limbs and bleak grey that had been Rogan's memory of Melbourne from when he'd visited last winter. Buds of pink and white proclaimed that the city was ready to impress with another display of delicate spring blossoms. So different from the brief week or two of Queensland's spring, with its plants slashing vibrant colours into a hot and often humid summer.

The streets were narrow, traffic slowed by small roundabouts, and it took Rogan longer than he had thought to reach the research institute. Security gates blocked the entrance through the high concrete fence. Rogan drove around the Institute first, getting the feel of the place. A series of interconnected buildings took up the entire block, and he noted that the rear entrance, like the main one, had security card controls and an intercom facility.

He stopped in front of the main gate intercom, pressed the button, and waited. A soft, feminine voice asked him to please state his name and business. Careful not to give away Liam's real identity, he stated he was Liam Kennedy's brother and Keith Reynolds had sent him. At his reply, the gates swung open. This cream sandstone building appeared to be a wing of the original, which, from what Rogan guessed, might still be used as a residence. The other buildings were modern, streamlined and functional.

The carved wooden door was locked, but Rogan spoke into the adjoining intercom and heard a soft click. He walked in.

The smiling face of the young woman rising from behind the reception desk froze into a startled mask. The colour rose in her cheeks. 'Liam.' She breathed the name in a way Rogan couldn't interpret. Disbelief? Hope? Perhaps both.

'I'm Liam's twin brother, Rogan.' He made no move to offer her his hand, and he doubted she would have taken it anyway. She seemed more stunned than he would have anticipated. Her gaze flicked behind him, and he turned as a man walked across the waiting area towards him.

'Mr Kennedy,' he gestured to the doorway behind him, 'I'm James Montgomery. Please come in.' He stood aside and waited for Rogan to walk into the room. Rogan was surprised when the receptionist followed them, then he realised that she must be Paige Montgomery. She perched on a chair near the side wall as though she expected to leave at any minute.

'I'm sorry to hear about your brother,' James said as he sat behind his desk. 'It must be very worrying for you. We'll do everything we can to help.'

'When did you last hear from Liam?' Rogan asked. He looked at James, but noticed Paige's top teeth nip into her bottom lip.

'Well, that would have been over a week ago, wouldn't it, Paige?'

'Yes, Uncle James.' The dutiful reply had a hesitancy in it that worried Rogan, but James appeared not to notice. Paige's wavy brunette hair fell across her forehead as she lowered her head, but Rogan caught her expression and got the feeling she wasn't telling the truth. He wanted to question her, but suppressed the urge. Liam's life could be at stake here; he couldn't afford to risk putting either of these two people offside.

'Can you fill me in on what's happened? Keith Reynolds only gave me a brief rundown.'

James nodded sympathetically. 'Of course. I understand how worried you must be. A little over two weeks ago, my niece, Breeanna, didn't show up for work, so I accompanied Paige to Breeanna's house to look for her.'

'Where does Breeanna work?' Rogan interrupted.

'Here at the Institute. In the laboratories. Breeanna's always been a little . . . strange, but she's a *brilliant* research scientist. When we looked through her house, Paige discovered drugs and a syringe that Breeanna had been using. We were shocked, but . . .'

'So you hired Liam to look for her.'

'That's right. Last Tuesday we received a message from him saying that he had a lead but it might take some time to follow up so if we didn't hear from him for a while we weren't to worry.'

'Do you know what that lead was?'

James shook his head. 'No. I'm sorry. I wish we did. We're very worried about Breeanna and most anxious to find her. As you must be about your brother,' he added. 'If there's any way we can help . . .'

Rogan hesitated. This wasn't his scene. He was way out of his depth in Liam's world. But he had to try. 'Do you have a photo of Breeanna I could have?' he asked. At least he would know what she looked like in case he came across her.

'I have one.' Paige spoke quickly as though anxious to contribute. She walked from the room.

Rogan stood up and offered his hand to James. 'Thanks for seeing me. I'll let you know when I find Liam.'

'Please do. I feel responsible for this terrible mess. If I hadn't encouraged Paige to use a private detective, your brother wouldn't have been involved.' He shook his head and walked with Rogan to the office door. 'I hate to think what may have happened to Breeanna,' he sighed.

Paige was searching through her handbag, a frown creasing her pale forehead. She shared James' slim build but not his narrow face, and Rogan noted the soft prettiness in her high cheekbones and rosebud lips. With a breath of relief she brought out a small thin folder and flipped it open. She took out a photo, handed it to Rogan, and stood hovering, like an anxious butterfly, while he looked at it. He guessed the photo was several years old as Paige's hair was now longer, but the woman standing next to her, arm protectively curved around Paige's shoulders, focused his attention.

Not beautiful, not pretty, with strong facial bones, flyaway black hair and dark eyes that looked as though they held secrets a man would like to get to know. Her full lips were slightly parted, not smiling, but hinting that something humorous just might happen that she could laugh at. Breeanna Montgomery was a striking woman.

'Can I keep this for now?' he asked.

Paige hesitated for only a second. 'Of course.' Her mouth opened as though she wanted to say more, but quickly closed again.

'Thanks.' Rogan put the photo in his shirt pocket. His instincts told him Paige was hiding something, but he didn't know how to go about getting her to tell him without scaring her off. Diplomacy was Liam's forte, not his.

'I hope you find your brother soon.'

Rogan nodded and walked to the front door. As his fingers touched the handle he turned back to Paige. 'If you remember anything that will be of help,' he said, 'can you please give me a call?'

Paige nodded, looking almost relieved, and wrote quickly as Rogan gave her his mobile phone number.

The gnawing unease in his gut stayed with Rogan as he walked out and got into his Rodeo. The electronic gates swung open as he drove up to them, and clanged behind the Rodeo as it crossed the footpath.

Before he could turn into the street to drive away, a red Falcon shot out from a parking space up the road and screeched to a halt in front of his vehicle.

CHAPTER FIVE

The blonde who emerged from the Falcon with a slam of the door and a toss of her head was built like every sailor's dream. If the blue figure-hugging knit top wasn't lying, she had breasts that had enough uplift to make a bra superfluous. Her waist didn't so much curve as flow, and Rogan would have placed bets that her jeans-encased derriere was equally delightful.

A reaction of pure lust shot through him and reminded him how long it had been since he'd been to bed with a woman. The look on this woman's face indicated the situation wasn't likely to change.

She marched up to his window and wrenched open the door.

'Where the hell have you been, Liam?' Her eyes narrowed. 'Sunning yourself on some tropical resort by the look of that tan. I thought we had a deal?'

Rogan wasn't sure if he needed to cop the flak this woman

was intending for Liam, but at the moment he had no leads on Liam's disappearance, and he'd pretend to be the pope if it would give him even one clue to his brother's whereabouts. 'And what deal was that?'

'Don't get smart with me, Liam. I got you the lead on Breeanna Montgomery; now, where's my exclusive interview with her?'

'What makes you think I've found her?' Rogan countered.

Exasperation showed on the woman's face. 'You told me you were following through on the lead. Then you disappear for a week! *And* you don't answer your phone. It was only good luck that I spotted you driving into here,' she nodded towards the research institute. She frowned at his Rodeo. 'Whose vehicle is this? It has a Queensland number plate. Is that where you've been?'

Rogan thought quickly. If what this woman said about giving Liam the information he needed to find Breeanna Montgomery was true, he had to keep her thinking he was Liam. At least for long enough to find out what it was so he could trace Liam's movements.

'Yes,' he replied. 'But I didn't find her. It looks like we'll have to go over that information of yours again and see if there's something we missed. At the moment,' he nodded towards the street where a car was negotiating its way around the Falcon, 'you're holding up traffic.'

The blonde smiled, a seductive curve to lips that just missed being labelled 'pouty'. 'All right. We'll go to my place. Just follow me.'

Rogan watched, fascinated, as the blonde returned to her car. And changed his mind about 'delightful'. Firm flesh undulating beneath clinging denim was definitely 'delectable'.

As he followed the Falcon through a maze of streets that left him knowing which direction they had taken but confused as to what suburbs they passed through, his mind raced to work out a way to find out one, her name, and two, the information that had caused Liam to disappear.

The Falcon pulled up outside a block of old red-brick flats. The blonde got out, swung a small bag onto her shoulder, and waited at the low fence for Rogan to park. She then began walking along the path at the side of the building. Rogan caught up to her as she rounded the corner and went into an internal stairwell. When they reached the top of the stairs she picked a key from the set in her hand and stuck it in the lock of the first door.

Rogan followed her into a living room that promised concussion to the proverbial swinging cat. Even the two cloth armchairs and timber coffee table appeared to be snuggling together to escape being crushed by the walls. The blonde must have seen Rogan's expression. 'It's only a bedsit,' she snapped. 'Freelance journos don't make the same kind of money as lawyers and private investigators.'

She moved into the kitchen, where two chairs and a small table took up the tiny floor space left by benches, stove and refrigerator. To the side there was a partitioned alcove that Rogan thought must masquerade as a bedroom, and a door that led into a bathroom.

'Coffee or tea?' the blonde asked as she plonked her bag on the table, switched on an electric kettle and reached into a cupboard for mugs.

'Coffee's fine, thanks. Milk, one sugar.' Rogan glanced around, desperately seeking something to give him a clue to her name. Several unopened letters sat at one end of the table, and he edged casually around, trying to read the details on the front. The first letter was addressed to C Otten. Halfway there, he thought, and 'accidentally' bumped the stack. As the top letter fell to the side and revealed her full name on the next, he breathed his relief.

With a nonchalance he was far from feeling, Rogan slid onto one of the vinyl-seated metal chairs. 'So tell me, Carly, have you come across any other leads?'

Carly Otten shook her head. 'I've been keeping an eye on the sister and uncle since you made like a magician and disappeared. As you know, Paige is between boyfriends and she doesn't seem to have much of a social life. I guess it wouldn't be easy bringing a fellow home to that mausoleum of a house and have James and George give him the once-over. And James seems to divide his time between the Institute, the family's private hospital and the Crown Casino.' She laughed, and the lines between her eyes relaxed for a moment. 'You just have to hope his losing streak at the casino doesn't extend to his medical practice, don't you.'

Rogan's mind raced. He was going to lose control of this situation unless he found out a lot of information in a hurry. One thing he'd learned in the navy – sometimes going on the offensive saved you having to dig yourself out of the shit when you were floundering.

He picked up the mug of coffee Carly placed in front of him and pretended to be deep in thought for a moment. 'Carly,' he looked at her. 'I think I must have missed something. There must be a clue I'm not seeing. Tell me everything you know about the Montgomery family and especially Breeanna.'

'Hell, Liam, we've gone through this before. But,' she flicked her hand up, 'if it will help. George Montgomery, wealthy doctor, builds research facility after his first wife dies of cancer four months after their daughter, Breeanna, is born.

Remarries when Breeanna is two years old. Second wife gives birth to Paige, then divorces George five years later and moves to Perth with the child. George sticks Breeanna in boarding school during the week, has her home on weekends.'

Rogan waited silently as Carly took a sip of her coffee before continuing.

'Breeanna Montgomery. Thirty-three years old. Did two years of university, took two years off to travel the world. Not,' Carly punctured the air with her forefinger, 'as you might expect someone with her money would do – you know, luxury hotels, guided tours, etc – but bloody backpacking to some of the most miserable places on earth, like Delhi.'

'Doing the rebel bit, was she?'

Carly frowned. 'I don't know. From what I can gather she was a fairly solitary child, had few friends, but never went wild like some teenagers. Anyway, when she returned she finished uni and joined the family firm. A couple of years ago she moved out of the family mausoleum into the house her grandparents had owned.'

There was something disquieting in the picture Carly was painting. Growing up in a large, loving family, Rogan could only guess how the motherless Breeanna must have felt about being pushed into boarding school at such a young age. 'Did Breeanna see much of her stepmother and sister after the divorce?'

'School holidays, apparently. Which brings us to Paige. She visited her father in Melbourne each year, and two years ago also joined the family firm in a secretarial capacity.'

'Breeanna and Paige, how did they get along?'

'From what I've found out, reasonably well. But perhaps Paige is making sure she doesn't miss out on the Montgomery millions.'

Rogan thought about Paige's reaction to his question about Liam and wondered if she had anything to do with Breeanna's disappearance. 'If Breeanna died, would Paige be the only relative left to inherit?'

'Apart from James.'

'Tell me all you know about him again.'

A grim twist to the side of Carly's lips told Rogan she was swiftly losing patience with his questioning, but she resumed her profiling. 'James. Also a doctor. Went to the US, worked in a lab over there, came home, joined the rest of the family in the mausoleum and the research institute but in an administrative capacity.'

'You mentioned the family private hospital before. Does James practise there too?'

Carly faltered a moment, and Rogan saw a crack in her super journo veneer. 'I'm not sure. I think he must – he visits there a fair bit. But then, that's where the professor is hospitalised.'

Rogan remembered what Keith Reynolds had said. The professor had had an accident. 'How's his condition?'

'How you'd expect for someone who had a stroke then got thrown from his car and snapped his neck – lousy.' Carly's tolerance was clearly at an end. 'Now tell me,' she pushed her empty mug aside and leaned towards Rogan, 'did you really not find Breeanna?'

It was a relief to answer truthfully. 'No.'

'Damn. I need that interview. I have bills to pay.'

She stretched back in the chair and put her hands behind her head. The knit top pulled tight over her breasts, and Rogan's next question flew from his mind. He'd had more than enough experience with women to know that Carly was deliberately using her very ample charms to excite his interest, and he wondered if she had been sleeping with

Liam. A dismaying thought struck him. Surely Carly wasn't the person Liam had said was the woman of his dreams? Then sanity reasserted itself. If Carly and Liam had had any more interaction than that of business associates, she wouldn't have had to wait for Rogan to follow her into her flat – she would have expected him to know where to go. And Rogan knew that Liam would never take a new woman home to his unit, especially a woman he was seeing in a work capacity.

He leaned back, moving his hands from his mug. As he did so, his elbow knocked Carly's bag to the floor and the contents spilled across the vinyl. 'Sorry,' he muttered, and bent over to pick them up. Carly slid from her chair to the floor at the same time, and their hands met over her opened wallet. As Carly scrabbled to grab it before he did, Rogan noticed the photo behind a plastic cover inside.

'Nice-looking kid,' he commented on the miniature version of Carly in the photo. 'Your daughter?'

Pain flickered briefly in her eyes and she quickly gathered the wallet, notepad, pen and tissues and shoved them back in the bag. When she sat back on the chair her face was once more set in the self-contained, almost hard, expression she'd worn since he'd met her. But Rogan was intrigued. He had caught a glimpse of vulnerability that seemed at odds with her brash, confrontational manner. Perhaps she wasn't quite the pain in the arse she appeared to be.

Before he could explore the idea further, his mobile phone rang.

The surveillance camera refocused from the back of Carly Otten's head to the face of Rogan McKay as he spoke on his mobile phone.

Vaughn Waring watched intently. It was interesting to see Rogan McKay pretending to be his twin. Hopefully the man's deception would lead to the revelation of Breeanna Montgomery's hiding place. But failing that, they might discover where Liam McKay had been taken. Vaughn had a gut feeling that Liam had found the woman, and if so, it wouldn't take much to persuade him to tell them. Vaughn's methods were far more refined than the two thugs' had obviously been. And a lot more effective.

Rogan snapped his mobile phone back onto his belt and got to his feet. 'I have to go,' he told Carly Otten.

'You've got a lead,' she accused.

Rogan realised she was trying to force him off-balance so he would reveal the contents of the call. Before he could reply, she stood up and grabbed her shoulder bag. 'I'm coming with you.'

'You're not.' Hell, he didn't need her finding out he wasn't Liam. Not yet. She might still be useful for extracting information.

Smiling, she dangled her car keys. 'Then I'll follow you.' The smile dropped. 'Liam, you're not going to shake me this time. I need this interview. I need the money it will bring me. The newspapers and the mags will pay well for the story of the disappearance of an heiress, especially as she comes from one of Melbourne's most prominent families.' A fleeting desperation touched her eyes. 'If we work as a team we'll have a much better chance of finding Breeanna. And I have a lot of contacts you don't have.'

The truth of her words hit Rogan. He had no access to any of Liam's connections, and his knowledge of Melbourne and its citizens wasn't extensive, certainly not like Carly's. Perhaps he could utilise her knowledge, but keep her in the dark as much as possible. With Liam's life possibly at stake, he wasn't about to throw away any contact that could prove helpful. Even one as annoying as Carly. 'All right. You can come with me on the condition that you do what I tell you. No arguing.'

'Agreed. Now, what have you found out?'

Rogan didn't answer as he walked out the door.

Rogan thanked his lucky stars that he had a keen sense of direction. He'd visited Melbourne a few times over the years and had a fair idea how to get back to Keith Reynolds' office from Carly's bedsit.

Half an hour later he realised that in battling the now peak-hour traffic, he'd overshot the Moorabbin street by two blocks. But then he figured that wasn't such a bad thing because he didn't want Carly to know his destination. At the moment he didn't know who he could trust, so the fewer people who knew what he was doing, the better.

He parked the Rodeo, told Carly to get out, and locked the doors. Having her wait in his vehicle and poke around in his glovebox wouldn't be a wise move either. At a cafe further up the street he told her to wait there until he returned. By the time he walked into Keith's office he was sure she hadn't followed him.

The receptionist had gone and Keith was standing at her desk, glancing through paperwork. As the front door swung closed, he walked over and locked it behind Rogan. 'Come into my office.'

He motioned for Rogan to follow him behind his desk,

then sat down and typed a password into his computer. A few keystrokes later, he gestured for Rogan to look at the screen. As Rogan read the statements listed there, he heard Keith cracking his knuckles in measured beats. After a few minutes he looked at Keith.

'Where did you get this?'

'I didn't want to tell you on the phone, just in case someone could overhear,' Keith explained. 'My partner's away on holidays, but I phoned him this afternoon about a case I've been handling for him, and I mentioned what had happened to Liam. That's when he told me that Liam had come into the office about a week ago and asked if we could hold this CD for him. I was in court at the time, and my partner was flying out that afternoon, so he told Liam he'd put the CD in the safe in his office.'

Rogan looked back at the screen. 'Should I give this to the police?'

Keith didn't reply immediately, and Rogan guessed he'd placed him in an ethical dilemma.

'It's up to you,' Keith finally said.

'Well, it certainly appears as though Bruin isn't making any effort to find Liam, so I can't see any point in handing it over.' He was quiet for a minute, his worry for Liam churning up a notch. 'I'll have to follow it up myself.'

Keith nodded. His eyes were sombre. 'I was hoping you'd say that.'

'Just keep it in your safe for me, would you?' Rogan asked, and turned to leave. At the door he stopped. 'Do you know anything about a Carly Otten?'

Eyebrows knitting together, Keith cracked another sonata of knuckles. 'There's something familiar about the name. Should I know her?'

Quickly, Rogan related his run-in with Carly. Face clearing, Keith snapped his fingers.

'Of course! Investigative journalist. One of the best in Melbourne several years ago, but ended up in rehab with a severe alcohol problem. Husband divorced her, won custody of the child. Haven't heard of her for years.'

Pieces of Carly's puzzle now falling into place, Rogan said his thanks and left the office.

As he walked back to the cafe where he'd left Carly, Rogan debated the pros and cons of ditching her and following the lead by himself. Where he was going he didn't need her Melbourne knowledge, and he'd prefer to work alone.

But he finally decided he'd let her think she was going to work with him, just to throw her off the track.

CHAPTER SIX

The pall of cigarette smoke hadn't yet reached its usual nightly proportions as Frank Delano finished his inspection of the bar and lumbered into his office.

Doggie was waiting for him, not sitting in the spare chair like anyone else would have, but leaning against a filing cabinet as though he couldn't stand upright without a prop. It irked Frank more than usual and he shoved past, causing Doggie's eyes to open to an uncharacteristic fullness.

'What have you got for me?' Frank barked.

'Nothin', boss. The Montgomery woman's still missing, and there's no word back on who the blokes were who shot me mate. Don't know whether they've gone to ground or they're just so good we can't find 'em.'

Frank had come to that same conclusion. The more he'd thought about it, the more he'd realised they appeared to be dealing with people who were different from the professional criminals he knew.

'Pity about the private dick,' Doggie added.

'I didn't know he had a bad heart,' Frank growled. 'Do you still have someone watching the professor's house?'

'Yeah. But nothin's happened there. The wife goes to the hospital every day, stays home every night. A few visitors, not many. The old guy mustn't have been very sociable.'

Mrs Raymond's day-long visits to the hospital straight after her husband's accident had provided Frank with ample time to search their house. A thorough, non-intrusive search, not the furniture-destroying procedure they'd carried out on Liam McKay's place. But by the time McKay had arrived back in town, Frank's patience had worn too thin for prudence.

It had been easy for Frank to find out the private investigator's real name and address. Doggie had followed Paige Montgomery when she met with McKay, and it was a simple matter to note his vehicle registration details and pay for the information.

But with McKay out of the way, Frank had no leads left to follow, and the frustration was eating at him.

When his phone rang, he thumped his meaty hand down on the receiver as though it were the source of all his annoyance, but his frown lessened slightly as he listened to the relieved voice on the other end.

'We have a new player,' he said to Doggie as he replaced the receiver. 'McKay's identical twin brother is in Melbourne searching for him.' He scribbled on a notepad, ripped off the sheet and handed it to Doggie. 'That's his vehicle and the rego. First thing in the morning I want you to check out McKay's unit and any other place he might look for his brother. When you find him, follow him.'

Doggie levered his body from the cabinet and took the

piece of paper. 'Okay, boss.' His shoulder did its independent shrug. 'Any idea what he looks like?'

Frank wondered what the current sentence was for mercy killing.

'Do you have a relative you could go and stay with?' Rogan placed his hand on Janey Dearmoth's bony shoulder. Although not exceptionally tall, Rogan towered over the tiny ex-schoolteacher, and he was extremely concerned about her vulnerability. 'I don't want you staying here on your own. Whoever hurt Liam could think you know something and come after you.' Even though Bruin hadn't contacted him to confirm the blood on the carpet was Liam's, Rogan was sure it was.

'I'm not afraid, Rogan. At my age dying isn't the threat it once was. And if they thought I knew anything they'd have paid me a visit before now. I'm more worried about Liam.' She looked up into his eyes. 'It doesn't look good, does it?'

Rogan couldn't answer her. Saying the words would be too painful, and he hadn't given up hope yet. He glanced around Janey's living room at the mementos of a lifetime of caring for other people's children – class and school photos, wedding photos of former students, others with their children. In the corner of one bookshelf, a sepia portrait of a young man in air force uniform, World War II vintage.

Janey followed his gaze. Her face softened. 'We were to be married on his next leave. He never came back from New Guinea.' She squared her shoulders and turned away, gesturing for Rogan to follow her back to the dining room. 'Now, tell me what was on that CD of Liam's.' She held up a placatory hand. 'I realise you think it's better for my own protection that

I don't know, but sometimes it helps to discuss it and get another viewpoint.'

To Rogan's surprise, Janey took two glasses and a bottle of port from an old-fashioned china cabinet. She placed the glasses on the table, poured a generous nip into each and sat down.

With reluctance, Rogan followed suit. The port was excellent, gliding smooth and rich over his tongue.

'Apparently, Liam hires a woman to do research for him in cases where it's better for a female to ask probing questions. She sends the info to him by encrypted emails so it's secure. Liam had bombed out when he'd inquired at Breeanna's high school about any friends she would have made there, so he asked this research assistant to try her primary school. It seems one teacher remembered that Breeanna had been very friendly with another student, but her parents moved to Queensland when the girl was twelve. On a hunch, the researcher tracked this girl down. She's married to a grazier in Central Queensland. Her details were included in the report.'

'And you think Liam went looking for her?'

'The CD contained all Liam's notes on the case so far, including the email from the researcher, and it looked as though he'd had no luck with any other leads he'd followed. Breeanna had, quite literally, disappeared. She had a small circle of friends, but none of them had seen her for several weeks. And the cruncher is, when Liam searched through Breeanna's house, he found a box of Christmas cards that were a few years old, and one of them was signed with the same Christian name of Breeanna's old school friend.'

'So you're going to Queensland to see this woman?'

Rogan nodded. 'If I find Breeanna I might find Liam. His disappearance mightn't be connected to her case, but it's the only lead I have. I'd prefer to fly to save time, but the only flight west from Brisbane is booked out for the next two days.'

'And this Carly Otten, the one who says she was helping Liam, do you trust her?'

'I don't know who to trust, Janey. I told her I'd pick her up tomorrow morning, but I'll leave here at 3 a.m. That way I'll miss the peak-hour traffic and be in New South Wales before she knows I've left her behind.'

'If she really was working with Liam,' Janey said, 'she might be able to help you. Investigative journalists usually have contacts within the police force and government agencies that you may need. If this lead is another failure, where do you go then? She might be the only person who can help you.'

Janey was right. But he'd made his decision, and besides, he told himself, if this led him to Liam, he didn't want to drag Carly into any danger.

Ten minutes later, as he headed off to the spare bedroom to snatch a few hours sleep, Janey said, 'When Liam moved into his unit four years ago, I didn't believe him when he told me he was an insurance salesman.'

Rogan paused, curious. 'Why not?'

'Because he never tried to sell me a policy,' she smiled.

It was a practice Rogan had perfected in the navy. No matter what time he told himself to wake up, he was never more than a few minutes out.

At 3 a.m. he woke from a deep sleep and got up. In the bathroom he splashed cold water on his face and went to the toilet. A minute later he closed Janey's front door behind him and walked to where he'd left his Rodeo in Liam's driveway.

His face tingled in the crisp cold air that still held a

lingering hint of apple blossom. A streetlight broke the darkness further up the footpath, and trees in the adjoining property played shadows over his vehicle. He pressed his remote, the Rodeo's lights flashed and he heard the faint unlocking sound. With a swift yank, he opened the back door and threw his duffle bag onto the seat.

A muffled yell of surprise startled him as much as the jerking mound of blanket revealed by the interior light. Carly's blonde hair emerged from beneath the duffle bag.

'What the hell are you doing here?' Rogan growled.

Carly rubbed the back of her knuckles across her eyes. 'I learned years ago to follow my hunches. Looks like I was right again.'

'Did your hunch also tell you that I'm going to haul you out of there and leave you on the footpath?'

For the first time since Rogan had met her, Carly was silent. She sat, the fallen blanket revealing a blue sweatshirt that moulded closer than sweatshirts were supposed to, and gazed at him with something akin to fear in her eyes.

'The doors were locked,' he said. 'How did you get in?'

Pink tinged her cheeks. 'I've learned a few tricks over the years.'

Rogan remembered that rehab centres weren't only for alcoholics. She could have learned other tricks that he didn't want to be the victim of. 'Out!' he demanded.

'Please, Liam.'

The words were soft, and Rogan saw her throat work, as though she wasn't used to asking favours. Her unwilling show of weakness made him hesitate. It was easier to be blunt with her when she was in her super journo persona. He waited.

'I . . .' she cleared her throat, 'I don't get many opportunities like this. I have a very important reason for needing this interview.' She stopped and waited, obviously hoping that Rogan would say something, but he stayed silent. 'I need to prove,' she resumed, 'that I can write like I used to.' The breath sagged out of her. 'I've been out of the industry for a while. This interview will gain me some credibility. Some kudos.'

Damn, but she was making it hard for him. 'Is that all?' he asked.

The look she flung him said he was the devil and did she have to sell him her soul to get what she wanted, but she whispered now, as though almost afraid to say the words, 'I need my daughter to respect me again.'

If she had said 'love', Rogan would have assured her that kids love their parents no matter what, but he thought of his mother, of the esteem in which he held her, and realised just how much Carly had lost. Now that she was climbing her way back from the alcoholic pit Keith had said she'd been in, he didn't want to be the one to kick her back down. But he sure as hell wasn't going to tell her anything until she absolutely needed to know it.

'Put your seat belt on,' he muttered, closing the door. 'I don't want the cops giving us a fine.'

He opened the driver's door and got in. Carly scrambled across into the front passenger seat. 'Thanks,' she murmured, then some of her previous manner surfaced. 'This lead of yours better be good.'

'Give me any trouble, Carly,' he growled, 'and you'll be sitting on the road so fast you won't have time to get gravel rash.'

She stayed silent, and Rogan prayed she would go back to sleep.

*

They'd driven into New South Wales by the time the sun dispersed the snatches of mist still clinging to the night-damp ground. Carly had slept for long stretches, waking only briefly when street and building lights flickered over her face as they drove through country towns.

Rogan had occasionally glanced at her, noting the lines around her still-young mouth, the darkness under her eyes that make-up hadn't successfully concealed. He guessed her age to be around thirty-five, the same as his, and it made him question how much she had lost and how desperately she would fight to get it all back.

Since they'd crossed the mountains north of Melbourne and passed through the lush orchard country of Shepparton, the terrain had slowly changed to flat plains sweeping towards the horizon. Sheep grazing behind wire fences had given way to small herds of cattle cropping the highway's edges and milling across the bitumen in search of more feed on the other side.

Motorcycles and utilities had become the modern drover's transport of choice, though some still rode on horseback as they tried to keep the cattle moving to prevent them stripping the vegetation to its roots. Here and there hastily erected one-strand electric fences kept the cattle from straying into prohibited territory. Not that they'd find much feed on the other side of the fence, Rogan thought. The drought had eaten into the land, creating dust from pastures, leaving bones where animals once fed contentedly.

Rogan silently cursed the delays. It was more than twenty-four hours since he'd found the destruction in Liam's apartment, and his anxiety increased with each passing hour. The aching sense of loss still sat in his gut like a rock. He dreaded the effect on his family if Liam were dead. His own pain would be unbearable, but he was more afraid for his mother. He'd seen how Ewan's death had devastated her.

His Rodeo was a work vehicle and not as comfortable as a sedan, but to his surprise, Carly complained only a little, even giving him an occasional break from the driving. The Rodeo's airconditioning eased the heat brought by an October sun, and he took the opportunity to doze while Carly drove the route he'd directed her.

Their breaks were few, food and toilet stops mainly, and they approached the Queensland border as rose pink streaked a cloudless blue sky that was swiftly changing to grey.

'Liam, I'm stuffed,' Carly said. 'I need a shower and I need to sleep in a horizontal position.' They drove through the tiny town of Boggabilla, and she pointed her thumb to an old hotel on a corner. 'That's how my legs are going to feel when I finally get out of this rattle-trap.'

Rogan looked at the pub, and laughed at the name emblazoned on the front – *The Wobbly Boot*. His bones felt far too stiff to be wobbly. His lifestyle was normally an active one, but he'd spent a great deal of time behind a steering wheel in the past seventy-two hours. He needed a run and a swim as much as he needed a good night's sleep.

Last night he'd consulted his maps and memorised the route he needed to take, and he figured they now had about three hundred and fifty kilometres left to reach their destination. He glanced at his watch. No point driving there in darkness. He'd been lucky not to encounter any kangaroos on the road when he'd driven down to Melbourne, and he didn't want to take the risk of hitting one now.

'We'll stop at a motel in Goondiwindi and get a meal and a decent night's sleep,' he said.

'You paying?'

If her bedsit was any indication, Rogan thought, Carly was barely keeping above the poverty line. 'Yes,' he replied, 'but don't expect the Hilton. I can't afford it.'

Carly looked at the flat, sparsely vegetated country on either side of the vehicle. 'I don't think we're likely to find one here,' she said dryly. Stretching back into the seat, she added, 'As long as the bed's not lumpy.'

Rogan asked for twin beds but had to settle for a room with a double and a single bed. He didn't know if Carly had any ideas about them sharing a bed, but he had no intention of complicating the situation by sleeping with her. Especially as she thought he was Liam. Before he could offer her the double bed, she threw her overnight bag on the single. 'If I get first shower,' she said, 'I'll shout dinner.'

'Steak with the trimmings?'

She unzipped her bag and laughed, and it was the first genuine warmth Rogan had seen from her.

'More like steak burgers,' she said.

Carly bought steak burgers, chips and soft drinks from a nearby cafe while Rogan had his shower. He fancied a cold beer, but knew he'd feel a real bastard drinking in front of her when she was trying to stay sober.

To his relief, she made no attempts to prise any information out of him about where they were going.

To her relief, she discovered he didn't snore.

CHAPTER SEVEN

Breeanna's school friend had managed to make contact with one of the medical institutions George Montgomery was visiting in the United States, only to discover that he had left that morning for Europe and his hotel destination was unknown.

Now Breeanna stood, watching moonlight turn the nearby white cliffs to silver. She hugged her jacket closer, cutting out the chill that seeped through the bush, quieting all but the nocturnal creatures.

In a way, she was ashamed of herself for running away, but it had seemed her only option at the time. She'd spent the past couple of weeks writing down everything that could possibly give her a clue to what had forced the professor to resort to such a bizarre act as destroying his laboratory computer hard drive, and what records he had that made people want to kill to get them. Nothing they were working on at the laboratory had reached a stage remarkable enough for anyone to want to steal. The professor's implication that James and Paige were to blame had seemed equally astounding. Perhaps when she was finally able to make contact with her father she would be able to sort out this terrible mess she found herself in. Relying on other people . . .

A twig snapped, startling her, and she had to stop herself from running back along the track. She waited quietly, and eventually heard the sound of a small animal shuffling through the undergrowth. She sighed her relief, and let the tension ease from her body.

Her eyelids felt heavy, and she hoped she might finally be tired enough to sleep. She switched her torch on and turned around.

Rogan and Carly left early the next morning and headed north. As Rogan drove, he ran through Liam's reports in his mind, trying to think of anything there that could give him a clue to what had happened to him. When his brother Ewan had been murdered, Rogan had tried to find the killer, and had ended up helping an undercover cop named Chayse Jarrett to accomplish that. But Rogan knew his skills were not the kind that were needed now. He lacked the patience and subtlety that were Liam's stock-in-trade, as well as the knowledge of where to go to track down records and specific information.

In the end he decided that a woman with Carly's attributes might be an asset in ferreting out such information. And he wasn't just thinking about her investigative skills.

Several hours later they reached the town of Miles, and turned left onto the Warrego Highway, a long, straight sliver of bitumen surrounded by open plains and lined with scruffy trees and huge orange-flowering prickly pear. Scattered along the highway were enormous concrete grain silos, shimmering in the heat like monoliths from a bygone era. Fields of grain gave way to grazing plains and small towns with names like Dulacca and Wallumbilla. Rogan wondered at the origin of what seemed to be Aboriginal place names, and his mouth curved in a smile when he remembered one of the towns further west was named Muckadilla. It sounded like the sort of strife he and Liam would have landed in as kids.

On their way into Roma, they passed the Big Rig, a tourist attraction commemorating the discovery of Australia's first gas and oil. 'Didn't they discover gas here by accident?' he asked Carly.

'They were drilling for water,' she said, then grumbled, 'with my luck, I would have hit the sewage run-off.'

Rogan glanced at her, expecting to see a smile that would indicate she was joking, but her mouth was set in a morose line. He wondered if her soft centre would be any easier to reveal than that of the prickly pear, but he didn't fancy trying.

His problem now was finding Breeanna's school friend. He doubted that Liam would have phoned her first – he'd once told Rogan it was better to catch people face to face and unawares: that way he could tell if they were lying. Rogan's map had shown the names of many of the area's grazing properties, but not the one he needed to find.

When he stopped for fuel he asked the attendant, but she had only recently moved into the area and didn't know.

As he drove away, Carly said, 'Let's grab some lunch.' Her brusque tone indicated that her mood appeared to be deteriorating, and Rogan felt a flash of impatience. Letting her tag along hadn't been in his original plan, and he was beginning to wonder if she'd played on his sympathy to convince him to let her come.

Roma had the easygoing atmosphere of many country towns. Its buildings were a mix of old timber and new brick or concrete, and traffic moved slowly through the wide streets. Halfway up a block on McDowall Street, Rogan spotted a sign that said 'Irish McGann's Hotel'. 'Counter lunch suit you?' he asked Carly, and was pleased when she nodded. A pub was often a good place to gain information. There was usually a loquacious local drinking in the bar who could be relied on to tell you what you needed to know.

The hotel's cool, high-ceilinged interior was a relief from the midday heat, and they walked through to the lounge with its wooden chairs and tables and huge flat-screen television playing a re-run of *Lord of the Dance*. The lively Irish music was soft enough to be enjoyable, but loud enough to seep under your skin and make your foot want to tap in rhythm. Carly looked around. 'I'd rather sit in the dining area.' She indicated the white-clothed tables in the adjoining room.

Rogan would have preferred the lounge, with its collection of Irish memorabilia sitting on shelves and propped against the smoky-timbered walls. Stern-faced women in black dresses peered down from several black-and-white photo portraits, contrasting with smiling colleens on old-time musical posters. A piano accordion and a fiddle on a table looked as though they had been laid aside so the players could refresh themselves with a quick ale. His parents would love the place, Rogan thought.

After he'd ordered and paid for their meals, Rogan walked into the bar. With more than half the men there dressed in jeans and check shirts, riding boots and Akubras, he felt confident that someone would be able to give him the information he needed. He ordered a beer and a soda water from the sprightly grey-haired barman, leaned on the padded leather arm rest, and turned his attention to the sinewy man sitting on a stool next to him. After a couple of minutes he realised that his attempts at conversation were gaining him no more than the odd laconic monosyllable, so he quickly finished his beer, picked up Carly's drink, and walked back to the dining area.

Carly had gone to find the ladies' toilet, and thirst and impatience had Rogan walking back to the bar for another beer. He walked back to the bar for a refill.

'Just passing through?' the barman asked as he placed the icy glass in front of Rogan.

'I'm looking for the Kinnetty property.' Rogan took a mouthful of beer and smiled in appreciation. He'd barely tasted the first glass. 'Can you tell me where it is?'

'Of course I can,' came the reply.

CHAPTER EIGHT

Janey Dearmoth peered through a tiny gap in her living room curtains.

Normally she wouldn't consider herself a stickybeak, but since becoming aware of Liam's disappearance she had kept a close watch on the comings and goings in her quiet street. Four times yesterday the same car had driven slowly past, and today it had come back twice.

Although she knew Rogan had placed little hope in Sergeant Bruin being able to find Liam, Janey still had an old-fashioned respect for and faith in the police force. With a determined tread, she walked over to the antique stand that held her phone and picked up the detective's card.

Carly tapped her foot impatiently. The smell of beer and spirits had tantalised her as she and Rogan had walked into the hotel, and she'd deliberately chosen to sit in the dining area to be as far away from temptation as possible.

So much depended on how well she handled herself. She wasn't about to ruin her best chance in years of getting back into the big time. But her craving for a drink was almost unbearable. In desperation she gulped down the last of the soda water. Wet it might have been, but it couldn't match the glorious intoxicating warmth that alcohol would spread through her veins. She pushed the memory aside.

Carly had learned years ago that an ability to bend the truth, if not the ability to lie outright, could gain her more than sticking to the facts, but she felt strangely uncomfortable about lying on this job. Perhaps winning back her daughter's respect meant she first had to find her own.

Rogan was tempted to leave Carly in the pub and go to the Kinnetty property alone. If Liam had made contact with Breeanna's school friend, Rogan would have to reveal he wasn't Liam, and he didn't want to do that in front of Carly. Her moodiness made it difficult to gauge how she would react, and he didn't want to risk alienating her. Although he didn't completely trust her, at this stage she was the only link he had to Liam.

He showed Carly the beer coaster with the barman's directions written on it. 'As soon as we eat we'll drive out and see if this woman knows where Breeanna Montgomery is. But I want you to stay in the car.'

'Why?'

'She might open up to one person, but I doubt she would tell a journalist anything.'

'She doesn't have to know I'm a journalist.'

'You wouldn't be able to help yourself, Carly. You'd interrogate her the moment you walked in the door.'

Carly flung him a dirty look, but reluctantly nodded her agreement.

The call came when Breeanna was cleaning the last room on her roster. She pulled her cloth hat down so that only the bottom half of her face was clearly visible and hurried out, locking the cabin door on her way. Thirty timber cabins with canvas upper walls were scattered through the resort and connected by pathways back to the building that housed the restaurant, shop and office.

A small grey kangaroo moved in indolent hops across the cement path, then sprawled in the dust under a shady tree. Her chest tightening with apprehension, Breeanna lengthened her stride. Although the message had said the call was urgent, she didn't want to draw attention to herself by running.

The sound of childish laughter from the swimming pool sparked a momentary envy, and she took a handkerchief from her shorts pocket and wiped the perspiration from her face. She skipped lightly up the steps onto the verandah, walked through the bar adjoining the restaurant and into the office. The manager handed her the phone, smiled, and walked into the small shop beside the reception area.

'Yes,' Breeanna breathed into the phone. She concentrated on the rapid flow of words from the caller, and closed her eyes as they formed pictures in her mind. Was it possible? Was she responsible for another death? What worried her now was the danger she had probably placed her friend in by asking for her help. She had to deflect that possibility.

'Send him out here,' she said. 'Tell him to book into the Lodge and wait for me to contact him.'

She heard the concern in the reply. 'Don't worry. I can

look after myself,' she said, 'but I am worried about you. Could you take the kids and visit your sister at the coast for a while?'

Relief flowed through her at the affirmative reply.

'How much further do we have to go now?'

Carly was clearly becoming impatient, and Rogan had to admit he didn't blame her. Finding the Kinnetty property hadn't been as easy as he'd thought. He'd forgotten that a country kilometre didn't always equate to a city kilometre. Perhaps the barman should have described the distance as 'as the crow flies', Rogan thought, then he would have realised just how far off the main road they had needed to go.

'The turnoff is about an hour's drive from Injune.'

'The turnoff to where?'

'Carnarvon Gorge.'

Carly spun around to face him. 'Is that where she's hiding?'

'The woman at Kinnetty told me to book in at the Carnarvon Gorge Wilderness Lodge and wait until Breeanna contacts me.' Rogan glanced at her. There was a predatory gleam in her eyes that he found a little unnerving. Whatever determination had made her a top investigative journalist hadn't been extinguished by her alcoholism.

North of Roma the countryside had changed, becoming undulating, with brush box trees varying the constant eucalypts, then back to flat clay plains. Emus were everywhere, picking their way through the dry creek beds, foraging for food, standing on the road and reluctantly giving way to traffic with their defiant, unblinking stare. Unlike kangaroos, the emus had featured rarely in the numerous roadkills Rogan passed.

As they approached Injune, they could see several mountain ranges on their left. They stopped at the Information Centre for coffee, and Rogan picked up brochures on the Gorge. His navy training might ensure he never went into a situation unprepared, he thought, but knowing the territory was only half of it. He had no idea what meeting Breeanna Montgomery would bring, but he hoped it would lead him to Liam. He took out the photo Paige had given him. Breeanna's dark eyes seemed to stare into his as though assessing his worth, and he had the oddest sensation that she might find him wanting.

The road cut through hills now, some ravaged by bushfires, the new growth on the trees vibrant against the blackened trunks.

When they turned onto the Gorge road the sun was lower in the sky and glared through the windscreen. Strange, stick-like trees grew in the fields on either side, and cattle grazed on the flat plains. In the distance lay huge mountain ranges, blue with eucalyptus haze and what Rogan thought might be smoke.

As they drove closer to the Gorge, it was as though they were entering an enormous funnel. There was something primeval about the land here, as if its spirit breathed under the dirt and in the craggy cliffs that drew them with the force of a magnet. Rogan felt his pulse quicken. He was not given to flights of fancy, but the feeling that something momentous was going to happen seeped through him.

He glanced at his mobile phone in its holder on the dashboard and frowned. No signal. He didn't like being out of range in case news came of Liam and he couldn't be contacted.

Brolgas shared paddocks with Brahman cattle, the vegetation got thicker, then they were in the National Park. The road changed to dirt, crossed creek beds, dipped down gullies, and was interspersed with cattle grids. And all the while Rogan tried to shake the feeling that had settled on his spine like a clamp.

CHAPTER NINE

It was easy for Breeanna to observe Rogan and the woman with him. In her staff uniform she blended in, becoming part of an established situation, expected and therefore overlooked.

A conference was being held at the Lodge and most of the cabins were occupied. Breeanna was pleased to see Rogan had been allocated one of the cabins closest to the road. It would make it easier for her to watch him. While he and the woman were putting their gear in the cabin, she went to the reception desk and checked the details he'd given. When she saw his signature and credit card details, a relieved smile hovered at the corners of her mouth. Still, until she heard his story, she wasn't going to trust him. Perhaps not even then.

She walked back to the staff quarters – demountable buildings set several hundred metres on the other side of the road from the resort. Her room was small, with a single bed, wardrobe and desk, but at least she had privacy. As she showered and changed into shorts and a blouse, she debated where and when she should talk to Rogan. The woman with him was an unexpected problem. Breeanna's friend hadn't mentioned her presence, but . . . Damn, it was getting more complicated.

Still with no plan formulated, she tied a scarf around her thick dark hair and returned to the resort. The sun was setting, but its heat still hung heavy in the air. She bought a drink and sat on the roofed deck outside the bar. From that vantage point she could observe a fair section of the resort, but in particular she could keep watch on Rogan's cabin.

A rustling in the adjacent bush garden had her glancing over. An echidna lumbered over the log surrounds, its slender snout seeking insects to devour. A piece of bark dislodged under its claws, and the spiny mammal tumbled onto the grass, rolling into a ball to protect its soft underbelly. Then, with a decidedly huffy twitch of its spines, it scuttled back into the safety of the garden. Breeanna felt her lips curve in an involuntary smile, and she realised laughter had become a rare thing for her in the past couple of weeks.

The conference activities were late finishing, and she was grateful. Normally by this time of the day the tables were crowded, and she kept away, savouring the isolation of her room in the staff quarters or walking one of the tracks around the resort.

After a few minutes, she saw Rogan's companion leave the cabin, a towel draped around her shoulders. Breeanna expected her to head straight for the swimming pool, but instead she walked around to the public phone in front of the reception office.

If the area wasn't so open, Breeanna would have been tempted to get closer and listen to her conversation. The woman spoke swiftly, almost urgently, glancing about as she did, and hung up with a brief smile. She walked back to the pool inside a fenced-off area, slipped off her shorts and blouse, and lowered herself into the pool. Breeanna raised an eyebrow at the skimpy bikini and what it revealed, and wondered at her relationship with Rogan. A keen observer of body language, Breeanna hadn't seen any affection between the two, but she knew not all couples overtly displayed their attachment. She was about to stand up when Rogan walked down the path to the pool, his sneakers, jeans and T-shirt making it obvious that he wasn't joining the woman.

He stood at the gate, watching her as she swam lazily. Then she stepped from the pool, and Breeanna saw Rogan's reaction as his gaze followed the luscious curves. The woman bent over to pick up her towel from a chair, the movement deliberately exposing the swell of her breasts to Rogan's gaze. Breeanna could see his arousal, the tension in his body. Without a word to the woman, he turned and walked away. The woman mouthed something Breeanna couldn't hear, wrapped the towel around her body and walked back towards the cabin.

To Breeanna's surprise, Rogan didn't follow her, but strode past the deck where she sat, and walked swiftly up the road. He'd almost reached the resort boundary when he stopped abruptly. He kicked at a rock, then turned around and came back. When she saw he was making for the deck, Breeanna rose swiftly and walked into the shop.

Rogan's temper had been sparked by Carly's deliberate attempt to arouse him. She might be attractive, and under other circumstances he might possibly be willing, but at the moment he didn't need the complication of a sexual relationship with her. He was already on edge with worry about Liam.

Once in the cabin Carly had told him she was going for a swim. He was surprised she didn't want to wait with him for Breeanna to make contact – after all, wasn't this the scoop she needed to get her career back? But she'd just shrugged and said she wouldn't be gone long. After a while he'd begun to get suspicious, and went down to the pool to check on her.

Now he took a long swig of his rum and Coke and wondered what kind of game she was playing. Her mood swings over the past two days he'd put down to the strain of her situation, but that hadn't made them any easier to cope with; he wondered again if he'd done the right thing in letting her come with him. He also wondered how Breeanna was going to make contact with him. When he'd checked in he'd asked the receptionist to let him know the minute any messages came in. Rogan looked at his watch. He guessed it wouldn't hurt to check, just in case.

He finished his drink, stood up, and walked around to the front steps. Before he could open the glass front door, a woman stepped behind him and called his name.

He spun around. It took only a moment for him to realise the woman was Breeanna Montgomery.

Carly took her time in the shower. She realised she'd made a wrong move with McKay. He was attractive in a rugged sort of way, with a lean, muscular body, but the problem was she actually liked him. He was the first man who'd been kind to her in a long time and not expected something back. As her career had dived in ratio to her escalating alcoholism, she'd discovered a lot of men were happy to buy her drinks if she accommodated them sexually. Her marriage had already broken up, her daughter had chosen to live with her father, and in her haze of denial and self-pity, Carly had taken whatever comfort was offered.

Now she cursed her eagerness. In a day or two all this would be over, and she'd probably never see him again. She'd hoped . . . Not that it mattered now. The Montgomery woman would make contact, Carly would offer her the chance to put her side of the story forward, and the woman would jump at the opportunity. Especially the way Carly intended to make the offer. She'd been given the inside story on Breeanna Montgomery, and was confident she could gain the woman's trust. One good story, and she'd be back where she belonged, not forced to do the crap work that had paid the rent for the past few years. The thrill of the chase was like an adrenaline rush, and Carly felt the craving for a drink so badly her throat ached with it.

She turned off the shower and reached for a towel. Coffee, she told herself. Coffee. She had to stay sober. Her hand trembled as she wiped the water from her face. So much depended on it.

If she hadn't grabbed the verandah rail, Breeanna would have stumbled backwards. The man who stood before her was the image of his brother, but so different it had startled her. She was expecting a Liam clone, a man of deep thought and controlled emotions. But Rogan was barely suppressing the feelings that hit her with the force of a whirlwind. She'd often debated whether her ability to feel the emotions of others was a gift or a curse, but never had she felt as unsettled as she did now.

Here was a man who lived life with passion. The raw energy emanating from him was almost palpable. And so was the amazing awareness that he was responding to her on a level no other man had before. The realisation shocked her. And scared her. For the first time in her life, she felt as though someone had seen into her soul.

His eyes were blue, a brilliant piercing blue, as though he spent a lot of time searching far horizons. Now he was searching her face, seeking . . . exactly what, she wasn't sure.

'Breeanna Montgomery?'

His voice broke the silence that had engulfed them. Breeanna tried to clear her mind and focus on what she needed to say.

'Who's the woman?' The words were out before she became conscious of uttering them. It wasn't what she had intended asking first, but on a subconscious level she knew the answer was vitally important.

She felt him struggle with the words, as though he was afraid she wouldn't like his answer.

'Carly Otten. A journalist. Freelance.'

At least he was honest. And yes, she didn't like what she heard.

'Why did you bring her? I thought your only concern was finding your brother.'

'She worked with Liam in trying to find you in return for getting an interview. I thought she might be useful.'

He wasn't lying, she could sense that, but she couldn't believe Liam had agreed to allow Carly Otten access to her. A swirl of laughter and conversation interrupted her thoughts. She glanced at the mini-bus that had pulled up in the parking area close by and offloaded a group of conference attendees, and felt suddenly exposed. And vulnerable.

'Meet me at the Moss Garden in the Gorge at half past six in the morning,' she told Rogan, and saw surprise flare in his eyes. 'I can't talk to you now,' she explained. 'There's a map at the Rangers' Information Centre. Come alone, and don't tell the journalist where you're going or that I've spoken to you. If I see her there, I'll leave without telling you what you want to know.'

She walked down the steps to the ground, and paused. 'And don't follow me now.'

As Rogan watched Breeanna walk away into the quickly falling dark, he had to use every bit of self-control not to run after her and force her to tell him about Liam. Because it was only as she'd reached the road that he realised when she'd called out to him that she'd used his real name.

CHAPTER TEN

The evenings were beginning to lengthen into what would become summer twilight in Melbourne. Sergeant Ed Bruin wasn't sure if he appreciated the longer days, or resented the fact that the hotter weather often led to an increase in crime, and therefore his workload.

He'd received Janey Dearmoth's phone call that morning, and had felt seriously chastised for his lack of enthusiasm in pursuing the information she was providing. Talk about the proverbial rock and a hard place. He'd told her he was in the process of 'pursuing several leads' but it was obvious she didn't believe him. He knew the Inspector would have his hide if he thought he *was* doing any more investigation on the Liam McKay case, but he felt he would be remiss in his duty if he didn't respond to the plea of an old lady worried about a prowler. At least, that's what he intended telling the Inspector if he was caught out.

The streetlight near Janey Dearmoth's unit was just

flickering on when Bruin pulled up outside. No curtain fluttered in the window near the front door, and he wondered if she was waiting in the semi dark, afraid to reveal her presence. But as he walked up the path, he concluded that she wasn't the fearful kind.

The doorbell's melody echoed through the unit. Bruin waited for several moments, then turned to go. Halfway to his car he stopped. Still wondering if he was acting out of childhood conditioning of respect for his elders, he retraced his steps and pressed the doorbell again. His fingers tapped his car keys against the palm of his hand as he waited.

He was about to leave a second time when he decided, just to placate his conscience, to try the back door.

The waist-high shrubs provided a neat border between the two units. As he rounded the corner of the building, a security light blazed in his face. He raised his arm, shielded his eyes, and moved forwards.

Janey Dearmoth's small, thin legs were preventing the security screen door from closing.

Bruin raced up to where she lay on the tiled laundry floor.

With a muttered oath, he pulled back the door and bent down to check her pulse.

The evening menu in the restaurant was comprehensive but Rogan had no interest in the variety on offer. He chose a rump steak, surmising that it would be local, and hopefully tender. Carly ordered the same. Her conversation had been sparse since his return to their cabin, but she'd been pleasant enough. She'd seemed a little nervous, but he'd been too preoccupied with his own thoughts to be concerned.

Whatever he'd expected from meeting Breeanna

Montgomery, it certainly wasn't the shock of recognition on a level beyond the physical. Her dark eyes had been almost mesmerising in their intensity, and the sensation of something momentous about to happen had gripped him again.

'When do you think the Montgomery woman might get in touch?'

Carly's question broke into Rogan's thoughts, and he had to stop himself from responding that she already had. 'It better be soon,' he replied, and was relieved when the arrival of their meals prevented the next question Carly had opened her mouth to ask.

The steak *was* tender, the mushroom sauce excellent, but Rogan barely noticed. Since he and Carly had entered the restaurant, he'd felt someone was watching them. He glanced around quite a few times, but the other diners were preoccupied with their own meals, the staff busy with their duties.

After coffee, he and Carly selected reading material from the Lodge library and retired to their cabin. Carly had again insisted that Rogan take the double bed, and she settled on the couch that folded out into a bed.

Breeanna stayed in the shadows, watching Rogan's cabin, until the lights went out. Much as she would have preferred to talk to him tonight, she knew it would be almost impossible for them to meet unseen and she didn't yet want to risk the journalist knowing she was there. Tomorrow was her day off, so it would seem quite normal for her to explore the Gorge. And if she was seen chatting with one of the guests also walking the track, it shouldn't arouse suspicion.

At least by meeting him in the Gorge she could see if he had come alone. Although she'd sensed he was telling the truth about the journalist, she wasn't sure if he could give her the slip. Carly Otten looked like a very determined woman. With the conference attendees staying at the Lodge for their sessions tomorrow, it would also mean fewer people on the tracks. She wasn't sure how she felt about that. Fewer curious eyes, but less help should she need it.

In two days time it would be a full moon, and already the night sky was bright with its promise. The temperature wasn't as cold as it was normally, and Breeanna wondered if they were in for one of the thunderstorms that were prevalent in the Gorge at this time of the year. She walked the dirt road back to her room. Once inside, she carefully gathered her meagre belongings into the backpack her friend had given her. From her handbag she extracted her purse, and pushed it into a pocket of the cargo pants she intended wearing in the morning, then put the handbag in the backpack. If she had to run again, she wanted to be prepared. She thought of something else she might need tomorrow. Her hand slipped under her pillow and grasped the butt of the small handgun her friend had given her.

Five days ago she had agreed to the plan that Liam McKay had proposed, and now he was missing. Missing . . . and perhaps worse.

Maybe it was time for her to confront her uncle and sister and get to the truth behind the professor's accusations. If she could stay alive long enough.

Vaughn's mobile rang as he and Mark stepped out of the small plane he'd hired to fly them to Roma. He listened intently, issued instructions, then hung up.

A substantial amount of money had persuaded a car rental

firm to agree to meet them at the airport in the middle of the night. Although the expense account allocated to him was normally limited, Vaughn had been given authorisation to use whatever funds and resources he needed on this job.

He pulled his suede coat closed against the cool evening air and walked across the tarmac. Mark Talbert followed, carrying their overnight bags and a narrow black case. Vaughn glanced back at the case. His mouth twisted with grim satisfaction. Once Rogan McKay had led them to the Montgomery woman, he, too, would be superfluous.

The magazines in the waiting room outside the medical ward were older than his kids, Ed Bruin reflected.

He didn't have to be there. His partner, a senior officer, had declared that the old lady had simply slipped and hit her head on the tiled floor. But Bruin felt obliged to get Janey Dearmoth's version.

The doctor had told him that she had a skull fracture but was now awake, so he had driven to the hospital, only to be told she had just taken a turn for the worse and slipped into unconsciousness.

The elderly woman had looked so frail lying on the pale tiles that memories of his grandmother as she lay dying in her bed had sprung to Bruin's mind.

He decided to wait a little longer, just in case.

Rogan rolled over in bed. He thought he'd heard a sound like a door closing. He raised himself on one elbow, and looked around. Moonlight filtered in through the screened windows in the canvas.

Carly's bed was empty.

Suddenly alert, he flung back the sheet and blanket, then relaxed as he heard the toilet flush.

He rolled back under the covers.

Rogan had memorised a map of the Gorge, and knew that it was only a few kilometres from the Lodge to the Rangers' Information Centre. But he'd set his internal alarm for 5.30 a.m., and woke while the cabin was still shrouded in darkness. He dressed quickly in jeans, shirt and sneakers, pulled on a light jacket and quietly let himself out of the cabin. Within moments he'd reached his Rodeo.

The sound of the engine turning over seemed harsh to his ears, and he hoped it wouldn't wake Carly. He drove slowly away from the Lodge. Around the first bend, he switched on his headlights, and sped up.

The light-grey haze of dawn revealed areas of burned grass alternating with long thick growth near dry gullies and sparse vegetation on rocky hillsides. The dirt road was rutted in places, but the Rodeo easily handled these and the ditches carved by rainwater runoff.

Several vehicles were already in the car park when Rogan arrived. He pulled in, and walked past the picnic area towards the Rangers' Information Centre. His impatience was eating into him, and he wished he'd been able to have a cup of coffee. Bringing Carly along wasn't turning out to be one of his better decisions. The humidity was rising rapidly, and he took off his jacket and tied it around his shoulders. Prickles of unease inched up his neck and he knew they had little to do with the weather.

★

Mark Talbert woke at the first insistent knock on the car window. They'd parked a hundred metres before the Lodge so as not to risk being seen by Breeanna Montgomery when she turned up there.

Mark wound down the window as Vaughn grunted into wakefulness in the back seat. Carly's face peered back at them.

'Rogan's driven into the Gorge,' she said. 'About fifteen minutes ago. He was checking the map of the Gorge last night, so I wouldn't be surprised if he's meeting the Montgomery woman there.'

Vaughn was instantly alert. 'Get in,' he told Carly. 'I might need your help again.'

Mark started the car.

CHAPTER ELEVEN

Rogan read the signs on the Rangers' noticeboard, then checked the small map that had come with one of the brochures. The track leading into the Gorge started near the Centre, and various smaller gorges branched off on either side, with the Moss Garden three and a half kilometres up on the left.

He glanced back down the road, and wondered what sort of vehicle Breeanna would be driving, or whether one of the vehicles already there was hers.

Only ragged sunlight streaked between the trees as he began walking. Ferns and flowering shrubs grew in scattered clumps beneath cabbage tree palms, ancient cycads and eucalyptus trees.

The creek ran clear and swift, shallow where large rocks had been placed to create single file crossings, then deepening into wide pools lined by boulders on one side and ferns, grasses and palms on the other. Like woven strands, the track and creek traversed each other. In some areas the grass and plants on the creek banks had been haphazardly dug up, exposing the dark soil, indicating feral pig activity.

Rogan glanced at his watch. He was making good time. After the seventh creek crossing he took the side track to the Moss Gardens, and his speed diminished. The path became narrow and rocky with metal handrails in the steeper parts and the cliff face rising sharply above. By the time he walked down the stone steps into his destination he was grateful he'd given himself ample time.

An overhanging wall of bright-green moss dripped water onto rocks which led down to a pool of crystal-clear water. Tree ferns and fig trees shaded a waterfall above the pool.

Rogan sat on a boulder, thankful for the cooler temperature, and savoured the tranquillity for several minutes. He couldn't see Breeanna, then realised that he was still too early, so was caught by surprise when she walked up behind him. She didn't speak, but he had that same *watched* feeling he'd experienced the previous evening, and whirled around and saw her.

The awareness of her sparked in his blood again. She was average in height and build, with a relaxed stance that belied the tension he could feel emanating from her. She'd dressed for hiking in cargo pants, shirt, hat and sturdy boots, and the backpack slung over her shoulder was similar to those Rogan had seen some of the Lodge guests handing back yesterday.

For a moment she stood, just watching him, as though she wasn't sure she wanted to be there. Then she indicated the track with an inclination of her head. 'Come on.'

'Where are we going?' Rogan asked, but she ignored his question and began walking.

'What has Liam told you?' she asked instead.

'I haven't seen him. I only found you because he left a CD with his lawyer that said he was going to try to make contact with your old school friend.'

She slowed down. 'So you know nothing about why I left Melbourne?'

'Your uncle mentioned your drug problem, Breeanna, but that's not my concern. I just want help in finding my brother.'

Her laugh was short and cynical, and she stopped and looked at him. 'My so-called drug addiction was a cover-up by my uncle to explain away my disappearance. I don't know why James concocted it, but I think Professor Raymond holds the key to all this, and he's in no condition to tell anyone.'

Exasperation rose in Rogan like a wave. 'I don't know what game you're playing, Breeanna,' he told her, 'but I don't have time to humour you. I only want to know if you saw my brother and if you have any idea what's happened to him.'

The force of his feelings hit Breeanna, and she felt instantly remorseful. Wasn't he doing the same thing she was? Trying to protect someone she loved? Guilt pressed down on her. She couldn't protect Paige, not if it meant an innocent person's life was at stake.

'I'll explain,' she said. 'I work with Professor John Raymond. Last month he had a stroke while driving home from the Institute, crashed into a truck and was left a quadriplegic. When he was out of intensive care I went to see him. Like some stroke victims, he's lost the power of speech, except for one word that comes out whenever he tries to talk. It's very frustrating for him, because all he can say is *duck*, and it makes no sense to me, or to his wife.'

'What about your uncle? What does he think?'

Breeanna hesitated. Then she chose her words carefully.

'I didn't ask him. The professor seems to . . . feel . . . that James . . . and my sister . . . are trying to harm him in some way.'

A gust of wind swept leaves and dust around them, and Rogan looked up to see dark clouds rolling in from the north. Breeanna followed his gaze, and he saw her frown. She began to walk along the track again, turning her head slightly to talk to him.

'I wouldn't have put any credence in what the professor had insinuated except that the day after the accident James spent hours going through the professor's office. He said he was trying to ascertain the professor's workload so he could look for a replacement for him, but he only had to ask me if that's what he really needed to know. Then he said the professor had been working on a special project for him and asked if I knew anything about it.'

'And did you?'

'I was aware he was working on something he was very secretive about. He'd ask me to witness and date his lab notebook, but he seemed to wait until I was very busy and didn't have the time to read what he'd written.'

'Was having the notebook witnessed usual procedure?'

'It depends on the experiment. The lab books have to be formatted in a particular way so they're covered by patent law, and in theory, each page should be witnessed and dated, but we don't always do that. Records on computer aren't considered evidence for patent law, so I think the professor was being very sure that whatever he was working on would have no problems getting a patent if it reached that stage.'

The track opened out a little and Rogan moved up beside her.

'That same day,' Breeanna continued, 'Allan Walters, one of

the other researchers in the lab, told me that he'd come in during the early hours of the morning to attend to an experiment and seen the professor's computer with the cover off and the hard drive smashed on the floor. Nothing else was disturbed, but when he phoned James to tell him, he apparently flew into a rage. Allan was astounded because James is usually so controlled. Then we heard about the accident and the computer wasn't mentioned after that.'

She told him about the intruder and the man who'd killed him, and about hiding when she realised she was being pursued. For a while Rogan was torn between the plausible scenario of drug theft and use that James had painted and the almost unbelievable story Breeanna told, but then he thought of the blood and chaos in Liam's unit.

'I believe you,' he said, and saw a flash of relief on her face.

'It was only when I came up here,' she said, 'that I realised there must have been a connection between what James was looking for and what the other men were after.'

Rogan considered what she'd told him. 'How did the professor let you know his fears about James and Paige if he can't talk?'

For a second Breeanna's teeth bit into her bottom lip, and there was a fleeting resemblance to her sister. Then a young couple walked up the track towards them, preventing any further conversation.

Breeanna wasn't sure if Rogan would accept her explanation of how she had communicated with the professor, so she ignored his question and quickened her pace. The humidity had risen, and sweat dampened her shirt.

They soon reached the creek and traversed the crossing. The air had become so oppressive she knew they were in for a thunderstorm, but there would be enough time on the walk back to the car park, she thought, to tell Rogan about Liam.

When they were almost at the tracks' junction, she glanced through the trees to see a man walking up the main track. No suit this time, just casual clothes, and although he was nearly twenty metres away, she recognised the resolute features, the solid build, and the determined walk of the man who had followed her into the service station the night the intruder had been killed.

CHAPTER TWELVE

Vaughn drew in deeply on his cigarette and questioned his wisdom in allowing Mark to go into the Gorge in an attempt to locate McKay, and hopefully Breeanna Montgomery.

With Vaughn waiting at the car park, McKay and Montgomery would be caught between the two of them. Vaughn struggled not to let his greed and eagerness cloud his judgement. He stubbed out his cigarette and reached over to the back seat. 'Hand me that case,' he instructed Carly.

He manipulated the combination lock and pushed up the lid. Within seconds he had assembled the pieces in the case into a high-powered rifle. He heard Carly's small sound of concern.

'What do you need that for?' she asked.

'Insurance.'

'Insurance against what?'

'Anyone in the way of me getting the Montgomery woman.'

Fear iced into Carly's stomach. 'Look, I know I've only done a few casual jobs for you, Vaughn, and I know you can't tell me all the details of this case, but Rogan McKay appears genuine. He really *is* looking for his brother. I know he went along with pretending to be Liam when I called him that, but that doesn't prove he's a criminal. He was just smart enough to take advantage of the situation.'

She looked at the expression on Vaughn's face and experienced the horrible sensation of realising she had been manipulated. Vaughn was a lot smarter than she had given him credit for. He had played on her vulnerabilities and needs and she'd been caught like the proverbial fish. Flathead, she thought bitterly. Liam and Rogan McKay weren't criminals hunting down Breeanna Montgomery for her secrets, with Vaughn on their trail to try to protect her. The lie had seemed so plausible, and nothing Vaughn had done in the past had given her any indication that he was anything other than an agent with one of Australia's intelligence services. His temptation of a scoop for her at the end had been a carrot she hadn't been able to resist.

It dawned on her that the astuteness on which she had once prided herself had diminished considerably.

Her legs moved forwards, but Breeanna's mind felt disassociated from her body. She couldn't believe that the man had found her here. Then she reminded herself that Liam and Rogan had done so.

The man kept walking, getting closer. She fought back panic; tried to think. Then she realised that *he* didn't know she was aware of his involvement. She had to find a way to use that to her advantage.

A rumble of thunder rolled down the Gorge. The black clouds were approaching faster, the sky before them darkening.

Breeanna thought quickly. If this man was here, the other one probably would be too, perhaps waiting further back along the track. She would have to go *up* the Gorge, and try to find somewhere to evade them. She glanced at Rogan. He hadn't lied about anything he'd told her, but then she hadn't asked him anything incriminating. Had he led the men here? Could she trust him?

'There's something further up the Gorge I have to show you,' she told him, taking a side track that branched to the left. Her stomach a flutter of nerves, she tried to remain outwardly calm. She didn't want, by any glance or movement, to tip off the man that she was aware of his presence.

Breeanna's strides ate up the ground, and Rogan felt they gave a hint of her personality: not impatient, just eager to be wherever it was she needed to go.

'Tell me about Liam,' she ordered after they'd traversed the next creek crossing.

Rogan did so, omitting to mention why he'd first become worried about him. Breeanna didn't interrupt, but when he'd finished she stopped walking, and looked him in the eyes. 'How did you know Liam was in trouble?' she asked.

He could sense the implicit admonition not to lie, but he gave a scant version of the pain he had endured and the loss of connection with Liam that he had felt, trying to give the impression that it had been a dream. Breeanna frowned in sympathy. 'It hurts, doesn't it,' she said, dark eyes deep with meaning, 'feeling someone's pain. Like someone grabbed your organs and tried to rip them from your body. You and

Liam have that sort of bond, don't you? That feeling that sometimes you're a part of him and he is of you.'

It was so much a rhetorical question that Rogan was stunned. How could she know how it was with him and Liam? He'd read of other twins who shared what they did, but never to the same intensity. And she spoke as if she really understood how they felt.

She began walking again, head bent, as though deep in thought. Exasperated, he fell into step beside her. This wasn't getting him any closer to finding Liam.

Breeanna sensed Rogan's frustration. And sympathised with it. But she didn't know how far she could trust him. Liam had been different. She'd known from the moment she'd met him that he would understand her need for discretion. Rogan appeared more impulsive, but . . . She sighed. Maybe that's what the situation demanded now. Or maybe her concern about him was more to do with the way he affected her.

They were passing a tranquil pool when Breeanna stopped suddenly. She motioned for Rogan to be quiet, then to follow, and she stepped softly about a metre off the path and pointed to the water. Two small brown bumps broke the pool's surface, spreading ripples back to the further shore.

'Platypus,' she whispered, pointing.

Rogan had stopped so closely behind and slightly to the side of her that he caught the traces of fruit and toothpaste on her breath, and the smell of shampoo fresh in her hair. Her body scent, warmed by rapid walking, struck him, creating an instant churning of desire. Surprised by his reaction, he stepped back and a stone spun from under his sneaker.

The water splashed as the platypus dived, and Breeanna turned around. She didn't need to read Rogan's feelings. The fierce hunger in his eyes echoed the tension in his body. What astonished her was the wave of uncertainty coming from him, something she was sure was almost foreign to his nature. And threaded through that was sympathy. It took another few seconds for her to realise that the sympathy was for *her*.

Perplexed, she retreated to the path.

Her 'innocent' detour hadn't worked. The man was still following them. Five metres away, he stood at the side of the track, his foot on a large rock, tying his shoelace. He kept his head bent, apparently concentrating on his task.

Anxiety curled tighter in Breeanna's stomach. He had narrowed the gap between them but was making no attempt to catch up, and she wondered what he intended doing. Watching the platypus had given her a valid reason to stop and see if the man would overtake them, but it appeared that, for now, following them was his only plan. The thought brought little relief.

'Where are we going?' Rogan's tone mirrored the tension she was feeling.

An idea formed in her mind. 'The Amphitheatre,' she replied, pitching her voice so it would carry to the man.

As Rogan fell into step beside her, she quietly told him about their shadow. 'If we can get him to follow us into the Amphitheatre,' she said, 'I think we can overpower him.'

Rogan listened to her plan, then made some suggestions.

The smell of leaf mould and eucalyptus had intensified with the increasing humidity. Mark didn't like the way the weather was building up. Thunder rolled through the Gorge, deep and intense. Lightning splintered through the black clouds roiling across the darkening sky. Sharp gusts of wind pummelled him with tiny branches whipped off trees.

Breeanna and Rogan had quickened their pace, and Mark had to hurry to keep them in sight. Twice more they crossed the creek, then took a path signed 'Amphitheatre' to where an enclosed steel ladder led to a narrow cleft in the white striated cliff face. He stopped behind a clump of cabbage palms and watched as they climbed up and disappeared into the cleft. They hadn't looked around, and Mark hoped they didn't suspect he was following them. He hadn't passed anyone returning on this track, and wondered if the Amphitheatre led through to somewhere else. Perhaps the Montgomery woman was taking McKay to where she'd hidden the records book Vaughn was looking for.

The wind strengthened, whipping the fine, dry soil into the air and stinging his eyes.

He unbuttoned his shirt so he could easily slip his gun from its concealed holster, walked down and began climbing the ladder.

The narrow passageway through the cliff was about forty metres in length, its uneven floor sloping upwards, leading to steps cut in the rock. Further in, and a set of steps higher, the floor fell away on one side, leaving only a thin wedge of rock on which to walk. Breeanna clung to the handrails attached to the walls as she hurried through, eyes down, careful not to lose her footing, Rogan following close behind.

Metres above their heads the rock joined again, the only light coming from the passageway entrance and the opening ahead. Breeanna negotiated the last tricky section, and found her breath catching in her chest as it always did when she walked into the bowl-shaped Amphitheatre.

Most of the floor was covered in tree ferns that had been roped off to prevent visitors from damaging them. Grey silt covered the rocky path around the left-hand side, sloping higher to where two timber benches offered a resting place. Breeanna stopped and gazed upwards. Sheer sandstone walls towered fifty metres high, slanting inwards, creating the effect of gazing up at a cathedral spire. Muted light seeped through the opening as black clouds rolled across the sky. She could feel the walls resonating with the power of nature that had caused the erosion of dirt and stone trapped within these massive vertical faults and forced them out through the narrow passageway to create the area in which they now stood.

A church-like hush filled the cavernous area. Breeanna shook off the awe that always gripped her here and turned to Rogan. He, too, had stopped, and the expression on his face, the almost reverential stance of his body, surprised her. She was sure that if she touched him she would feel the vibrations of the earth through his skin. He returned her gaze, and the silence between them was palpable with meaning.

Then thunder shook the tree ferns and lightning cracked brightness across the opening above.

'We'll have to hurry,' she breathed.

The walls of the passageway seemed to vibrate as thunder roared down the Gorge. Mark looked upwards, trying to ascertain through the gloom if there was potential for a rock fall. His eyesight had adjusted to the darkness, but he trod carefully, only occasionally looking up to see if his quarry was coming back.

He was getting bad vibes from the situation, but now the storm had hit fully he wasn't sure if that might be influencing his attitude. As he neared the end of the passageway he slowed, his right hand straying across his chest to the opening of his shirt. He took another step and looked into the Amphitheatre.

At first he couldn't make out anyone in the dimness. Then thunder boomed and a lightning flash illuminated the stand of tree ferns, and he saw Breeanna near a wooden bench gesturing towards the greenery where Rogan McKay's jacket was partially obscured.

He took another step forwards, out of the passageway.

CHAPTER THIRTEEN

'Put your hands behind your head.'

The words were steel, and Mark could sense no bluff in the tone. The voice had come from behind him but to the right of the passageway opening, and Mark cursed himself for his momentary distraction with Breeanna.

'I have a gun. And I *will* use it,' the voice continued, and this time there was a hint of anticipation, as though the speaker would relish the opportunity to carry out his threat.

Although their surveillance microphone didn't always catch exact tonal nuances, Mark recognised the voice of Rogan McKay. Mark had memorised the file Vaughn had gathered on McKay, and he knew that not only had his navy background trained him in small arms, but his part in the capture of his brother's killer last year had demonstrated his willingness and ability to use them. Rogan McKay was not a man Mark would prefer to take a chance with, but the risk mightn't be too great. After all . . .

The thought went unfinished as the end of a gun barrel pressed against his head.

'It has a hair trigger.'

The barrel moved away. 'The hands. Now. Slowly.'

Mark obeyed.

'Walk up to Breeanna.'

Again Mark obeyed. When they reached her, the gun pressed into his skull. 'Search him for a gun,' Rogan ordered Breeanna, and within moments she was removing Mark's Glock from his holster.

McKay stepped away, then took the gun from the woman. 'Turn around and sit on the ground. Then remove your shoelaces and belt and hand them to Breeanna.'

With grudging respect, Mark did so, and cursed when he saw the weapon McKay had used to get the drop on him. A .25 calibre Phoenix, the kind of gun a woman would have in her handbag, with the kick of a lamb rather than a mule. Still, at such close quarters it could do a lot of damage. And although it irked his professional pride to be trussed up like a turkey with his own shoelaces, he knew that, for the moment, finding out the information he needed was more important than his embarrassment.

'You can't keep running, you know,' he said to Breeanna as she tied his hands behind his back. She didn't respond, so he added, 'Why don't you hand it over? Then you could go back to your job and your life.'

'Hand what over?' she asked, pulling tighter on the shoelace.

Mark hoped she hadn't cut off his circulation. 'The professor's record book. That's all we want.'

He felt the hesitation in her hands, then McKay pushed the gun against his forehead. 'Why do you want it?'

'We're retrieving it for the government.'

'The professor wasn't carrying out any experiments for the government,' Breeanna interjected.

'It was a secret experiment.'

Mark saw the uncertainty in her eyes, then the disbelief. 'My father would never take on any project like that.'

'He's undertaken commercial work before. Why not for the government?'

'Because his focus has always been on the betterment of mankind. Any secret experiment for the government would hardly come under that category. Besides, the government has its own labs; they wouldn't need the Montgomery Institute.'

Mark could see that he wouldn't be able to convince her. Then McKay hauled him to his feet. 'Where's my brother?'

'I don't know. Our only interest in Liam was that he might lead us to Breeanna but he gave us the slip. So then we focused on you.'

'Is the woman, Carly, with you?' Breeanna asked.

'We use her occasionally, but she's never been told full details of any case.'

McKay's grunt of scepticism ended Mark's attempt to persuade them he was telling the truth. Then McKay reached into Mark's back pocket and took out his wallet.

'Driver's licence, credit cards, gun licence, all in the name of Mark Talbert,' McKay told Breeanna as he looked through the contents. 'And an ID badge that says he's working for the Department of Defence. It wouldn't be hard to fake, though.' He shoved the wallet back into Mark's pocket. 'You smell more like an intelligence spook than Defence personnel,' he said, then pushed Mark towards the far end of the Amphitheatre where the rope fence stopped visitors from entering a small cave. 'Get over the fence,' he ordered.

The cave was shallow inside, but McKay pushed Mark down against the back wall so he couldn't be seen by anyone who stopped at the fence. After Breeanna tied Mark's feet with the belt and gagged him with his own handkerchief, they left.

Mark tried frantically to pull his hands out of their bonds. He knew the mood Vaughn was in. He also knew he had to try to keep Rogan McKay alive.

As they neared the top of the steel ladder, Breeanna and Rogan could hear the wind outside the Amphitheatre howling like a banshee. Thunder roared, a great rumbling beast of noise that pulsated in their bellies and did little to prepare them for the jagged streaks of lightning that flashed negatives of trees and rocks across their pupils after its passing.

Wild gusts of rain pelted them during their descent, the ladder shaking against its rock foundations. Breeanna bent her head against the wind as they ran back along the path. She stumbled once, felt Rogan's firm grip on her arm preventing her falling, then he was urging her forwards.

At the creek crossing she stopped and yelled at him that they would have to be careful, the other man could be waiting for them.

'Do we have to follow the track?' he asked.

'In some places we can avoid it. But I'm not sure about others.'

'We'll stay off it as much as we can.'

They ran as quickly as the terrain would allow. The storm seemed to increase in intensity, the thunder magnified by the steep sandstone cliffs forming the main gorge, giving it the feel of a living entity, a raging growl from the belly of a monster. Rogan had never heard anything like it, and he was almost enthralled by its power.

The rain eased as they raced through thick scrub. Rogan glimpsed a dark object coming towards them.

In the clarity of a lightning flash he saw a huge feral boar charging, black bristles raised on its back, the massive head and shoulders a formidable setting for its razor-sharp tusks.

The storm had increased Vaughn's impatience. He had trusted Mark to be able to find Rogan McKay and follow him in the hope that he would lead them to Breeanna Montgomery, but he still itched to do the job himself. Only the possibility that the Montgomery woman would recognise him had stopped him. He looked again at the map of the Gorge Carly had obtained from the Information Centre. One way in, the same way out. Besides, McKay would have to come back to the parking area to get his vehicle.

Carly waited in the back seat, disgusted with herself for allowing her craving for success to cloud her judgement. It had always been her weakness – her belief that she knew better, that she could do better, than everyone else. It was that same arrogance that had prevented her from admitting that she was an alcoholic, until she'd lost everything that should really have mattered to her.

Few vehicles remained in the car park, and no-one had walked up from the track since the storm had hit. Wind buffeted the rental car, and leaves and debris swirled in the eddies it created.

Since Vaughn had assembled his weapon, Carly had agonised about what would happen to Rogan and the Montgomery woman once Vaughn had what he wanted.

Because she was sure now that protecting the woman was the last thing Vaughn was interested in. Which also meant that Rogan could be an obstacle Vaughn would need to eliminate.

Whatever else she might have been in the past, and heaven knew her ethics had often been severely bent, Carly knew she could never be a party to murder.

The boar's speed was incredible.

Rogan pushed Breeanna to the side.

Eyes fixed, head extended, the boar charged at Rogan, dipping its head and slicing up with its tusks just as he jumped aside.

The boar's shoulder caught him mid thigh, pushing him off balance.

He sprawled against Breeanna, knocking her to the ground, then sprang up, only to see the boar continue its mad charge through the undergrowth. Breeanna scrambled to her feet, eyes darting in the direction they were headed.

'I hope he wasn't alone.'

'I'm just grateful it wasn't a sow,' Rogan replied, touching his thigh gingerly. He wondered if being hit by a truck would have had less impact.

'Why?'

Breeanna's look of incredulity almost made him laugh. The wind had whipped her wet hair into a mass of unruly curls, emphasising the paleness of her skin and wide, dark eyes. It struck him as oddly attractive. 'The boars will usually only charge if you're in their way or they feel cornered,' he explained. 'When the sows have piglets, they're the most vicious bitches you can come across. They charge with their mouths open, ready to bite, and even if you get out of their way they'll still go after you. If they get you on the ground, they'll keep biting chunks out of you until —'

'I get the picture!' Breeanna's stomach was almost heaving with the images she was picking up from Rogan.

'Let's keep going,' he urged and led the way, this time scanning the terrain ahead for danger closer to the ground than the man Breeanna was sure would be searching for them.

The call came from the hospital just as Ed Bruin's partner informed him they'd been called out on another case. Janey Dearmoth was conscious. Bruin thanked the duty nurse and said he'd get there when he could.

At the moment, a stabbing in Flinders Lane had higher priority than an old woman who'd slipped and knocked herself out. But he couldn't shake the feeling there was a connection to the McKay case, and having to abandon that case was still niggling at him. When he had some free time . . .

The storm had stopped as quickly as it had started, leaving broken branches and flattened grass patches in its wake. As Breeanna and Rogan neared the beginning of the track, they quickly detoured behind the Rangers' Information Centre so they could spy on the car park without being seen.

Although there were still some vehicles in the area, only one car stood between them and Rogan's four-wheel drive. A sedan with a man in the front passenger seat, and a woman in the back. A blonde-haired woman.

'Carly,' breathed Rogan, angry at her deceit, and mad at himself for trusting her.

'I don't know for sure,' Breeanna shook her head, 'but the man could be the other one who's looking for me.'

'Can we circle around to the other side of my Rodeo?'

'No, it's too open. He wants me, not you, so if I'm not with you, he should leave you alone.'

Rogan glanced at her, and saw the look of someone who was considering all possibilities and swiftly discarding them. 'I'm not leaving without you,' he said.

Suddenly she smiled. 'You are. But not for long.'

Vaughn stiffened in his seat.

Rogan McKay was walking towards the car park. Alone.

Where was the Montgomery woman? Vaughn turned around to see Carly, too, gazing at McKay, a frown creasing her forehead.

'He said she would contact him,' she murmured, almost to herself. 'Perhaps she didn't show up?'

Vaughn fingered the rifle on his lap, then decided that a handgun would be more suitable. He smiled grimly as his hand curled around the butt under his suede jacket.

Rogan was halfway across the car park when two rangers walked out of the Information Centre. They exchanged a few words, then one began walking in the same direction as Rogan; the other stayed near the building, watching. The irritation that flared in Vaughn increased when the ranger drew level to Rogan as he got closer to the car. Vaughn's hand moved from his gun. He shoved the rifle on the car floor and covered it with Mark's jacket.

The ranger walked up to the passenger window as Rogan walked around the back of the car. Nodding respectfully, the ranger looked down at Vaughn and introduced himself.

'I'd like to inspect what's in the boot of your car please, sir,' he asked.

'What!' This was something Vaughn hadn't expected. 'I don't have to show you anything.'

'I'm afraid you do, sir. We have reason to believe that you may have taken plant material from the National Park, and we have the authority to search your vehicle, with or without your permission.'

The thought of Vaughn even touching something green and growing would normally have made Carly smile, but the distraction of the ranger seemed to be offering her a way to escape from a situation that had become more than she felt she could handle. She also got the feeling that if Vaughn was happy to kill Rogan if he got in the way, her life would be worth even less to him. She watched Rogan walk past the car and head towards his Rodeo. Her fingers crept onto the door handle.

Vaughn cursed as he reached across and tried to pull the keys from the ignition. He couldn't afford to make a fuss. There was a limit to what he could get away with. He heard the back door open just as the keys slid into his hand. *What was Carly up to?* He got out of the car as she did the same. The ranger waited patiently as he walked around to the back of the vehicle.

Carly heard Rogan's Rodeo start. She walked casually behind Vaughn, then saw the Rodeo begin to reverse. Without looking back, she sprinted over, wrenched open the back door, and jumped up onto the seat as Rogan pushed the gear into first. He flashed her a look of fury, but continued driving out of the car park.

CHAPTER FOURTEEN

Breeanna's lungs were pounding fire as she raced the back way along the creek to the staff quarters. If her assessment of the situation was correct, the man in the car would cooperate with the rangers, and this would give Rogan time to get away. He'd argued about leaving her, but they both knew that they needed transport, and she couldn't let the man know she was in the vicinity.

She tried to rationalise what she'd felt from Mark Talbert. He was lying and telling the truth in equal measure, but there was no menace, no evil, in the emotions he projected. She shuddered. Not like the man he was working with.

A low branch slowed her pace. As she ducked under it, she glanced at her watch. Rogan had promised to wait seven minutes before talking to the rangers, so she knew that she would arrive back at the Lodge about the same time he did.

★

'Get out, Carly! I know about Mark Talbert and his mate. And that you've been working for them.'

Rogan pulled to the side of the road once he'd driven out of sight of the car park. The last thing he needed was Carly sticking to him like flypaper and reporting back to Mark Talbert and his cohort.

'Rogan, I'm sorry I lied to you. I believed what Vaughn told me. He said you and Liam were crooks who were trying to find Breeanna Montgomery so you could force her to give you something.'

Vaughn. So that was the other man's name. 'And what would that be?'

'He never told me. Said it was classified. But he said that he was working for the government and he and Mark were trying to protect Breeanna.'

Just who the hell was telling the truth? Rogan was beginning to wonder if everyone was lying to him. 'So you needing the interview was a lie?'

'No. I really do need to get my career back on track.' The desperation in Carly's eyes seemed genuine. 'Vaughn said that once Breeanna was safe and the government had given the all clear to go public with the case then I'd have an exclusive interview.'

'So why have you decided to tell me all this now?'

'Because Vaughn has a rifle that he intends using on anyone who tries to stop him getting his hands on Breeanna.' She hesitated. 'And I'm worried that any witnesses will get the same treatment.'

The clock on the dash clicked over another minute and Rogan cursed. He couldn't waste any more time arguing with Carly. He had to get Breeanna away so she could tell him about Liam. He put the Rodeo into gear and hit the accelerator.

A few minutes later they arrived back at the Lodge. Rogan pulled over, took out his wallet and thrust several notes at Carly. 'Get a bus back to Melbourne,' he told her.

'But . . . can't I . . .' she started to protest, then saw the look on his face, and nodded. 'I understand. You think you can't trust me.' She grabbed the money and jumped out of the vehicle. Stuffing the money in her pocket, she ran into their cabin.

As Breeanna had instructed him, Rogan drove down a nearby dirt road to several long low buildings. When he braked, she dashed from one of the buildings and hopped into the passenger seat, throwing her backpack onto the floor.

The ranger thanked Vaughn for his cooperation, apologised for delaying him, and walked away just as Mark sprinted up from the entry to the Gorge track. Vaughn got into the driver's seat, started the engine and spun the wheels as he raced across to Mark.

Stones flew as they sped back to the Lodge. Vaughn slowed briefly as they passed, checking for Rogan's four-wheel drive, then accelerated. The car shuddered across the corrugations in the dirt road, splashed quickly through the Mickey Creek crossing, then gathered speed as Vaughn pushed it to its limits.

Four-wheel drives weren't built for speed, Rogan thought as he slowed to take another tight curve in the road. The undulating nature of the land also made it difficult to maintain a decent speed, but he wanted to put as much distance as he could between them and the man Carly had called Vaughn.

The sedan's lower centre of gravity would enable it to make better time on the winding dirt road.

Although Breeanna had her small weapon, and he now had Mark Talbert's Glock, he didn't want to risk a gun battle with Vaughn. His twin's life might depend on him, and he wasn't going to take any chances. He also didn't want to put Breeanna's life in jeopardy, though he felt she was more capable than most of looking after herself.

Breeanna clung to the seat belt, trying to move with the bumps, forcing herself to relax as the vehicle hit several deep holes and bounced her against the door. The trees in this section of the park had taken a battering from the storm. Several branches littered the road, and one trunk had even been hit by lightning, with charred pieces of timber scattered across the ground.

The Rodeo slewed around the next bend, and as Rogan saw the road ahead, he slammed on the brakes.

The water flowing across the creek crossing wouldn't deter him, but on the other side where the road curved upwards, a large tree had fallen across the road, effectively blocking it.

'We've got them!' Vaughn growled in triumph as they rounded a bend and saw Rogan's Rodeo stopped in front of a fallen tree further ahead. Then he cursed as the Rodeo turned sharply and began to climb the embankment. It ploughed through the undergrowth, skirting the trunks of tall eucalypts.

Fury mounted in Vaughn as he realised that once the Rodeo reached the top of the rise and drove down the other side his quarry would be lost to him.

He sped down the crossing, veered sideways as the sedan

slipped in the water, then stopped. He grabbed the rifle from Mark, and, using the bottom of the open window to steady himself, took aim at the driver.

He pulled the trigger.

CHAPTER FIFTEEN

Just after Carly had thrown her belongings into her overnight bag and hurried to the Lodge office, she'd seen Vaughn's car pass by, heading out of the Gorge. Relief almost made her sag at the knees.

She told the receptionist that she'd had a fight with her 'boyfriend', he'd driven off without her, and she needed to get back to Roma as soon as she could. The young woman was sympathetic, and said that one of the staff members was driving into town that afternoon if she'd like to wait and catch a lift with them. Although she didn't relish staying any longer, Carly had no choice but to agree.

The aromas wafting from the restaurant made her realise that she hadn't eaten breakfast. She looked at her watch. The breakfast menu would be finished, but she could grab a toasted sandwich from the cafe section.

Sitting on the deck waiting for her order made her feel exposed, so she decided to return to the cabin to eat. At least there she could make herself a cup of coffee and relax in private. She checked her money again. And it wouldn't cost her anything.

By the time she'd finished the sandwich and coffee, the nerves in Carly's stomach had been quelled. She noticed that Rogan's duffle bag was still in the corner where he'd left it, and wondered if anything in it could give her a clue to where he might go next. Her courage had returned, and the interview with Breeanna Montgomery still loomed as the possible saviour of a career that was otherwise over. She walked across and picked it up.

The front door opened, and closed.

She whirled around.

'You won't be needing that.' Vaughn's words were almost a whisper, but the gun in his hand and the look on his face told Carly more than her nerves could stand.

Her body shook in spasms of fear.

Moisture trickled between her thighs.

Mark stood outside the cabin door and tried to listen. The mood Vaughn was in, Mark wasn't too sure about leaving him alone with Carly, but Vaughn had ordered him to wait on the small verandah.

In the past few months he'd been working with Vaughn, Mark had caught glimpses of the deep dissatisfaction with his lot that would sometimes surface. Just a word, maybe two, but he was astute enough to read the nuances in Vaughn's tone. With Vaughn, the professional mask had rarely slipped. Until this job.

*

The gun barrel slid down her cheek like a lover's caress. Cold steel on warm flesh. Even as the terror invaded her body, Carly's mind registered the feeling.

'I don't know why you went with McKay,' Vaughn almost whispered the words, 'but you won't go near him again, will you.'

'No.' Carly squeezed out the word.

'Good. Because that would be a mistake. For you.' The muzzle rested on the bridge of her nose. 'And your daughter.'

Rogan looked at the splintered hole where the bullet had exited the windscreen after penetrating the back window, and felt his anger subsiding. He would have preferred to have fought it out with the two men back at the Gorge. Running wasn't his style. Only the knowledge that Liam's life might depend on him had stopped him. But his stomach clenched at the thought that time was running out. He'd believed Mark Talbert when he'd said that Liam had given them the slip. Why else would they have arranged for Carly's deception?

'Tell me exactly what you found in Liam's apartment.' Breeanna looked at Rogan as she spoke. He was concentrating on driving as fast as possible, negotiating the gullies and bends with swift, sure changes of gear and rapid acceleration.

She saw the line of his jaw tighten, and felt the rush of anxiety coming from him as he told her.

'Why did you go to Carnarvon Gorge?' he asked a few minutes later.

'My friend got me a job at the Lodge so I could hide while I decided what my next move would be,' she explained. 'I knew my father would return to Australia soon, so I hoped to wait it out until that occurred. Then Liam found me. He'd already become suspicious of the story James had concocted, and he even used a hire car to come to Queensland because he'd had the feeling he was being followed.'

'Why was he suspicious about James?'

'Paige had told Liam that she couldn't believe I was a drug addict. She'd found drugs in my house apparently, but that hadn't convinced her. Even James finding the so-called proof that I'd stolen them from the lab didn't sway her.' Breeanna sighed. 'My sister had more faith in me than I had in her.'

'What do you mean?'

'After I'd escaped from the man . . . Vaughn, you said Carly called him?' Rogan nodded. 'Well,' Breeanna continued, 'after that, the professor's accusations seemed to be confirmed, and I thought Paige must have been involved. That's why I didn't go to the police. I was trying to protect her. I hoped that when my father returned he would be able to . . . I don't know . . . keep her out of it in some way.'

'She was acting pretty suspiciously when I talked to her.'

'I think you'll find she's worried about Liam.'

Rogan flicked her a questioning glance, then the intimation in her words struck him. Was Paige the woman Liam had fallen in love with?

'Liam said that when he returned to Melbourne he was going to warn Paige to be careful what she told James. But I don't think he got the chance.' Breeanna's stomach churned with the thoughts going through her mind. 'I'm sure if he had, Paige would have told you where I was. He was also going to investigate James for me. You might think he was changing clients mid stream, which would be rather unethical of him, but technically he was working for Paige, not James, and she had asked him to do whatever he could to help me.'

'Do *you* think James is responsible for Liam's disappearance?'

'It's a possibility. Several years ago James was working in a research hospital in the US and got into trouble. My father flew over and sorted it all out and brought James home to work at the Institute. I overheard them talking about it not long afterwards.'

'What kind of trouble?'

Breeanna hesitated slightly before she replied. 'Stealing drugs.'

Silence stretched between them as Rogan mulled over what she'd told him. When the road changed to bitumen, he asked, 'Do you have any idea how we get James to talk?'

'No. I'm sorry. James and I have never been close. For some reason he's always resented me, and I've never found out why. At times I thought it had to do with my mother, but . . . He's always emotionally closed off around me.'

Sadness tinged her voice, and Rogan looked at her intently. He saw the creases of worry on her forehead and the tiredness in her face, and sympathy surged through him. 'We're going to have to ask the professor some more questions,' he said. 'But you never told me how you managed to communicate with him.'

Breeanna watched him as she contemplated her reply. Would he believe her? So few people did. Liam had, but she felt Rogan was far more sceptical. 'I'm an empath,' she finally said. 'I can feel things about people. What they're thinking. What they're feeling.'

'Like telepathy?'

The doubt was there in his voice, just as she had thought it might be. 'It's not telepathy,' she explained. 'I can't read anyone's mind, not in words. I . . . I *feel* what they're feeling. I guess you could say I tune in to their emotions.'

'Don't you just home in on their body language? Pick up clues that way?'

'That's possibly a part of it. But it's more than that. It's a link, a connection, a transference. It's as though I become a sponge and I soak up what they're feeling. Some people are naturally empathetic, but with me it goes deeper. Emotionally and physically it can be very draining, and over the years I tried to block it because I couldn't always cope.' She sighed. 'Sometimes it can be rather frightening. Professor Raymond was terrified, and that was hard to deal with. I asked him questions, and I felt his answers. He was pleading with me to understand, and in the end I said I did because I was worried he'd have another stroke. He wasn't in physical pain, but his emotional trauma was severe. He kept trying to talk, but as I told you, the only word that would come out was "duck". All I could surmise was that he was trying to say he couldn't duck when he hit the other vehicle. Nothing else made sense. Or maybe it didn't mean anything at all.'

Rogan wasn't sure if he believed Breeanna, but it looked as though he would need her if he was going to see Professor Raymond and question him. He'd been hoping that he could leave her somewhere safe and go back to Melbourne alone. There was something about her that unnerved him. Something that posed a threat to his peace of mind.

'I'm sorry you feel that way about me, Rogan. It will make it harder for us to work together.'

Startled, Rogan looked at her, and felt drawn into the warm depths of her dark eyes. For the briefest of moments he was sure she was inside his head, pleading for his understanding.

'You have the same type of connection with Liam,' she said. 'You even feel the same physical pain he does, don't you.'

'How do you know?'

'He told me. I know that's something you two never normally discuss, but he wanted me to see that he really did understand about me being an empath.' She smiled. 'He also said that if ever I met you that you wouldn't be so easy to convince.'

It puzzled Rogan that Liam would talk about him to a stranger but before he could ask Breeanna why, she explained.

'It was an act of faith, you see. I was trusting him not to go back and tell James where I was, and he was trusting me with his real surname and his connection with you.'

Rogan found it hard to believe, but then, he'd seen the improbable things a man did when he was in love.

The road had levelled out, so he pushed harder on the accelerator.

It was lunchtime before Ed Bruin could get up to the hospital to see Janey Dearmoth.

The elderly woman lay still, white bandage blending into white pillowcase, pale skin emphasising the hollows in her cheeks and the shadows of pain beneath her closed eyes.

Bruin sat on the hard visitor's chair and leaned forwards.

'Miss Dearmoth,' he said, remembering how he'd been reprimanded before for not using her correct title, 'it's Sergeant Bruin. I've come to ask you about your accident.'

Her eyelids fluttered open, and she took a minute to focus on him. 'I'm a silly old woman, Sergeant. I should have been more careful.'

Bruin tried not to let his disappointment show. It was an accident after all. He'd had a suspicion . . .

'You'll have to find out what Darren was doing snooping around Liam's apartment,' she continued.

His head snapped up and his fingers sought and found his pen and notebook. 'Darren who, Miss Dearmoth?'

'Darren Kennett. I taught him in secondary school. Him and his scoundrel of a cousin. Thick as thieves, and just as larcenous.'

'And who was his cousin?'

'Francis . . . Francis . . .' her voice trailed off, and Bruin realised she'd slipped back into sleep. Or unconsciousness.

He went to find a nurse.

They'd nearly reached Roma before Breeanna asked Rogan something that had been niggling at her memory.

'When you were telling me about the feral sows biting people, you've seen it, haven't you?'

His face grim, Rogan nodded. 'In North Queensland. I went pig shooting with some navy mates. We were spread out. One of the blokes was attacked when he walked past some long grass where the sow must have had her nest. We heard her squeal,' he grimaced, 'then his screams. By the time we got there and shot her, half his calf had gone.'

Breeanna shuddered. 'I knew feral pigs could eat through a kangaroo carcass in a day, but I didn't realise they were that aggressive.'

'I guess the sows are like any mother when it comes to protecting her young.'

'I suppose.'

Breeanna's voice was doubtful, and Rogan remembered that she had never known her mother.

'When did you first learn you were an empath?' he asked, changing the subject.

'One day when I was eight years old I sat on my father's

lap and told him not to be sad about losing my mother, that I loved him. He thought I was talking about my stepmother leaving him, but I said that no, he'd been thinking about *my* mother. That's when he realised that all the other times I'd *known* things . . . it hadn't been coincidental. It seems my mother had been similarly gifted. My father warned me to be careful what I said to people, that they wouldn't understand.'

'I know that feeling.'

It was an off-hand remark, but no sooner had Rogan uttered it than he looked at her, and a flash of understanding passed between them. Then Breeanna saw uncertainty in his eyes as he turned quickly away.

The surges of conflicting feelings that emanated from him confused her, and left her nerves even more on edge than before. She had felt comfortable with Liam, but Rogan affected her very differently. It was as though they had an *awareness* of each other. An awareness that made them both wary.

Frank Delano considered himself an old-fashioned crook – not for him the shootouts in fancy restaurants. Cement boots and the odd knee-capping were more his style. Which was why he was becoming impatient with the way things were unfolding with this Breeanna Montgomery fiasco.

Perhaps he'd been too easy on James Montgomery. He snorted as he picked up his glass of Scotch from the desk. The lure of big bucks must have softened him, he thought. His original threat of physical mutilation had had James running scared, then James had phoned to say that soon money would be no object; all he needed was a little time.

Two days later James had come to see him and told the

seemingly improbable story about a scientific discovery that would be worth millions, if not hundreds of millions. The only problem was that the professor who had made this discovery had taken off with the proof and must have hidden it before he was involved in a car accident.

Frank had been born a sceptic, but he'd also developed a talent for sniffing out when someone was lying, and James Montgomery wasn't lying. Frank smiled as he remembered how a little well-applied pain had confirmed that.

In the past few days, though, Frank had felt the bastard wasn't playing square. He wasn't lying exactly, but . . . Frank's beefy fingers reached into the cigar case on his desk.

A few moments later, as he leaned back in his chair and let the exotic aroma seep through his nostrils, he decided that his patience had been stretched thinly enough. It was time to apply more pressure to James Montgomery.

CHAPTER SIXTEEN

Rogan pulled up outside a small cafe. His stomach was rumbling, and he thought Breeanna probably hadn't had time to eat breakfast either.

'I'm getting a burger,' he told her. 'Would you like something?'

She nodded. 'Thanks. A burger would be fine. And chips. And a milkshake. Vanilla.' She took a scarf from her backpack and tied her hair up, revealing the slimness of her neck and further defining her high cheekbones. Her shirt gaped a little as she lowered her arms and Rogan glimpsed pale olive skin on a full, rounded breast. Desire sparked in him, but it was tempered by something he hadn't experienced before. For too many years he'd entered into relationships without ever sharing the inner part of himself that he protected, the core of his being that he had exposed to no-one, not even Liam.

What scared him now was that he suspected this woman, this *stranger*, could not only see into his soul, but that he wanted her to. He'd tried hard to ignore the effect she had on him, but he could feel his control slipping. Every self-preserving instinct screamed at him to push her away, but instead he found himself grinning and saying, 'Getting shot at hasn't dulled your appetite,' before walking into the cafe.

Breeanna sat, watching him, stunned by the sensations coursing through her. Rogan's grin had transformed his face, revealing more to her than he knew, and probably more than he would ever intentionally tell her. And what she had perceived had created a yearning inside her that she tried hard not to acknowledge. She pushed the feeling aside.

There was an aching core of loneliness in her that had never eased, but she'd be damned if she'd let a man like Rogan give her what she craved. No man had ever completely accepted her for what she was, and she'd witnessed the doubt in Rogan. She'd also seen him with Carly, seen his physical response, and wondered if he had slept with her, a woman he barely knew. Above all else, she needed a man who would be hers and hers alone.

James dropped the phone into the cradle and slumped back in his office chair. Sweat dampened his hands and forehead. What Frank Delano had asked him to do was tantamount to murder.

James had never liked killing. When they'd dissected frogs in school he'd paid another student to carry out the coup de grâce. Even the laboratory animals in medical school had caused him a problem. But operating on human beings was a different thing entirely. Having the ability to save lives gave him a feeling of power and control that wiped away the inadequacies of his youth.

Bitterness twisted his mouth as he realised that this time he was in too deep for his brother George to buy his way out. Last time, George had stipulated that James work partly at the Institute and partly at their private hospital so that he would be kept almost constantly under George's watchful eye. But James had made sure that George hadn't been able to keep track of his leisure activities, and it was those activities that had led to the predicament in which James now found himself.

With an effort, he reined in the panic that threatened to consume him. If he lied convincingly enough to Frank Delano, perhaps he could earn himself a day or two's reprieve. After that . . . James hated to contemplate his choices. Unless Breeanna returned, he might have to book himself a flight out of the country. He realised, though, that murder was an option that might be forced upon him.

'Where are we going?' Breeanna queried Rogan as they drove east along the Warrego Highway. 'You should have turned off back there.'

'We're not going to Melbourne just yet.'

'And why not?' Breeanna heard the suspicion in her voice, but she didn't care. Getting back to Paige was her first priority. And she'd thought Liam's welfare was utmost in Rogan's mind.

Several seconds passed before Rogan replied. 'Just how long do you think we'd last in Melbourne before Vaughn and his mate found us? From what you've told me, he seems to have the police in his back pocket, and if he is with a government agency, we don't know just how far his power extends. We'd be better off with disguises, and I know where I can get another identity. And a disguise for you.'

Nothing in his tone gave his feelings away, but Breeanna waited patiently for him to continue. She was beginning to relate to him a little better now, and it made it easier to pick up his underlying emotions.

'My youngest brother, Ewan, was murdered last year,' he said at last. 'He was often on the periphery of the crime scene, but this time he played outside his league. A few months ago, his wife, now his widow, found a driver's licence, credit card, and bank account details that he'd hidden. The licence had his picture, but there was another name on it and the other documents. I think that they were his safety net, and he'd planned to use them only if he needed to.'

'So now you're going to use them.'

'That's right. Most of my money is tied up in the charter boat that I own with my partner, and I don't have a lot of cash lying around. We might just need the ten thousand dollars that's in that bank account if we're going to find Liam.'

'Isn't the money rightfully Ewan's wife's?'

'Meryl won't touch it. I told her to take it to the police but she seemed a little reluctant. I think it was the last link she had to Ewan and she also wasn't prepared to admit what a lying sod he was.'

Breeanna was about to comment that Rogan's words were a little harsh, when she sensed the anguish he still felt about his brother's death. 'So where are we going?' she asked.

'Beechmont, in the hinterland behind the Gold Coast. Then back to Melbourne to question your uncle. He's the only link to you and the professor. Vaughn and Mark Talbert were after the professor's lab book, so perhaps James told them you had it.'

'I'd like to speak to Paige first. James has a lot of influence on her, but if I can get her alone I'm sure she'll tell me whatever it is she was reluctant to tell you.'

'Okay. But you'll have to do it without alerting James, which might be difficult with them both living in the same house. It's not like we can knock on the front door, is it.'

Her mind ticked over the possibilities. 'There might be a way.' Her instincts told her Paige was innocent of any involvement in whatever the professor had tried to communicate, but Breeanna couldn't ignore the adoration she had for their uncle. She only hoped that Paige would be honest with her.

Vaughn watched as the park rangers dragged away the last section of tree trunk they'd cut with a chainsaw. At his urging, Mark drove over the thin branches and shredded leaves lying on the road.

A small sigh escaped Vaughn's lips as the car picked up speed. He'd put the long delay to good use. A light plane would be waiting for them at Roma airport, and the police at Mungindi, Goondiwindi and Texas had been directed to radio in if they saw McKay's four-wheel drive crossing the border into New South Wales. As an extra precaution, he'd also ordered surveillance on McKay's parents' home and the access roads into Beechmont. He and Mark would fly to the Gold Coast airport, and if McKay turned up at Beechmont they would drive straight there. But if McKay was spotted crossing the border they would continue on to Melbourne.

Involving the police again was a risk he'd decided to take. His agency's status gave him the authority, but it also meant he would have to account for that use once this was over. If he succeeded in getting the professor's records it wouldn't matter.

For some years now he had had an escape route set up for

himself in the hope that something worthwhile would come his way. And this was the jackpot. Or rather, two pots of gold in one.

And nothing, or no-one, would stand in his way . . . and live.

Darkness had fallen by the time Rogan and Breeanna reached the outskirts of Brisbane and it was only as they left the well-lit Gold Coast freeway and began their ascent into the mountains that Breeanna saw just how clearly the full moon illuminated the countryside.

She placed her hands on the small of her back and stretched. The kinks in her spine reminded her that they'd driven almost non-stop from Roma. She'd dozed briefly in the afternoon, then questioned Rogan about his life. He'd touched briefly on his navy service and charter boat business, but when he'd talked about his family she was warmed by the genuine love he felt for them. There was a solid core of strength in him and she hoped it would be enough for whatever lay ahead.

The road twisted and turned, making its way to the black smudges of mountains rearing into the bright night sky. Then it began to climb the mountainside, two-cars wide but narrow, skirting houses perched on the hillside, their lights shining into the heavily treed darkness.

When they reached what appeared to be a tiny village, Rogan turned off onto a side road. He drove up to a log cabin and parked in the small accessible area between the back of the building and the uncleared scrub behind. The cold night breeze struck them as he and Breeanna opened the vehicle's doors. Rogan went to the cabin's back door and knocked. An outside light came on and the curtain at a nearby window fluttered. Seconds later the door was pulled open.

'Rogan! What's —' Before Meryl could say any more, Rogan hurried Breeanna into the kitchen and closed the door after him. Meryl took one look at their tired faces. 'Take a seat.' She gestured to the adjoining living room where a small fire crackled warmth from a stone fireplace. A colourful rug covered the timber floor, and a book lay open on the plump cushions of a wood-framed lounge.

'Have you eaten?' she asked, pushing back the sleeves of her deep-pink tracksuit.

Rogan shook his head. 'No. But we could do with a coffee.'

'I'll put the kettle on.' Meryl walked towards the kitchen bench, glancing back at Breeanna, then shooting a questioning glance at Rogan.

Rogan followed Meryl into the kitchen and Breeanna could hear him explaining their predicament and asking her for Ewan's fake driver's licence and credit card. Before Meryl could get them, the phone on the bench rang, and she went to answer it. Rogan spooned coffee into two cups, poured milk and hot water, and took them into the living room.

Traffic leaving the Gold Coast airport had been heavy, and Vaughn fumed at the delay. McKay's vehicle had been spotted on the road into Beechmont, but the police observer was under instructions not to follow and arouse suspicion. So far McKay had not made contact with his parents, but Vaughn guessed he would do so soon. Why else would he have driven there?

Vaughn looked at the information on his laptop again. The

widow of the dead brother still lived in the village. Perhaps McKay had gone there?

'That was your mother,' Meryl told Rogan as she hung up the phone. 'Apparently, when your father was out in the far paddock late this afternoon he noticed a police car hidden across the road. The only reason he saw it was because the sun glinted off the binoculars one of the policemen was using, and he realised they were looking at your house. He didn't think too much about it until a friend further down the road phoned about ten minutes ago and told your mum that the police had set up a roadblock near his place and were checking cars heading south.'

'Shit!' Rogan cursed himself for not anticipating that. 'Why did Mum phone you?'

'Because she hasn't heard from you for a few days and you're not answering your mobile. She's worried. She said you told her Liam's working undercover on a case which is why she can't reach him, but she has the feeling something's wrong and wanted to know if I'd heard from you.'

'I haven't answered her calls because I didn't have anything positive to tell her. She doesn't need any more stress at the moment.'

'Perhaps we should just tell Vaughn and Mark that we don't have what they're after?' Breeanna suggested.

'Do you think they'd believe you?' Rogan asked.

Breeanna thought about the vibes she'd picked up from Vaughn after he'd shot her assailant. 'No. Vaughn is obsessed with getting the professor's lab book and I must be the only lead he has to it. From what Carly told you, we can't be sure that he wouldn't kill to get to me.'

'And if they are government agents,' Rogan's tone indicated he thought it was possible, 'they've probably had us under surveillance since we drove through Brisbane. After all, we came the most direct route.'

'There was no roadblock at the foot of the mountain,' Breeanna commented.

'They probably didn't want to make it obvious they were looking for us. I'll bet there's one there now.'

'We'd better make sure that you two leave the mountain before these men find you,' Meryl said as she walked into an adjoining bedroom. A few moments later she returned and handed Rogan two plastic cards. 'There's enough family resemblance for you to pass for Ewan on the driver's licence photo, but you'll have to dye your hair.' She looked assessingly at Breeanna's dark hair and strong facial features, and said, 'Come with me. I was in a feature film once and we ended up not being paid so I kept the costume.'

Meryl grabbed a box from the top of her wardrobe, opened it, and took out a short, badly cut, brassy-blonde wig. She showed Breeanna how to pin up her hair and secure the wig in place. Then she took a small container from a drawer and within seconds green contact lenses covered Breeanna's dark eyes.

Breeanna frowned as she looked in the mirror. 'I'm not ungrateful, Meryl, but just what sort of part did you play in that film?'

Rogan's chuckle made her look back at him, and that same grin that had opened him up to her before was back on his face, crinkling his eyes and making them appear even bluer. Again that deep yearning started deep inside her, this time accompanied by a startling rush of desire. As though he had read her feelings, the grin froze on Rogan's face. He held her gaze for a few more seconds, then turned abruptly and walked away.

Meryl watched the silent exchange, saw Breeanna's puzzled expression, and kept her own counsel. 'I'll get you that hair dye,' she said to Rogan as she walked back into the living room.

Rogan took the packet that Meryl handed him.

'We'll have to leave now,' he told her. 'It's too risky to stay here any longer. We can't use my vehicle, and they'd search yours if we tried to hide in that. Besides, I don't want to drag you into this any further. It's too dangerous.'

'So what are you going to do?'

The grin was back. 'Easy,' he replied. 'We jump off the mountain.'

CHAPTER SEVENTEEN

Breeanna had never considered herself a coward, but as she climbed up into the four-wheel drive she began to question her acceptance of Rogan's scheme to get them off the mountain.

'We'll hide the Rodeo near my parents' farm and sneak into their shed for the gear,' he told her as they drove away.

'Have you ever done this before?' she queried.

'I'm a qualified instructor.'

Qualified. Over the years she'd heard different definitions of the word. 'What sort of training does carrying a passenger entail?'

'At least three years of flying and an extensive training course.'

'But have you ever done this *at night* before?'

'No. It's against regulations. Paraglider pilots operate under visual flight rules so we don't carry instruments or navigation lights. But at the moment we don't have much choice, do we.'

Apprehension swept Breeanna. She had felt that Rogan was a man more keen on action than talking, but she wondered if he might be a bit too gung-ho. 'Then how are you going to see where you're going?'

Rogan slowed down to negotiate a bend. On a straight stretch of road he turned off the Rodeo's lights. Moonlight bathed the countryside in silver so bright that trees cast shadows on the undulating paddocks. As though deciding words were superfluous after so effectively illustrating his explanation, Rogan switched the lights on again and remained silent until they turned off on a dirt road some kilometres further on. Trees lined either side of it, and thick scrub contrasted with the open fields they'd previously passed.

Several hundred metres down the road, Rogan drove off to the side and hid the vehicle behind a stand of trees. He switched off the engine, and grabbed his jacket and Breeanna's backpack. 'Come on. We have to walk from here,' he told her.

The breeze was colder where they were, and stronger, and she wished she'd taken her jacket from her pack. Rogan suddenly stopped walking and swung the pack towards her. She pulled out her jacket and put it on, then took off the blonde wig and stuffed it into the pack. Rogan hauled the pack back onto his shoulders and kept moving. When they came to the bitumen road, he checked there was no passing traffic, then led her across the road and into the bushes on the other side.

He set a good pace, but Breeanna had no problems keeping up. Her youthful travels overseas had given her a love for walking, and she tried to get in at least an hour each day after work. When they'd gone a fair way, Rogan ventured out into the paddock, but kept to the side of a ridge running across the property. When one of the shadowy shapes grouped under a large spreading tree raised its head and mooed, Breeanna realised they were sharing the paddock with cattle. Although the moonlight made it easier to negotiate the uneven ground, she decided to keep a wary eye out for dark patches. She didn't relish the thought of stepping into fresh cow dung.

Soon they came to a wire fence separating the paddocks. Rogan pulled down the top strand for her to climb over, then followed. The crisp air bit into Breeanna's lungs, and although warmed by her exertions, she had to shove her hands into her pockets to keep her fingers from getting cold.

'The house is just past those trees,' Rogan pointed. 'We're going to have to go around behind it so we can't be seen from the road.'

Breeanna's gaze followed as his hand changed direction. Surely he was joking. It looked as though the paddock ended where he was indicating. In the distance she could see the dim outline of another mountain range. Apprehensive, she walked after him, eventually reaching and climbing over another fence.

Ten paces further on, the paddock ended abruptly. The land, its sides covered in thick scrub and precariously perched trees, fell steeply away to the valley below.

'Tell me we're not going down there.'

'Sorry. No choice. We don't want to be seen. Just keep close to me.' He jumped lightly to a small shelf a metre and a half down from the edge, then held up his hand to her. She took it, on a subconscious level feeling the instant satisfaction of touching him, and jumped down to join him.

He held her hand a second longer, then released it, crouching slightly as he picked his way slowly across the hill-side. His boot dislodged a rock, and Breeanna heard it tumble down into the darkness. She emulated his hunched posture, careful not to let her head show above the top of the rise.

The vegetation grew thicker, and they had to work their way around trees now, whose overhanging limbs cut off the moonlight, making it harder to see. Breeanna was just about to reach out to Rogan for guidance when a cloud covered the moon and turned everything black.

She took another step forwards . . . into nothing.

Headlights swept across Meryl's cabin as a car did a U-turn out the front. The engine died and two men got out. Meryl hugged her arms across her tracksuit as a sudden chill shook her. She had refused to obey Rogan's plea to stay with a neighbour for the night, but now she wondered if she'd been a little rash.

She looked quickly around the living room. Nothing there to indicate she'd had visitors. She'd washed Rogan's and Breeanna's coffee mugs and put them away. All she had to do now was convince the two men that they hadn't been there. Then an idea struck her, and she hoped she would have the time to pull it off.

Hurrying into the bathroom, she quickly searched through some packets in a drawer and picked one out. She opened it, took out two containers, mixed the contents together, and poured the liquid down the sink. Grabbing a towel, she wiped the containers, making sure some of the contents smeared across the towel, then dampened it with water splashed from the basin tap. She tossed the towel into the dirty-clothes basket, dropped the packet and containers into the bin, threw a tissue on the top and walked to the kitchen as a knock sounded on her front door.

★

Fear tightened Rogan's chest as he heard Breeanna's stifled cry. He realised she hadn't fallen too far, but he hoped she wasn't hurt. Telling himself that his concern was only because an injury could delay their escape, he scrambled down, picking out her shape as she struggled to her feet. She swayed a little and he reached out and pulled her to him. As her breasts crushed against his chest and he breathed in the sweet scent of her, he finally admitted to himself that he'd wanted her in his arms from the moment he'd first seen her.

For a few seconds she melted into him, then, as if by mutual consent, they drew apart.

'Are you okay?' His voice was rough with concern and more than a little desire.

'My back hurts a bit, but I'll be fine.'

There was a slight quiver to the words, and he wondered if it came from pain or if she felt the same almost overwhelming need that still clawed at him. 'Hold onto my belt,' he told her as he turned away, 'it gets a little rougher before we make the shed.'

Meryl refused to open her front door, and spoke to the men through the window. It was only after the older man expressed his 'concern' for Rogan's welfare that she pretended to believe his claim to be working for the government and let them in. The Defence Department ID in the name of Vaughn Waring that he showed her looked authentic enough, but after finding Ewan's fake driver's licence several months ago, she knew how easily such things could be forged.

The younger man closed the door behind them, and Meryl asked them to sit down. Vaughn sat on the lounge, forcing her to choose the single chair and lose sight of the other man as he drifted silently further into the room.

'What's happened to Rogan?' she asked. 'He left here last week to see his brother in Melbourne. Has something . . .' She almost wrung her hands but decided that might appear to be overreacting. She suppressed a smile. Over*acting* might be more like it.

'His brother was helping us with a case, and now they both seem to have disappeared.' Vaughn's lips thinned as he pressed them together and paused for emphasis. Meryl wondered who was the better actor as she let a slight 'Oh' of shock escape her mouth. 'We hoped they may have come here,' he continued, then leaned forwards. 'I'm sure you'll understand that this is very confidential.'

'Of course.' She widened her eyes and nodded her head, sending a slight jiggle through her breasts and rippling the soft tracksuit fabric. With satisfaction she watched the rapid throat movement as he swallowed. Then his deepset eyes narrowed, and a brief flare of alarm shot through her. She glanced around, but the younger man was no longer in the room. Then she saw him come out of her bedroom, and she frowned.

Vaughn quickly soothed, 'My associate is just checking to make sure that no-one has broken in without you being aware of it. The people Liam was investigating are quite dangerous.'

'Should I stay with friends until you find Rogan and Liam?' she asked. 'Oh, their poor parents. I was speaking to Mrs McKay just today and she asked me if I'd heard from Rogan. She can't get through to him on his mobile.' She heard the back door open and saw the younger man walk outside and close the door. 'Please don't tell them. They'll be terribly worried.'

'Then perhaps you'll contact me if they turn up here?' He

handed her a card stating his name and mobile phone number and stood up.

Meryl rose quickly to her feet. 'Of course. And please, let me know as soon as you have any news.'

After she locked the door behind him she walked over to the back window and peered out. The younger man was using a torch to search the backyard. A minute or two later he walked around the side. Meryl ran to the front window and watched him get into the driver's side of the car.

'Four-wheel drive tracks in the backyard,' Mark told Vaughn as he fastened his seat belt, 'and they're the same tyre patterns as McKay's.'

'So they've been here. I thought that bitch was lying. But they haven't gone to the parents' place,' Vaughn frowned. 'So where the hell are they?'

Mark turned the key in the ignition. 'If they guessed we'd follow them, they could be hiding out somewhere, waiting for us to give up looking. But I think they'll head back to Melbourne.'

'Why?'

'Because I think they came to see McKay's sister-in-law for disguises. She's an actress, so she'd have some idea of what to do. In the bathroom I found a towel that appeared recently used and an empty hair-dye packet and containers that she'd tried to hide. So either McKay or Montgomery now has hair coloured *Autumn Auburn*.'

The look Vaughn threw him expressed his growing impatience. 'What?'

'The russet colour that leaves turn in autumn, according to the box.'

'Then it's probably her. Neither of them has the right skin colouring for it, but it would show up fake on a bloke, whereas women are always changing their hair colour and no-one takes much notice.'

'So what do we do now?' Mark asked as they reached the main mountain road.

'We'll pay a visit to the parents. For all we know McKay might have swapped vehicles and gone there. He grew up here and he'd know the country well enough to evade any roadblocks, so we might be wasting our time if we hang around too long. If the police surveillance hasn't spotted them by morning, we'll fly back to Melbourne.'

Mark heard the frustration in Vaughn's voice. He knew they had little to go on back in Melbourne. Breeanna Montgomery was their only link to Professor Raymond's record book. Periodic checks had revealed that the professor's condition hadn't altered, so no communication was possible there.

'McKay hasn't found his brother yet, so it's a fair bet he'll go back there and keep looking. And the woman might go with him.' He held out the slim hope to Vaughn.

'Perhaps we'd better have another look at that surveillance tape of Liam McKay getting carried out of his unit,' Vaughn mused. 'If we find him before Rogan does, we might have a bargaining tool. If he's not already dead.'

The clouds had cleared by the time Rogan and Breeanna reached the shed at the back of the McKay home. While Breeanna waited behind the shed in the shadow cast by a large avocado tree, Rogan crept around to the door and slipped inside. Moonlight coming through the window enabled him to find what he was looking for without too much effort, and soon he re-joined Breeanna.

'We still have more walking ahead of us, I'm afraid,' he said as he led her back to the scrub. 'We have to get to Rosins Lookout before we can take off.'

'Why can't we do it here? Isn't one cliff as good as another?'

'The Lookout's the only spot on the Beechmont plateau that's safe.' He started a little in surprise as his mobile vibrated in his pocket. Checking the number, he quickly put the phone to his ear. He listened intently, said, 'Okay' and returned the phone to his pocket. 'We won't have to walk so far after all.'

'Why not?'

'That was Meryl. She's borrowed a friend's car and will pick us up around the corner where the cops can't see us.'

He smiled, and Breeanna's heart skipped a beat. There was a certain daredevil air about him that appealed to the rebel in her, and the reaction she'd had when she'd first met him came back in force. Much as she didn't want it to happen, not now, and not with a man she sensed didn't want to share himself with any woman, she realised her feelings towards him were changing.

Her acting ability had enabled Meryl to cope with dealing with Vaughn, but as she sat in the car at the side of the road and waited for Rogan, tendrils of fear inched up her neck. Vaughn had scared her. Something lurked inside the man, and if she were given to flights of fancy, which she assured herself she wasn't, she would have said he had an evil streak.

When a knock sounded on the boot of the car, she almost

jerked into the steering wheel. Heart pounding, she glanced around to see Rogan holding a large pack and indicating for her to open the boot. She found the button and pressed it as Breeanna slid into the back seat. Rogan joined her seconds later.

'Vaughn and his mate came to see me,' Meryl said as she drove up the road. 'I tried to persuade him not to see your parents, but I doubt he listened.'

Rogan cursed, and she shared his anger. His parents didn't need any more stress in their lives. 'The younger guy, probably the one you two tied up, searched my house and yard. I'm sure they know you've been there.' She quickly explained about the hair dye. 'Hopefully he found it and they think one of you is now a redhead.'

No cars passed them, and she stopped only briefly at the Lookout to let Rogan and Breeanna out before driving off.

Rogan walked down to the top of the slope from where they would launch. An east-south-east breeze was blowing at about ten knots, and he was grateful. At least launching and soaring would be easy. As he'd never flown at night before, he didn't want to take any more risks than he had to. He took a pair of overalls from the pack and handed them to Breeanna. 'Put these on. It gets cold up there.'

'What about you?'

'You'll keep me warm,' he quipped. While she was pulling on the overalls, he secured his safety helmet and clipped on his harness. Then he did the same for Breeanna.

'It's like a lounge chair without legs,' she commented, feeling the padded foam harness around her back and bottom. Rogan secured her backpack in the storage area in the rear of her harness.

He spread the wing-shaped canopy over the ground. The

breeze began to puff it up. 'Sometimes we fly for over five hours,' he said as he attached her harness to his, 'so you need to be comfortable. That's why the straps are loose; you're secure, but nothing pulls. Now, just do what I tell you.'

He felt the canopy fill and rise above him, and the familiar expectant rush of adrenaline kicked in. 'Take a couple of steps forwards,' he told Breeanna, following as she did so.

Then there was only air beneath their feet as they soared upwards.

CHAPTER EIGHTEEN

Mark Talbert felt like a real bastard as he and Vaughn left the McKay farmhouse.

When Vaughn had started his spiel about Liam McKay disappearing, Mrs McKay had collapsed into a chair, and Mark had watched Vaughn's face as he had elaborated with descriptions of the apartment being ransacked and finding the bloodstain. The McKays were so distressed that Mark was sure they had missed the vindictiveness with which Vaughn emphasised those points.

Then Vaughn continued, saying that Rogan had started looking for his brother and he, too, was now missing. By the time he finished, the McKays' anguish was so evident that Mark was worried about their wellbeing.

'Don't you think you overdid it in there?' he asked Vaughn as they got back into their car.

'At least *they* were telling the truth when they said they hadn't seen Rogan McKay,' Vaughn sneered, and pulled a pack of cigarettes from his pocket. 'Perhaps if they have a heart attack that bitch of a daughter-in-law will drag Rogan out of hiding. And if we get him we should get Breeanna.'

Mark frowned as Vaughn flicked his cigarette lighter and lit up. The smoke wafted across his nostrils, and tempted him. It might have been two years since he'd given up smoking, but at times like these it would be easy to slip back into the habit.

He was beginning to wonder if Breeanna Montgomery really did have what Vaughn was after, but he wouldn't like to be in her shoes when Vaughn got hold of her.

No wonder God gave angels wings. The thought sprang from nowhere, but Breeanna realised she was paraphrasing a story her grandmother had read to her when she was little.

After her initial burst of fear when they'd left the safety of the mountainside, she had been exhilarated by a euphoric feeling of freedom as they soared higher. Rogan's knees were below her elbows, his hands on the steering lines beside her shoulders, and she looked out at a surreal world of puffy white clouds suspended against the dark sky and flickering stars, and the mountains and valley bathed in silver moonlight. In the farms below them, lights from scattered houses shone like fireflies.

The breeze stung her cheeks with its coldness, and her eyes watered a little, but she marvelled at the serenity she felt. Birds experience this all the time, she thought in awe. She closed her eyes, let her body relax, and gave herself up to the sensation. Sitting there, suspended, soaking up the quiet that was broken only by the sounds of the nocturnal animals in the trees below, all the tension stored in her body from the past few weeks evaporated.

Rogan kept manoeuvring them close to the slope, catching the breeze rising up the mountainside, and using it to gain height and glide further north-east. Breeanna opened her eyes and caught glimpses of water way ahead of them, and felt a twinge of apprehension. Then she relaxed again, confident in Rogan's ability to land them on the other side of the dam where he'd arranged to have a friend pick them up.

She was glad Rogan didn't try to talk to her. It was almost as though he could sense her need to savour this strange combination of elation and tranquillity. Then again, she thought, he had more empathetic capability than he liked to admit.

Too soon, it seemed, they were over the water and heading for the landing field.

Rogan frowned. The offshore valley wind was creating turbulence in the area he'd planned to land. He'd been caught in turbulence before and managed to scrape out of it, but now he had Breeanna to worry about.

Suddenly, half the wing folded under.

The canopy pitched forwards in a spiral dive towards the trees, rocks and water below.

CHAPTER NINETEEN

Rogan pulled hard on the opposite control line to try to stop the rapidly worsening spiral dive, but the wingtip had lodged itself in the suspension lines.

'Hang on,' he yelled, and yanked both brake lines.

The big canopy finally stopped rotating, stalled, and dropped behind.

Breeanna's fingers clung onto Rogan's legs, but she stayed silent.

The wingtip came clear of the lines.

Rogan let up on the brake handles and the canopy inflated fully and soared above them again.

The abrupt cessation jerked them back into their harnesses, and Breeanna's soft sigh of relief echoed in Rogan's chest. He was grateful he hadn't had to use the reserve chute. With no directional control over it, ending up in the dam was a distinct possibility.

Their landing wasn't quite as gentle as Rogan would have

liked, but he quickly unclipped Breeanna's and his harnesses and his helmet, and gathered in the canopy. Now that the danger had passed, reaction kicked in, and he took a deep breath to allow his pulse to return to normal.

He watched Breeanna ease the harness from her shoulders and step out of the overalls. Hell, but she was gutsy. She hadn't panicked, not even for a second. Tensed up, maybe, but that was only natural. The attraction he felt for her now became tempered by a new respect.

She took off her helmet and ran her fingers through her hair, then looked up at him and smiled broadly. 'Except for the hiccup at the end, that was a fantastic experience.'

Her eyes were dark and mysterious in the moonlight, and a different type of adrenaline surged through him. As though sensing the change, Breeanna's expression altered, becoming intense, and almost expectant. Her lips parted, and although her feet didn't move, her body swayed slightly towards him.

With one step he stood in front of her, only a silent breath of need separating them. Then his lips claimed hers as she reached up and wound her fingers into his hair, pulling him closer, moulding her body against his.

Desire blazed, hot and demanding. One hand captured her head as he deepened the kiss, the other slid beneath her shirt, savouring the silkiness of her skin, the firm flesh, the promise of greater delights. He tried to keep control, to stay in charge, to go slowly, but the force of his feelings threatened to overwhelm him.

The sound of footsteps coming closer finally penetrated the swirling pulse of need in his mind, and he pulled back, just as Breeanna did the same.

'You nearly kill her, then you kiss her?' Laughter edged the incredulity in the voice that came from behind them.

Reluctantly, Rogan let his hands drop to his sides. Breeanna's face was flushed and somewhat dazed, but there was a question in her eyes that puzzled him.

He turned around to look at the man who had spoken. His appearance matched the gruffness in his voice. Burly, bearded, and unkempt in a way that appeared more a result of hard work than laziness, Pete Laszinsky stood a half-head taller than Rogan. He clapped Rogan on the shoulder.

'Shit! I thought you were done for then, mate. When I saw you get trashed in that rotor I was sure I'd have to pick up the pieces.'

'Me too, for a minute,' Rogan agreed, then introduced Pete to Breeanna. Pete smiled, then picked up the packs and led them back along the track to where his car was parked. When Rogan told him that he and Breeanna would have to hide in the car boot until they reached Pete's house, the big man guffawed. As the laughter rumbled across his frame, he tossed the packs into the boot and told them to get either side.

'Better keep you two apart so the cops don't think my car's on fire,' he chortled.

In spite of herself, Breeanna had to smile. But she noticed that Rogan didn't share Pete's humour.

Twenty minutes later they were in the dining room of Pete's low-set chamferboard home. Breeanna mixed the dark-brown hair dye while Rogan took off his shirt.

'You'd better put the towel around your shoulders,' she told him, pointing to one Pete had given her for the purpose. As Rogan reached for the towel, she watched the muscles ripple across his chest, and felt her body respond.

Her emotions were still raw from the depth of passion he had roused in her, and she needed a barrier between them to prevent her giving in to the temptation to run her hands across his back, his chest, his . . . She almost shuddered with the effort it took to stop her mind straying to where it wanted to go. She may have chosen celibacy for the past few years as a self-protection measure, but it certainly wasn't because her libido was dead.

She pulled on the plastic gloves provided in the box, and told Rogan to sit on a stool. It shouldn't have taken long for her to apply the mixture, but her hands were quivering as she combed his thick hair into sections. The taste of him was still in her mouth, and she searched for some distraction to divert her desire to repeat the kiss.

'How come Meryl had such different hair dyes?' she asked in desperation.

'Meryl's always changing her hair colour,' he replied, and she felt the vibrations of his voice through her fingertips and nearly dropped the comb. 'She likes to be *in character* when she goes for an audition.'

Just then Pete ambled in from the kitchen. 'Got stir-fry cooking,' he announced. 'Better feed you up before I take you to the airport.' He winked. 'Just hope you don't get caught in any more turbulence.'

That's already where she was, Breeanna thought wryly, but in a different way from what Pete was intimating. It wasn't dealing with the intense attraction to Rogan that worried her, but rather the intuition that told her if she allowed herself to fall in love with him, he would end up breaking her heart.

*

As he walked across the marbled floor, James Montgomery caught the first muffled notes of electronic music. Although they didn't match the refrain that had been repeating itself in his head for the past hour, it didn't matter. The sounds and smells enveloped him like warm liquid. Already his worry about Frank Delano was beginning to fade, replaced by a compulsion too strong and too ingrained to fight.

Anticipation flooded through him, and his step quickened.

The lights of Melbourne spread out like a fairyland under the plane's wings as they descended into Tullamarine Airport.

Rogan had become used to the brassy wig Breeanna had worn since they'd left Pete's place, but still got a shock when he caught a glimpse of his reflection in the small oval window. With his hair darkened, his resemblance to Ewan was more pronounced, and it emphasised the unceasing knot of anxiety in his gut that Liam might also be dead.

The hire car Rogan had arranged at the Gold Coast airport was waiting for them, and they joined the smooth-flowing traffic on the freeway.

They'd discussed the problem of where they would stay in Melbourne, and agreed that a hotel in the city was the best choice. It would provide a certain anonymity and, as Rogan said, it was sometimes better to hide in the open. Breeanna chose the Chifley Old Melbourne, and Rogan had to give her top marks for panache when she sailed past the concierge in her shirt, pants, jacket and boots, with the backpack slung over one shoulder, and waited while he booked in. Rogan explained that the airline had 'misplaced' his luggage, and the receptionist visibly relaxed and accepted his credit card.

They were allocated a room on the second floor,

overlooking Flemington Road. Breeanna opened one of the windows and looked out through the budding limbs of the trees on the footpath and across six lanes of traffic to the Royal Children's Hospital on the opposite side. She often hoped that one day her research would result in lessening the suffering of children, in particular. She'd tried to remember anything in the professor's notebook that would give her a clue to what he'd been so careful to hide, but the snippets she'd glimpsed as she'd witnessed the pages didn't add up to anything. Well, nothing that made sense.

Although it was the second month of spring, the night air was bitingly cold, and she pulled her jacket closed. After her weeks in the bush, the smells of the city seemed almost alien, but at the same time comfortingly familiar. She turned from the window to see Rogan lying propped against the pillows on one of the beds, grinning at her. 'What's up?' she asked him.

A twinkle lit his eyes as he tried to control the grin. Then he gave up and laughed. 'You look like a hooker who's been hiking. Or maybe the end result of a drunken hairdressing convention.'

Breeanna looked at herself in the mirror and had to smile. She wouldn't have thought it possible, but the plane journey had tousled the wig into an even more dishevelled state. She pulled it off and tossed it on the bench, then unpinned her hair and shook it free. Taking out the small container Meryl had given her, she popped the contact lenses from her eyes and stored them.

'You should do that more often,' Rogan commented.

'Do what?'

'Smile.'

She thought about that for a while. The events of the past

few weeks had turned her life upside down, but they hadn't threatened the image she had of herself. Rogan had done that. He'd aroused something in her that she thought she'd put aside, and she'd found herself longing to allow it back again.

With swift movements she pulled off her boots and sat cross-legged on the other bed, facing him. 'Do you think that sometimes we become what people expect of us?' she asked.

'It's possible. Why?'

'When I was nineteen I dropped out of university and backpacked around the world on my own. I was trying to find my identity, who I was deep inside. I'd hidden my ability as an empath as much as I could, but I still felt alienated from my peers. I was searching for something, but I wasn't sure what.'

'Happens to a lot of teenagers,' Rogan said, and she nodded.

'I visited American Indian shamans,' she continued, 'modern-day druids in England, and ashrams in India. Then I worked in one of the hospices for the dying that Mother Teresa set up in Calcutta. I was amazed by how serene the nuns were in the midst of all the disease and poverty. They seemed to have found what I'd been searching for. So I asked one of them how they coped every day and she said, "We do what we can with the talents God has given us".'

She shrugged. 'It sounded so simple, perhaps too simple. But I thought she was right. I was good at science, so I came home and finished uni and joined Dad and Uncle James at the Institute. And I've been content. I love my work, but the last couple of weeks have made me realise that I've become the person my father has expected me to be, rather than . . .' she struggled to find the right words, 'who I actually am.'

He looked at her keenly. 'And who is that?'

'An empath. There are a lot of people who are good at science, but I have a gift that I should be using to help people. For too long I've viewed it as a hindrance to having a normal life. I have to stop being afraid to be different.'

'It's okay to be different if you believe in yourself.'

His words gave her the courage to ask a question that had puzzled her. 'Why are you afraid of me, Rogan?'

'What? Afraid of you?'

Even as his words denied it, his fear slammed into her psyche like a fist. 'Not physically afraid,' she explained, 'but emotionally.' She watched the closed expression on his face and decided not to push him any further. She got off the bed. 'I'm going to have a shower, then get some sleep.'

She slipped off her jacket and reached for her backpack.

'Hold it!' Rogan was beside her in an instant. 'There's blood on the back of your shirt.' Before she could react, he lifted the shirt, and she sensed the sympathy that shot through him.

'When you said you'd hurt your back I thought you'd bruised it.' His voice was gruff. 'But there's a gouge where a stick must have dug under your jacket, and it's been bleeding. Didn't you feel it?'

'It wasn't bad,' she told him, 'and we had more important things to worry about.' His fingers skimmed around the injury, and she quivered at the gentleness of his touch. She turned, and his hand brushed around her waist, leaving trails of heat. She looked into his eyes, now a deeper blue than before, and felt the need spark between them. The force of it burned into her, and she knew that if she gave into it and allowed herself to melt into him, to feel the heat of him against her flesh, then the ache between her thighs would overwhelm her. And a gut intuition that was as old as time itself told her that once that happened she would be linked to him in a way she had never been to another man.

There had been relationships in her past, loving, caring relationships, but none with the passion that had blazed as intensely as the kiss she'd shared with Rogan. Making love with him, she feared, would be like a snow goose finding its mate. It would bind her to him for life.

It took a strength of will she hadn't known she possessed to move away from him. Backpack in hand, she walked into the bathroom.

Growing up in the mountains had given Rogan a dislike for the noise of city traffic. On his teenage trips to the Gold Coast it had always taken him several hours to adjust to the constant assault on his senses. Now as he looked out through the window Breeanna had opened, exhaust fumes, bright lights, the clattering of trams and rumble of trucks and cars seemed to crowd in on him.

This was *her* environment, he reasoned, not his. He loved blue sky, sunny days, endless ocean, tall mountains and rolling meadows of sweet grass. He didn't belong here with the cacophony of traffic and rushing people. It was easy to convince himself of that, because it was true, but he also knew he was groping for excuses why he shouldn't become involved with Breeanna. Because *involved* was a poor word for what he wanted to be with her. But he was determined that it wasn't going to happen.

He closed the window and took out the Melbourne phone book. Seconds later he was dialling Janey Dearmoth's number. When it rang out he hung up, then wrote the number on a page of the hotel stationery. He would try again in the morning.

The bathroom door opened and Breeanna walked out, dressed in red flannelette pyjamas. She must have washed and blow-dried her hair. It cascaded in lustrous waves, sweeping across her forehead and framing her face. For a moment the breath caught in his chest, then he said, 'Guess it's my turn.' She nodded, and walked over to the far bed.

When he emerged from the bathroom some time later, Breeanna was lying in bed with her back to him, seemingly sound asleep. For a moment he felt rebuffed, then decided to be grateful that at least she wasn't still awake and providing a temptation to him. He switched off the light, slipped the towel from his waist and climbed into bed.

Fifteen minutes later he realised that just being in the same room with her was sufficient temptation, and as he listened to her tossing fitfully in the other bed, he was frustrated enough to hope she was feeling the same way.

When his mobile phone rang, James took a good minute to orientate himself and answer it. He was rostered on call at the Montgomery Private Hospital, and the condition of one of the patients had deteriorated, so he had to go there immediately.

Although he resented the intrusion, euphoria sang in his veins. Tonight had been lucky for him, so tomorrow night he could go where the stakes were higher and he was sure the odds would be even more on his side.

With a spring in his step, he walked to the car park.

As he drove away, he didn't notice the car that followed him.

CHAPTER TWENTY

Over breakfast in their room, Rogan tried to be as composed as Breeanna appeared. This morning she wore the pants and jumper she had been wearing, she told him, the night Vaughn had shot her attacker. Without the wig she looked striking, but Rogan knew it provided a reasonable disguise. Right now she was worrying at it with a hair brush, trying to make it look a little more subdued.

'I don't think that's going to work,' he told her.

She tossed the brush onto the bed. 'I agree. I'll just have to reconcile myself to being a city hooker today.'

Rogan blinked, then saw the twitch at the side of her mouth. He answered with a smile, and the tension in the air dissolved.

Breeanna looked at her watch. 'Time to phone Paige.' She wrote down the mobile number and handed it to Rogan. He picked up the hotel phone and punched in the numbers. It only took a second for Paige to answer.

'Don't say my name,' Rogan began, only to have Paige cut him off.

'Liam! Where are you? Are you all right? Darling, I've been so worried.'

Rogan listened as Paige began to cry, then he heard her gulp and try to regain control of herself. 'I'm sorry, you said not to say your name. But I'm alone, no-one can hear me.'

'Can you meet me on the beachside bike track in half an hour?' Rogan asked, pitching his voice low and soft so it would appear that he didn't want to be overheard.

'Of course. What part?'

'You just walk towards the city. I'll find you,' he said, then hung up.

Mark Talbert was parked down from the Montgomery residence and the Institute when he saw Paige Montgomery press a code into the security pad on a small side gate and slip out. Although she was dressed for jogging, there was something furtive about her movements.

He debated whether to follow her or stay on watch for James Montgomery as he'd been ordered. Paige started running towards the bay, glancing back occasionally as though worried about being seen.

Using his mobile to phone Vaughn as he exited and locked his car, Mark set off in pursuit.

'Do you think I have the walk right?' Breeanna asked as she strutted along the bike path in front of Rogan. She knew the provocative sway of her hips was getting to him, and smiled inwardly. Good. He deserved to suffer after the night she'd had. It had taken ages for her to get to sleep. Just the sound of Rogan's breathing had made her ache to throw caution to the wind and join him in his bed.

When she'd woken early in the morning and made her way to the bathroom, she'd spotted his clothes and towel draped on the side table near his bed, and was tantalised by the knowledge that he was naked between the sheets. Her imagination gave her no peace after that, and it had taken a lot of willpower to smile pleasantly at him this morning in a bland, almost disinterested manner, while inside she was practically seething with desire.

'I'm going to hide over there behind those bushes,' Rogan grumbled. 'Remember, if she's not alone, don't talk to her.'

For the next ten minutes Breeanna walked up and down on a twenty-metre stretch of the path in front of where Rogan was hiding. The crisp morning breeze was heavy with salt, but invigorating, and her blood began to warm with the exercise. Scudding grey clouds covered the sun, spoiling what otherwise would have been a lovely spring day. When she saw Paige approaching, she slowed down and scanned the path behind her sister. Although several other people were using the path, and cyclists whizzed past at irregular intervals, Paige appeared to be alone.

After Paige passed her, Breeanna turned and followed. She quickened her pace and drew level, then 'accidentally' stumbled and bumped into her sister. It took only a second for Paige to recognise her, but Breeanna told her to keep walking while they talked.

★

It was only as he hurried to catch up to Paige after she'd stopped chatting to the woman who'd collided with her, that Mark realised who the other jogger was.

The hair may have been different, but the pants and jumper were similar to those Breeanna Montgomery had worn on the night he'd first seen her. Coincidence, maybe, but he didn't think so.

The two women rounded a curve and were hidden from view by shrubbery.

He broke into a run, then caught sight of Paige. But Breeanna was nowhere to be seen.

Rogan was becoming impatient, and he was worried that Breeanna was placing herself in danger by being with Paige. He had Breeanna's pack on his shoulders, and knew it would take only seconds to retrieve the gun inside it, but that might be too long.

He was also concerned that Janey Dearmoth hadn't answered her phone again this morning. It was possible she was away, but he had a bad feeling about it.

So it was with relief that he saw Breeanna striding back through the bushes next to the bordering houses.

'I told Paige to continue her run,' she said when she reached him. 'Thought it would look better.'

He nodded. 'Let's get out of here. You can tell me what she said while I buy some new clothes. These jeans stink of feral pig.'

'Paige has no idea what's happened to Liam,' Breeanna explained as Rogan drove away from the parking area.

'Apparently he phoned her when he got back to Melbourne after seeing me, but he must have been attacked almost immediately. He'd just told Paige that she wasn't to trust anyone when he made a strange noise and the line went dead.'

'They must have been waiting for him,' Rogan said grimly.

Breeanna laid her hand on his shoulder in comfort, then moved it away. 'She wanted to tell you, but because Liam said she wasn't to trust anyone, she thought she'd better not. I'm afraid she's a little naïve at times.'

'And what about James?'

'It seems he's not coping too well. *Unravelling* is the word Paige used. Very unlike our normally suave, in-control uncle.'

'Sounds like he might be ready to crack. Perhaps we should put a bit of pressure on him.'

'That might work. Paige said he's been keeping erratic hours. Not only that, but she overheard him talking to our father, and he was making out that nothing was wrong. When she questioned him, he said that Dad was in the throes of very delicate negotiations and he didn't want to worry him.'

'So where will he be today?'

'According to Paige he has appointments all morning, so he'll be staying in the office. That will give us a chance to see Professor Raymond's wife.'

It was a modest brick home in what was once a modest suburb but now featured amongst the 'Most Wanted' in real estate agents' books.

Mrs Raymond opened the door and gave a cry of delight at seeing Breeanna. Breeanna had insisted on taking the wig off before leaving the car, saying that the professor's wife didn't need any more trauma in her life and the wig would have been impossible to explain. She introduced Rogan as an old friend from university.

Within a few minutes Mrs Raymond had them ensconced in her sitting room, and bustled around placing fine bone china cups and saucers on a small lace-covered table before bringing in a matching teapot and milk jug.

After asking politely about the professor, Breeanna said that she wondered if Mrs Raymond had come across anything that the professor might have brought home with him from the laboratory.

'He used to bring notes home with him sometimes,' she replied, 'but he hasn't done that for a while. He did use his computer fairly regularly, but James has already checked that out. He has been most kind to me since John's accident.'

I'll bet he has, Rogan thought, but kept his expression neutral.

'There was something about the accident that I couldn't understand,' Mrs Raymond said as she handed around a plate of chocolate cake.

'What was that, Mrs Raymond?' Breeanna asked.

'Well, as you know, dear, John was very much a creature of habit. He always drove straight home from work. I know because sometimes when I needed the car I would drop him off in the mornings and pick him up in the evenings. He would drive home and it was always the same route, up New Street, across North Road, then up Warrigal to Surrey Hills. I used to tease him about it – gently, you understand, because John was quite sensitive. A week after the accident I was clearing out some newspapers when I saw the article that said he was on South Road when the accident happened. Why was he going so far out of his way?'

'Did he ever drive on South Road?' Breeanna asked.

'No. He . . .' Mrs Raymond frowned. 'Well, only once,

when he went to the post office near there. It wasn't on his route, but he said that parking was easier there than at the one closer to home.'

Rogan's gaze met Breeanna's. 'So he might have been posting something?' he asked.

'Well, I only thought of that the other day. When the nurses at the hospital gave me his clothing, I found one of those stickers from the post office envelopes in his coat pocket so I put it in my purse, but then I forgot about it. I'll get it for you. Perhaps it might help.'

It was a faint hope, but at the moment Rogan was desperate enough to clutch at anything that might give him a clue to Liam's whereabouts, and everything kept leading back to the professor.

On her return Mrs Raymond held out a small sticker to Breeanna, and said, 'I hope that can help you in some way, dear.'

An hour later, Breeanna sat in their hotel room and phoned Australia Post. Saying that she was calling on behalf of the Research Institute, she said that one of their staff had posted an Express Post parcel, but was worried he may have addressed it to the wrong town as it hadn't arrived at its destination.

She quoted the number on the sticker, gave a fictitious name and address, and smiled when she was told that no, the parcel had been addressed to a Mr Gary Birchsmith in Kerang and had been delivered.

Breeanna murmured her thanks and put the phone down.

It was a tenuous connection, but now the only word the professor had been able to say had fallen neatly into the hole in the puzzle.

CHAPTER TWENTY-ONE

Frank Delano had had enough of James Montgomery's excuses. He had given him a deadline, and Montgomery hadn't met it.

No, it was time to let him know that he'd had his last chance. And this time, he and Doggie would be there to make sure it happened. Hospitals were usually busy in the afternoon, and two visitors accompanying the part-time resident doctor to see a patient would not be remarked on.

This time there would be no slip-ups.

When Breeanna phoned Gary Birchsmith in Kerang, his wife said he was camping somewhere on the Murray River and wouldn't be home until the following day. Breeanna said she would come and pick up the log book from him then.

'When we get the professor's log book back from him we

can use it as a bargaining tool to get James to talk,' she told Rogan after she'd hung up.

'You sound pretty confident that's what he sent to this Birchsmith person.' Rogan poured hot water over the coffee and milk in two mugs. As he handed one to Breeanna and poured a sugar sachet into the other for himself, he realised he was beginning to acknowledge the probability that Liam was no longer alive. He had fought against accepting it, but with each day that had passed, and now each hour, he conceded that if Liam wasn't being held prisoner somewhere, then he must be dead.

'We won't give up looking, Rogan.'

He gave her a searching look. '*Can* you read my mind?'

'No,' she said softly. 'It was obvious that you were thinking of something else, and you looked so sad it must have been Liam.'

'Why would the professor post the lab book to this bloke?' he said, changing the subject. Her sympathy was almost too much for him to cope with, especially knowing how Liam's death would affect his parents.

'Some years ago the Institute undertook research on avian viruses,' she saw Rogan's frown and explained, 'bird viruses, especially those that mutate and have potential cross reactivity to humans. The influenza virus is the one scientists are most concerned about.'

'Like the SARS scare a while back?'

'Yes. Doctors were worried, and rightly so, that it could turn into a pandemic. In 1968 a global influenza pandemic began in Hong Kong, spread around the world in five months and killed 45,000 people. And don't forget more than twenty million people worldwide died of the Spanish Flu in 1918.'

'So how does this connect the professor to this bloke in Kerang?'

'After the Hong Kong Bird Flu epidemic in 1997–98, my father realised the huge profit potential in finding a vaccine for bird flu. When you consider the possibility, and some scientists believe the inevitability, of another pandemic, a vaccine would be worth billions of dollars. Money that could be poured back into his quest for finding a cure for even one of the various types of cancers.'

'Dedicated man,' Rogan observed, sipping his coffee and watching the animation on Breeanna's face. She was a fascinating combination, he decided.

'My mother died of cancer. It was discovered when she was pregnant with me, and she died several months after I was born. Anyway,' she continued, 'my father sent Professor Raymond to Kerang to collect samples from wild ducks which come to the wetlands there on their migratory path to and from Asia. He wanted to see if they showed evidence of avian disease and if so, was it mutating. He sent the professor because he knew he'd do the job properly. The professor worked with a local man, Gary Birchsmith. I wasn't aware that the two still kept in touch, but the professor's always been a rather secretive person.'

'Do you think this vaccine is what the professor was working on? If it's worth as much as you reckon, it would certainly be worth killing for.'

Breeanna took one of the chocolate packs from the mini-bar and opened it. She broke it in half and offered the rest to Rogan.

'That's what's puzzling. I worked on that research at various times, and from what I remember glimpsing of the lab book that everyone's chasing after, it wasn't the avian virus that he was conducting experiments on.'

'Perhaps Mark Talbert was right. Perhaps they were working on something for the government, something the professor was keeping secret from your father.'

She shook her head and bit off another piece of chocolate, then licked a bit from the top corner of her mouth. It was a natural movement, but one that Rogan found almost erotic. He tried to concentrate as she replied, 'John Raymond would never deceive my father. Some years ago he developed a drug that he received acclaim for, then it was discovered that he hadn't tested extensively enough for the severe side effects it turned out to have. He was disgraced and no-one would give him a job, except my father. He's fiercely loyal to Dad, but he's become almost paranoid about checking his work.'

Just then the phone rang. Rogan answered it, expecting some query from the hotel desk clerk, but instead heard Paige's voice telling him that James had left the office unexpectedly and she didn't know where he'd gone.

The smallness of her bedsit and the bleakness of the day only served to emphasise Carly's depression. She was bitterly ashamed of her cowardice in the face of Vaughn's menace, and wondered if her ex-husband was right. Perhaps she only had the courage to chase the dangerous stories when she was primed with alcohol.

She ran her finger gently across the photo of her daughter once more, then put it back in her bag. She really didn't have much left to lose, did she. Facing Vaughn wasn't a prospect she wanted to contemplate, but hopefully he was still chasing after Rogan and Breeanna. Perhaps she could get a story from Paige Montgomery's perspective. If she pretended to be a friend of Breeanna's, Paige might open up. From what her research had unearthed, Paige was a trusting, almost gullible type. Carly grimaced. She wondered if that description could ever have been applied to her. Perhaps when she was her daughter's age, but certainly not for a long time.

Five minutes later she turned the key in her car ignition, only to find it wouldn't start. After several futile attempts, she got out and slammed the door. She hated the thought of spending the rest of Rogan's money on a taxi, but she didn't have the patience to catch a tram and walk.

Vaughn cursed with frustration as he finished watching the last of the surveillance tapes. Not a hint of a clue to the identity of Liam McKay's balaclavaed abductors or where they may have taken him.

Everything about this case had been cocked up from the start, Vaughn thought. His employer hadn't received notification of Professor Raymond's discovery until almost a week after the professor's accident, so Vaughn had had to accelerate investigations into the people working with him and check out the possibility the professor might have passed his notebook on to one of them. Apart from George Montgomery, the only person who'd worked closely with the professor, knew him on a personal basis, and seemed to have his trust, was Breeanna Montgomery. And her frequent visits to the hospital and strange behaviour afterwards appeared to confirm that she was more than a probability. A search of her house had proved fruitless, so he and Mark had come back that evening to persuade her to hand the professor's notebook over to them.

He looked at his watch in annoyance. His employer

expected a regular email update, and considering the convoluted method by which it would reach him, it wasn't wise to leave it too late.

When he clicked on Send several minutes later, it was with the awareness of what his failure in this would mean. His predecessor had disappeared, and Vaughn knew it hadn't been voluntarily. Vaughn had every intention of disappearing, but at *his* discretion. He had a plastic surgeon lined up in South America, several bank accounts in different names and countries, and a plan that ensured no trace left behind when he went.

His mobile vibrated and he answered it. With a growing sense of disbelief, he heard his immediate superior inform him that he was to return to Canberra the moment his replacement arrived the next day. No explanation was given, but Vaughn knew this was the beginning of the end for him. The man who would replace him was the very person Vaughn had been grooming for greater responsibility, just as Vaughn himself had once been groomed twenty years ago.

The fear grabbing his gut was replaced by anger. He was no lamb to go meekly to the slaughter. He'd waited a long time for the one opportunity that would reward him for his years of dedication, and no-one was going to tear it from his grasp.

So when his mobile rang again and Mark told him that James had driven from the Institute and he was now following him, Vaughn smiled grimly.

That left Paige Montgomery alone. Good. Perhaps he could *convince* her to tell him where her sister was. He was running out of time. And he had nothing left to lose.

*

The young records clerk smiled as Ed Bruin half sat on the edge of her desk. She liked the detective – he didn't bark at her like some of the old ones did, but he didn't look very happy today. She picked two sheets of paper from the bottom of the pile in her tray and handed them to him.

'That Darren Kennett's a bit of a hopeless case,' she said. 'A list of petty crimes you couldn't jump over. The cousin of his you were looking for info on is Frank Delano, owns a bar, operates as a bookmaker and a loan shark. He has a few priors for assault, was a prime suspect when some of his competitors were murdered but nothing could be proven. The details are all there.'

'Thanks.' Bruin tapped her shoulder lightly with the paper. 'I owe you one.'

'Hey,' she called out as he walked away, 'how's the old lady who recognised Kennett?'

Bruin's face turned grim. 'She died this morning. Blood clot in the brain.'

CHAPTER TWENTY-TWO

'If James isn't in his office, perhaps we should search it,' Breeanna suggested as she tied up her hair and pulled the wig on again. She had agreed with Rogan that she would wear it when they went outside. 'There might be something there that will give us a clue to where Liam is.'

'Do you really think he'd leave anything incriminating lying around?' Rogan stretched and walked over to the window and stared at the never-ceasing traffic, grey bitumen and grey clouds. He scowled. The hotel room was beginning to make him feel claustrophobic. It was spacious enough, especially to someone used to the confined quarters of a boat, but he longed to be back where the horizon seemed limitless and the sun shone warmth in a clear blue sky.

Breeanna considered the possibility of James leaving anything for anyone to find. 'I doubt it. But if he *is* cracking, he could get careless.' She thought for a moment. 'He has an office at the hospital; maybe there's something there.'

'We can't do anything useful here.' Rogan snapped the window closed. 'So we might as well try.'

She watched him pick up her backpack. He'd wrapped the Glock in one of the new shirts he'd bought so it would disguise its shape, but she'd kept the Phoenix in her shoulder bag. Her friend had assured her it was in good working order, in spite of its age, but Breeanna hoped she wouldn't have to use it.

Mark found it difficult keeping track of James' car in the busy city traffic, but he wasn't surprised when James drove straight to the Crown Casino. Once they'd entered the floors of parking spaces, James found a park relatively easily, but Mark had difficulty and only a swift sprint allowed him to catch up as James walked through the throngs of people in the casino with the determination of a man who didn't want to be delayed. James scooted swiftly up a flight of wide marble steps, showed something to a security guard standing near a large set of doors, and was allowed to pass through.

When Mark tried to enter, he was politely asked for his Club Card, and when he said he didn't have one, was refused entry. He walked back downstairs, bought a drink at one of the bars, and positioned himself so he could keep watch for James to come out.

James Montgomery was late, and Frank Delano fumed as he hadn't fumed in many years. A phone call to James' office revealed that he had left over an hour ago. Another phone call told him James had gone where Frank suspected.

Stubbing out his cigar in the ashtray, he hauled himself to his feet and went in search of Doggie.

The anger building up in Ed Bruin increased as he parked outside Frank Delano's bar. Janey Dearmoth had been little more than a stranger to him, but he had admired the woman's spirit, and her death epitomised all the meaningless deaths he had encountered in his years on the force. So many good people dying while scum like Delano flourished.

Although the police line was that her death was an accident, the case was officially open until the coroner's inquest, and Ed told himself that he was simply making sure all the loose ends were tied up. He'd just opened his car door when he spotted Delano and Kennett driving out of a lane at the side of the building. Cursing his bad timing, he slammed the door shut. The little 'talk' he'd planned to have with Kennett would have to wait until another time.

But the expression on Delano's face made him pause. His instincts, honed by training and years of experience, told him that Delano was going somewhere with a purpose. Bruin thought that perhaps it might be useful if he could find out what that purpose was.

Keeping a discreet distance between them, Bruin followed Frank Delano through the rain that began drizzling greyness on the streets of Melbourne.

When the woman calling herself a friend of Breeanna's said she had a message from her, Paige's finger went straight to the button to open the security gate. Then stopped.

'How do I know you've come from Breeanna?' she asked.

'She's with Liam's brother at the moment,' the woman calling herself Carly Otten answered. 'And I'm helping them search for him.'

Paige pressed the button.

The receptionist on duty at the Montgomery Private Hospital unlocked the door to James' office when Breeanna explained that her uncle had left a file there he needed her to pick up. Reassuring her she would lock up when she left, Breeanna made sure the woman was back at her desk before she began searching.

After a minute she heard the door open, and looked up to see Rogan closing it behind him.

'Waiting rooms aren't conducive to waiting,' he explained. 'It will be quicker if we both look.'

Although she agreed with him, Breeanna hoped none of the medical staff would need access to any of James' patients' files while they were there.

Carly breathed in the rich aroma steaming from the cup of black coffee Paige had made for her. Hot and strong, the good stuff, too, she thought, not the cheap crap she'd been forced to use for the past few years.

'Please,' Paige sat on the seat next to her in the reception area, 'what is Breeanna's message?'

'I've been helping Breeanna and Rogan try to find Liam,' Carly lied, 'and they thought if we went through everything Liam told you, we might be able to come up with a clue.'

Paige frowned. 'Breeanna didn't say anything about that when I saw her this morning.'

So Breeanna was back in Melbourne. Carly had to think fast, but covering her butt was something she'd perfected long ago. 'I've only just received her phone call. I used to be a private investigator some years ago, so I think she's hoping I can use my contacts to help you search.'

Tears began to form in Paige's eyes. 'I'm so worried about Liam. I fell in love with him the moment we started talking. It had never happened to me before, and I never really believed in love at first sight, but . . .' Paige brushed at her cheeks. 'I'm sorry. I didn't mean to blurt that out, but I haven't told anyone before.'

Carly surprised herself by feeling a rush of sympathy for Paige. She knew what it was like to lose someone you love. Perhaps it might be possible to find Liam as well as get her scoop on what Vaughn was trying to take from Breeanna. A woman as gentle as Paige would once have earned Carly's scorn for being weak, but now, Carly thought wryly, she almost envied her.

'That's okay,' she reassured Paige. 'I just hope we can find Liam for you.'

A buzzer sounded. Paige took a tissue from the pocket of her skirt and blew her nose. 'Please excuse me,' she said to Carly, and walked back to her desk. She picked up the intercom phone that connected to the front gate.

'Please state your name and business,' she said softly.

'Detective Inspector Carraway, Victorian Police. I need to talk to Miss Paige Montgomery.'

Apprehension clutched at Paige. 'I'm Paige Montgomery. What do you need to discuss?'

'It's confidential. We should talk in private.'

Paige hesitated. She was sure that whatever the inspector wanted to discuss, it wasn't going to be good news. Liam, and now Breeanna, had told her not to trust anyone, but did that include the police?

Well, she decided, at least Carly was here to help her.

She pressed the security gate button.

The opulence of the Crown Casino was lost on Ed Bruin. He'd been there a few times in a work capacity, but rarely in a personal one. His pay packet stretched to a once-a-week takeaway with his family, and the occasional romantic dinner he struggled through for his wife's sake, but he had no urge to donate money to the ever-hungry pokies or games of chance.

As he watched the water fountains spurting and coloured lights rippling in rhythm with the music in the massive foyer, his thoughts drifted to the irrigation he still had to install in his garden, and the new set of fairy lights he'd promised the kids he'd erect this Christmas.

Delano and Kennett had headed straight to the Mahogany Room, where Bruin knew only high rollers were allowed. Membership was determined by the customer's ability to bet lavishly and often in the downstairs gambling rooms before they would be considered as members.

Bruin looked at his watch. No wonder he was hungry. Well, at least there was plenty of variety in the snack bars. He'd grab a bite then head back to the station.

Once he was in the almost narcotic state of bliss that gambling brought him, James felt his problems fade. His little win last night had already gone, and now he was borrowing against his credit card again. He knew Frank Delano would be waiting for him, but the urge to win, to dig himself out of the mess he'd created, had been too strong. Just an hour or two, he told himself, that's all he'd need if his luck held.

When his brother had left for the United States, James had succumbed to the temptation to prop up his failing finances by siphoning some of the Institute money into his own account.

It had taken many years for his brother George to trust him again, but James had developed a cunning that many addicts came to rely on to hide their habit. He would sometimes leave his credit card statement on his desk and make sure that George could see he made his monthly payments in full. And the same with his car loan repayments. But the money he gambled with came from Frank Delano, and the debt had grown over the years to an amount that James knew his brother would never agree to pay.

Years ago in the United States, when James had been caught stealing drugs to sell to finance his habit, only George's influence and money had kept him from being arrested and going to jail. But a worse fate was in store for him now if he didn't pay Frank off.

He looked at his cards, felt a rush of pleasure as they displayed an ace and a jack, then stiffened as a man moved behind him and jabbed something hard in his back.

The smile dropped from his face as he turned to his side and saw Frank Delano. He knew without looking that Darren Kennett would be behind him, holding a gun.

The dealer looked at James expectantly.

Frank Delano's lips smiled. 'Mr Montgomery has to leave.'

*

Mark nursed his second drink of lemon, lime and bitters and wished like hell it was something stronger.

At first he wasn't sure if it was the same person, but as he watched a man hesitate at the stairs leading up to the Mahogany Room, Mark recognised the detective he'd seen on one of the surveillance tapes of Liam McKay's apartment.

His photographic memory was one of the reasons Mark had been chosen for the assignment he was working on. The stakes were too high to risk using any recording equipment, either audio or visual, but when the time came that something incriminating enough was uncovered, he would do so. He'd waited too long to risk blowing it by becoming impatient.

Ed Bruin was walking away when he glanced back at the stairs leading to the Mahogany Room.

Frank Delano and Darren Kennett were walking down, an expensively dressed but very nervous-looking middle-aged man between them.

Ed slipped behind a group of high-spirited tourists and waited until the trio had passed.

Interesting. Very interesting. The space between Ed's shoulder-blades tightened. With feigned casualness, he began to follow the three men.

'There's a policeman coming in,' Paige told Carly. 'Will you please stay with me? I don't think I could bear to be alone if he has bad news.'

'Of course I'll stay,' Carly replied. Although her need for a story was predominant, she felt an urge to protect the young woman. Must be getting soft, she thought. She took another sip of her coffee as she heard the front door open. A familiar smell of cigarettes drifted to her. She rose and turned as the policeman's footsteps stopped a metre away.

Her hand holding the coffee mug shook, spilling the hot liquid over her suddenly numb fingers.

Standing in front of her was Vaughn Waring.

CHAPTER TWENTY-THREE

Years of training allowed Vaughn to keep his expression carefully neutral as the surprise of seeing Carly jolted through his body, only to be replaced by a deep, unreasoning rage.

Paige stepped forwards and introduced herself. Vaughn switched his attention to her, then asked, 'And this is . . .'

'Carly Otten,' Paige replied.

'And is Miss Otten a client?' Vaughn asked again, his eyes darting back to Paige, then concentrating on Carly. She appeared to have regained some of her composure, but he saw the stiffness in her body, the defensive tilt to her head. What the hell was she doing here? Surely she couldn't be telling Paige Montgomery about her involvement with him? Her silence seemed to suggest she hadn't divulged that information, or, if she had, that she wasn't going to expose his true identity at the moment.

'No, no. Carly is . . .' Paige looked a little flustered, 'a friend.'

'I see.' Vaughn dragged the words out, and the tension in the room increased. He kept his gaze on Carly. 'Perhaps Miss Otten could excuse us?'

'Paige asked me to stay,' Carly was relieved to hear no tremor in her voice, but she'd had to lock her knees so they wouldn't shake. In spite of her winter-weight pants and jacket and the warmth in the room, she shivered, and gestured with the coffee mug to conceal it. Vaughn's face was almost mask-like but his eyes in their deep-set sockets seemed to burn with hatred.

'Please, Inspector,' Paige interrupted, 'what did you want to talk to me about?'

With an effort, Vaughn turned his attention to Paige. He noted the redness of her eyes and the way her hands clenched as though trying to keep her emotions under control. 'As I said before, Miss Montgomery, it's confidential. We need to speak in private.'

Carly saw Paige hesitate. Paige was clearly uncomfortable with the way Vaughn was insisting, but she was wavering with her need to find out what he had to impart. 'Surely if Paige says it's all right for me to stay you should have no objections.' Carly tried to sound confident. '*Inspector*.'

Vaughn's control began to falter. Carly had intoned the title as though trying to let him know she would expose him if she was forced to. He looked at the defiant stance of her shapely body and realised he was going to thoroughly enjoy killing her when the time came. And he hoped it would be soon.

'Perhaps it would be better if you come down to the station, Miss Montgomery,' he suggested. If he had to abduct Paige to get Breeanna's whereabouts out of her, he would.

Carly almost panicked. If Vaughn got Paige in his grasp,

she was positive he would kill her. Hadn't he told her exactly that? That he would kill anyone who came between him and Breeanna Montgomery? Carly tried to tell herself it was none of her business, that all she had to do was let Paige go with Vaughn and go home and pretend the last few days hadn't happened. Once she could have done that. But something had changed. Rogan had been kind to her and treated her with respect, and even when he'd learned she'd betrayed him, he still cared enough about her welfare to give her the money to return home.

And Paige had trusted her. Such a little thing, but Carly felt she couldn't betray that trust. 'A good idea, Inspector,' she smiled at Vaughn, 'Paige and I can drive down and meet you there. That way you don't have to worry about giving her a lift home.'

Paige looked at Carly, then at Vaughn. Something was playing out between them, and the air almost vibrated with the strain. She recoiled when Vaughn suddenly swung his attention on her full force.

'I'm sorry to do this, Miss Montgomery, but I have to insist that you come with me.' He stepped towards her. 'Alone.'

'Paige, if he's not arresting you he can't make you go.'

Carly's voice was thin with alarm, and Paige saw the loathing in the man's eyes as he looked at her. Fear edged its way through Paige's nerve endings. Although she'd only just met Carly, she trusted her. She couldn't say the same for the police officer. 'I'll go to the police station, Inspector, but not *with* you.' The man's face tightened, and Paige felt her fear intensify. 'If you give me the address I'll lock up the office and meet you there.'

The rage that had built up in Vaughn reached its pitch. Tomorrow wasn't just another day; it was likely to be his last day. Even if he couldn't use the professor's discovery for himself, it would be the only possible bargaining tool he would have to save his life. His right hand slowly undid his coat button. Eliminating Carly would be a pleasure, and it would certainly be a good example to Paige of her fate if she didn't talk.

'Well, there's nothing here to give us a clue to Liam's whereabouts.' Breeanna closed the last drawer of the last filing cabinet in James' office. She looked at Rogan, and saw the deep despair in his eyes. There was nothing she could say, no hope she could offer, that could change how he felt.

'It's time to talk to your uncle,' Rogan said grimly. He flexed his shoulders and the backpack slid a little lower. 'He's the only link we have left to Liam.'

'Apart from the professor. While we're here I'd like to find out from him if he really was working on an avian virus vaccine. If he was, there could be other people involved who we're not aware of. People who might have known about Liam.'

'I guess we can't discount any possibility. Nothing we've done so far has helped.'

The bitterness in his voice tore at Breeanna's heart. She knew he felt he had failed his brother, and his parents. 'The professor's room is on the next floor in the other wing.' She walked to the office door and looked into the corridor. 'It's clear. Come on.'

Carly watched in frozen disbelief as Vaughn reached inside his jacket, but the moment light glinted on metal in his hand something snapped in her mind.

She flung the coffee mug at his face, and kicked out at his knee.

A shot sounded as he fell back on the floor, the gun in his hand arcing towards the ceiling.

Paige screamed.

Carly grabbed her hand, and pulled her along as she ran down the adjoining passageway.

Another shot ploughed into the end wall as they raced around the corner of the L-shaped corridor.

A door blocked the end, and Carly realised it was operated by an electronic lock that could only be opened with a swipe card. She started to yell at Paige about the lock, only to see the younger woman digging into her skirt pocket.

Plastic flashed in Paige's fingers as she ran her card through the lock.

Carly pushed the door open with one hand and shoved Paige through with the other.

A gunshot echoed in the confined area.

Carly cried out. She collapsed in the doorway, blood darkening the lower back of her jacket. Paige reached for her.

Footsteps pounded down the corridor.

'Run!' Carly tried to yell, but her voice was a hoarse whisper. 'It's you he's after.'

Paige ran.

The doors in the corridor were all locked, and Paige realised most of the staff would be at lunch, and would either be in the staff room at the far end of the building or have gone out.

Now she could smell the man's aftershave, and knew she wouldn't make it.

She swiped the lock on the next door and rushed in.

He pushed in after her before the door could close.

She stared around wildly.

Trapped. Like one of the mice in the animal room. Terror squeezed her chest as the man came towards her, less than two metres separating them. For each step he took, she took one backwards.

Paige's gaze never left his, but she knew the room they were in. Bench after bench was laden with lab equipment – micro-centrifuges, phials and tubes and beakers and Schott bottles and storage cases. Glass and stainless steel reflecting their movements in slow-motion roundness.

Then she remembered. This room had two doors. If she could get to the other one, she might have a chance.

She took one more step back, grabbed a half-full beaker and threw it at him. He ducked, and she spun around, ran to the other door, pulled it open and raced through. Straight to another door across the corridor. The bio-hazard room. She swiped her card again.

She dashed in, pushed back against the door to close it.

His hand slammed through the narrowing gap, close to her face.

She reacted instinctively.

The last joint of his little finger crunched between her teeth as she bit it with all her strength.

CHAPTER TWENTY-FOUR

The Montgomery Private Hospital had been converted from a double-storeyed, three-wing residence built at the beginning of the twentieth century. Cement render painted a warm cream with heritage-red accents had transformed the outside of the building, and flowering shrubs peeped colour through the surrounding wrought-iron fence.

Pale pastel wall colours gave the interior a feeling of spaciousness, and this was accentuated by the high curved ceilings. The patients' rooms each bore the modern touches of a built-in wardrobe and dressing table.

Mrs Raymond had been surprised but pleased to see Breeanna and Rogan enter her husband's room, and after a few minutes chat was happy to take advantage of their offer to visit with the professor while she went to do some shopping.

The electronic monitoring equipment attached to Professor Raymond blinked garish-coloured numbers and emitted the occasional beep. Only his eyes moved as Breeanna assured him that Rogan was helping her to find his notebook. As soon as she mentioned the notebook, he tried to speak, but only the word 'duck' came out, and the frustration in his eyes was extreme.

'It's all right,' Breeanna soothed, stroking wisps of white hair from the professor's forehead, 'we know where you sent it. And we're going up to get it as soon as we can. But we have to know, is Gary Birchsmith the only other person who knows where it is? Blink once for "yes" and twice for "no".'

Rogan watched the professor blink once and felt the last of his hope drain out of him.

The professor's head began to move restlessly on the pillow and he kept repeating the only word he could say. Breeanna looked worriedly at the monitoring machines and tried to calm him. 'It's all right. You need to tell me something, don't you.' He blinked again. 'You'll have to spell it out. I'll go through the alphabet, and you blink when I get to the letter you need.'

A quick blink, then his eyes moved back and forth in Rogan's direction.

'You can trust Rogan,' Breeanna assured him, but the movement continued.

'I'll wait outside,' Rogan said, and stepped out into the wide hallway. An anchor seemed to weigh in his chest. Every avenue of hope had turned out a dead end, and if the same thing happened with James Montgomery, he would have to tell his parents that Liam was probably dead. He baulked at the thought. How much grief could they take?

He began to pace, the carpet absorbing the sound of his footsteps. No other visitors or staff disturbed the silence. He reached the lift at the end of the long, empty hallway and turned around. All the doors on either side were closed, and he wondered just how many patients were like the professor, lying in a bed they would probably never leave. The thought was depressing, and he walked faster, grateful to reach the landing at the top of the stairs and look over at the people in the foyer below. Behind him the lights of the nurses' station shone brightly, and on the other side of the landing was another hallway, the rooms leading off it seemingly well occupied if the stream of visitors was any indication.

The sound of the lift door opening caught his attention. He glanced back.

James Montgomery exited the lift, carrying a medical bag.

Close behind him walked a heavily built man with a round, fleshy face, and another man whose face made Rogan think of his grandfather's expression, 'a half-sucked raspberry bar'. There was an air of determination about the men that made Rogan's stomach tighten. Were they going to see the professor? Although he and Breeanna intended questioning James, they didn't need witnesses. He'd have to warn Breeanna.

He reached into his pocket and took out a handkerchief. Pretending to wipe his nose, he sauntered back towards the professor's room, hoping his now-dark hair and half-concealed face would prevent James from recognising him.

To his relief, James opened a door not far from the lift, and the three men went inside and closed it.

Breeanna looked around as Rogan walked into the professor's room. She immediately sensed his tension, and, telling the professor she wouldn't be long, walked quickly over to him.

'James and two other blokes came up in the lift and went into a nearby room,' he whispered.

'He never comes to the hospital in the afternoon unless it's an emergency,' Breeanna said, then frowned. 'When I asked the receptionist if the professor was still in the same room, she said yes, but it was a bit lonely for him as he was all on his own in this section of the wing.'

'Look, you stay here and keep talking to the professor, and I'll go and see if I can find out what James is up to.' He closed the door again, and she went back to the professor. It only took a moment for her to realise that he was now too tired to continue. She told him to sleep and she would be back when he woke.

By the time she stepped into the hallway, Rogan had reached the door where he'd seen James enter. She saw him reach for the handle and turn it gently, only to have it stop after a quarter-turn. Puzzled, she walked up to Rogan.

'It's locked,' he whispered.

In keeping with when the building was constructed, the locks on the old-fashioned doors required rim lock keys, and Breeanna knew they were kept on a chain in the maintenance office, with a spare set in the main office. Normally the doors would never be locked, and certainly not if a patient was in the room. She gestured for Rogan to follow her.

At the next door along, she explained, 'All the rooms on this floor have shared bathroom and toilet facilities, and usually only bedridden patients are placed here, so it's just the nursing staff who make use of them.'

They crept into the room, a duplicate of the professor's, and walked to the bathroom door. Rogan eased it open and they went inside. A small window filtered light over a tiled and curtained shower, handbasin and toilet. Rogan moved to the door that would open into the room where James had gone. He very gently prised it open a fraction, and peered through the minute crack.

The tableau before him was so far beyond what he might have imagined that it was almost surreal, but the shock made his heart pound in his chest.

He froze, transfixed by the sight of Liam, pale, thin and unconscious, lying in the hospital bed while James held a syringe upright and tested it to ensure it held no air bubbles.

The two men who'd accompanied James stood close by, their demeanour reminding Rogan of undertakers waiting for a client.

Rogan moved a little, gestured for Breeanna to take a quick look, then eased the door closed. He slung the backpack off his shoulders, unzipped it and unwrapped the Glock. As he stood up, he saw that Breeanna now had the Phoenix in her right hand.

He swung open the door and stepped into the room, gun aimed at James' heart. Breeanna followed him.

Mark was sure something was wrong with Vaughn. The man's voice on the mobile had been distorted by an emotion Mark couldn't identify. It was almost as though Vaughn had played a vital game of football and even though his team hadn't won, he had scored an important goal. A heady mix of euphoria and anger was the closest Mark could come to describing it.

As he waited outside the Montgomery Private Hospital, Mark wondered if Vaughn was going to join him. He hoped so. In the mood Vaughn appeared to be in, he just might reveal more about this case.

The rain had stopped, but the sun refused to break through the clouds. Mark's fingers tapped on the bottom of the steering wheel, and he wondered if he should have followed James and the men inside the hospital.

★

Frank Delano was the first to recover from the intrusion into the hospital room where Liam McKay was held. In spite of the dark hair, the man with the gun was undeniably Liam's twin who James had told him about. But the woman with him was the jackpot. Breeanna Montgomery, the person they'd gone to such lengths to hunt down. In spite of the fact they held the guns, Frank felt he could negotiate with them. After all, everyone had their price.

He took a step towards Rogan, hands slightly raised in front of him, palms outward. 'No need for those guns,' he smiled, 'I'm sure we can negotiate something to keep us all happy.'

Rogan motioned with the Glock for him to get back, and his expression caused Frank's smile to fade.

Breeanna watched her uncle's face, saw the shock slip into resignation, and even relief. He put the syringe on the bedside table. She looked at Liam's face and realised the pale yellow-purple markings were fading bruises, and the thin red line on his forehead a recently healed wound. In the week since his disappearance he had developed the look of an invalid.

'What have you done to him?' she asked James, barely concealing her anger. The emotions in the room were bombarding her senses, but she found herself relating only to the icy fury and hopeful relief surging through Rogan.

James sank onto the visitor's chair next to the bed. He looked as though it was difficult for him to keep his body from sagging to the ground like melting jelly. 'Until now,' he replied, 'I'd been trying to save his life.'

'What's wrong with him?' Rogan's stance didn't waver, but his gaze lingered briefly on Liam's face.

'When Frank and Darren were interrogating him,' James

sighed, 'their methods were a little extreme, and he had a heart attack.'

'How could you be party to that?' Breeanna couldn't keep the astonishment and disgust out of her voice. 'You're a doctor! You're . . .' She wanted to say 'family' but couldn't utter the word.

James raised sad eyes to look at her. 'I didn't know they'd kidnapped him until he collapsed. When they suspected what had happened they called me in. I had him brought here so I could treat him and keep him sedated. I told them the heart attack was severe but when he was better they would be able to question him again. I was hoping,' he looked at Breeanna, 'that you would have returned by then and given me the professor's notebook. It wasn't in your house when they searched it, so we thought you must have had it on you. Frank told me you'd run away, so I planted drugs in your house and tried to make it look as though you'd lost control of your life. I had to prevent Paige from calling your father.'

'So was the attack severe?' Rogan's voice was harsh, bringing their attention back to the present. His finger perceptibly tightened on the trigger of the Glock as he aimed it squarely at Frank Delano.

'No. But it would have been very painful. They were using electric shocks to try to get him to tell where you were, Bree. I was trying to save his life by keeping him here. If they tried again he would certainly have had another attack, and it would probably have been fatal.'

'What were you going to inject him with now?' Breeanna indicated the syringe, but remembered to keep her gun trained on her uncle.

He told her.

'That would certainly counteract the sedatives,' she

muttered, 'but the stimulation could tip him into another heart attack if you weren't careful enough with the dose.'

'I know. I didn't want to do it, but I didn't have much choice.'

'You always have a choice,' Rogan said grimly. 'You could have gone to the police.' He looked at Frank Delano. 'What were you going to do with my brother then?'

Frank smiled as though he were an innocent bystander. Never admit to anything had always been his motto, and he wasn't about to change it now, but underneath he was furious at James for divulging everything. If he'd kept his mouth shut, they could have pretended to have 'found' Liam McKay and taken him to hospital. After all, Liam couldn't identify them as his assailants.

Once he gained the upper hand, and Frank was sure that would happen, he would now have to dispose of four bodies. That would certainly keep the sharks at Portsea busy, he thought.

Breeanna picked up a phial from James' bag. 'Sodium pentothal.'

'Isn't that truth serum?' Rogan asked.

'It has gained a reputation for being that,' she said, 'but it's actually a relaxant that seems to free up any inhibitions a subject may have about keeping something quiet. Which means they will often let something out that they might have wanted to keep secret.'

Suddenly, Liam moaned.

It was only a small sound, but Rogan turned towards him.

Frank saw his chance. With surprising speed for a man of his weight, he dived at Rogan.

Rogan recoiled, striking out with his elbow and catching Frank in the solar plexus. Frank crumpled over, gasping.

Doggie pulled out his gun.

Breeanna fired the Phoenix.

Doggie cried out in pain and astonishment, and grabbed his upper right arm.

Rogan reefed the gun from his hand. 'Good shot,' he said to Breeanna as he pushed the wounded man to a sitting position on the floor.

A dubious frown creased Breeanna's forehead as she looked at the Phoenix. 'I wasn't really aiming,' she said wryly.

'I think you'd better put that back in your bag,' Rogan grinned, 'and phone the police. There's a certain Detective Sergeant Bruin who might be interested to know where Liam is.'

CHAPTER TWENTY-FIVE

When the call came through on the car radio, Ed Bruin was sitting outside the hospital waiting for Darren Kennett and his cousin Frank to return to their car.

He replied that he would be there soon. Very soon, he thought as he locked the car and sprinted across the road.

Breeanna used Elastoplast tape to bind Frank Delano's hands together. As Frank's thick hair extended to his wrists, she knew it would be painful when it was ripped off, but the thought only made her apply more tape. Her hands were shaking with reaction from shooting Darren, but her stomach nerves were slowly settling. She had phoned for two orderlies to assist, and they now stood guard over Frank and Darren while James tended to Darren's wound.

Rogan stood next to the bed, looking down at his brother. Every now and again Liam would moan, and the sound of this tore at Rogan's gut.

'He'll be all right,' James assured him. 'He'll just need some recovery time.'

'How did you get involved with someone like *him*?' Breeanna asked her uncle while she looked at Frank.

'Easily. So very easily,' James sighed. 'At the casino one night I was losing heavily, and Frank bought me a drink and said he'd be happy to loan me some money. It escalated from there. I knew my gambling was controlling me, just as it had done in the States a few years back, but you don't see that when the possibility of a win is so close. And it's always close, believe me. It's as addictive as any drug.'

'How did Frank know about Liam?'

James bit at his lower lip, and his resemblance to Paige flashed through Breeanna's mind. Poor Paige. She was going to be devastated to know that her beloved uncle wasn't the saint she thought him to be.

'I told him,' James replied. 'When the professor came to see me one evening and told me about his discovery, it seemed like the answer to my money problems. When he left, I phoned a contact I had in the States to offer it to their research company for a couple of million dollars. I told my contact that I'd sell him the original data, then alter the professor's records here so the experiment would be flawed. The professor must have come back to the office and overheard me because later that night Allan Walters discovered the professor's hard drive had been destroyed and whatever records he must have had had disappeared.'

'But why would Professor Raymond come to you? You two could never agree on anything. You didn't even like each other.'

'He was desperate. His doctor had told him his blood

pressure was dangerously high, so he wanted George to be told before he had a heart attack or a stroke.' James finished bandaging Darren's wound and walked over to his bag. 'And I was desperate. Frank was going to have all my fingers broken if I didn't pay my debt to him.' He shuddered. 'And that would have been just the beginning.'

Breeanna looked across at Frank Delano. His expression said that none of this mattered and a good lawyer would show the jury it was all James' way of trying to push the blame elsewhere.

'But surely Dad would have given you the money?'

'He bailed me out last time,' James agreed bitterly, 'but I doubt he would have done so this time. I owe Frank too much.'

'Why didn't you get help?'

James rounded on her, face distorted. 'Why wasn't I born first? Why wasn't I the eldest son who could do no wrong in our parents' eyes? Why did George marry the woman I loved? Why did she choose to continue with the pregnancy when she knew the cancer would grow inside her and make her chances of surviving too slim to be worthwhile?'

Suddenly the emotions that had fuelled James' outburst dissipated, and he shook with the despair that had held him in its grasp for too many years. 'I resented you so much.' He raised tear-rimmed eyes to Breeanna. 'Morag might have lived, but she took the chance so she could have you. It was killing me inside knowing that she loved George, but even that was better than losing her forever, and not being able to see her every day, to hear her laugh, to . . .'

His pain lanced through Breeanna, and she walked over and hugged him. If only she'd known, if only . . . Reluctantly at first, then with increasing need, James returned the embrace. Thirty-three years of grief shuddered through his body as he cried the tears he'd never shed. Then he stepped back and took out his handkerchief.

'Did my father know how you felt about my mother?' Breeanna whispered.

'Yes. But we never spoke about it. I think that's why he always picked up the pieces when I fell from grace.'

'But why set these scum on Breeanna?' Rogan interrupted. 'One of them nearly killed her.'

James went very pale. 'I didn't know that. I'm sorry, Bree. We just wanted to get the professor's records from you.'

'I never had them,' she protested.

'But you were acting so strangely, and Allan Walters said you were the only one Professor Raymond would get to witness his notebook.' James looked bewildered. 'And Mrs Raymond said after you'd visited the professor he stopped being agitated and his blood pressure went down. So I was positive he'd somehow told you where they were.' He gazed at her oddly. 'I know you have your mother's gift.'

Before Breeanna could speak, Ed Bruin walked into the room.

The pain in his little finger was lessening as the aspirin he'd taken took effect, but Vaughn still seethed with rage. He hated being thwarted in achieving his goals, and someone was going to pay. Perhaps a death in the family would bring Breeanna Montgomery out of hiding.

He wasn't going to let Mark know his movements. The less to report back to his successor, the better.

*

As Breeanna watched James being handcuffed and led away by a uniformed police officer, she realised she hadn't asked him exactly what the professor had discovered. Not that it mattered now. Tonight or tomorrow she would go to Kerang and pick up the notebook. She wondered if Rogan would want to go with her. After all, his only reason for being here was to find Liam, and he'd done that. A pang of regret hit her when she realised that he would probably return to Queensland as soon as Liam was well enough.

She walked over to where Rogan sat watching his brother and placed her hand on his shoulder. She tried to tell herself that the gesture was one of comfort, but it was a lie. She needed to touch him. Wanted to touch him.

Wanted more than that.

Without a word Rogan stood and drew her into his arms. For a long, long moment they held each other. Then they sought each other's lips, their kiss deep, passionate and seeking fulfilment. Again Breeanna felt her senses overwhelmed by the intensity of Rogan's desire. His body was hot and hard against hers, his hands warm as he sought her flesh beneath her jumper.

She loved the taste of him, the unique smell of him that soap hadn't disguised. Impossible to describe, and her science-orientated mind told her it was only pheromones, but she wanted him so badly she ached.

He trailed hot kisses down the side of her neck, and her legs went weak. She was lost, and she knew it. He could take her now, standing against the wall, and she would have welcomed it. Anything, anywhere, to assuage the desperate need within her.

His hand brushed the abrasion on her back and she flinched, but held him tighter, not wanting the beautiful torment to stop. She realised she was grinding herself against him, and felt the groan that rumbled through his chest.

'Don't mind me.'

The hoarse, slurred whisper stopped their passion like a bucket of cold water. As one, they turned towards the bed and saw Liam, eyes half lidded, trying to smile. His bout of consciousness was brief, and before they could reach him he'd fallen asleep.

A small crowd had gathered by the time Ed and another officer brought James Montgomery out to the police cars. Although Breeanna had told the operator at the police station that they had the situation under control, two patrol cars had been despatched, sirens blaring, as backup for Ed.

Frank and Darren had already been placed into the patrol cars, and Ed said he would take James back to the station. He opened his rear car door and gestured for James and one of the officers to get in.

James turned, and looked despairingly at the shrub-softened façade of the hospital.

A rifle shot cracked the air, echoing against the surrounding buildings.

James' body thumped against the car and slid to the ground, leaving bloody streaks on the white duco.

Vaughn had almost given up hope of getting a clear shot at James until the man had stopped and looked back at the building.

Now Vaughn watched the crowd scatter in panic, and a car move quietly from its park and drive away. Good, Mark had

had the sense to get away before the cops cordoned off the area and questioned him.

The pain from his finger and hastily applied makeshift dressing cost Vaughn extra seconds when he disassembled his rifle and closed the briefcase.

Smiling in grim satisfaction, he walked quickly from the unoccupied room he'd located on the first floor of the hospital, and made his way to the staff car park at the rear of the building. It didn't take him long to get to where he'd left his car in the adjoining street.

Another loose end cleaned up, he thought. His employer had already arranged for the man James had contacted in the States to meet with a fatal accident, so, apart from Breeanna, that left only the professor with the knowledge of what was at stake, and he, Vaughn thought in disgust, couldn't talk.

And Breeanna. The elusive Breeanna. If he didn't get hold of her soon, *he* would become another loose end. And he knew just how effectively his employer tied those up.

After Liam's interruption of their intimacy, Breeanna had kept a reasonable distance from Rogan. She didn't want to risk that explosion of emotion happening again. Not here, and especially not now. Perhaps later, when all this had been dealt with . . .

And there were still Vaughn and Mark Talbert to contend with. Sergeant Bruin had seemed uncomfortable when she'd told him about them, and he'd asked few questions, even declining to question James or the other two about them. She sensed that the detective was hiding something, something that frustrated him. Rather puzzling, she'd thought.

'When do you think Sergeant Bruin will arrange for that

police guard for Liam?' Breeanna asked Rogan as she walked over to the window and looked out at the staff car park and the houses in the next block.

'Pretty soon, I'd imagine,' Rogan replied. 'He seemed sure that Delano and Kennett would get bail easily enough, and he was equally certain that Delano would arrange to have Liam killed. Apparently, anyone who's been a potential witness against Delano in the past has either developed amnesia or disappeared.'

Rogan looked down at his brother. Breeanna had read the patient chart at the foot of the bed and reassured him that Liam was in no danger, but he hoped Liam would wake again so they could talk. The terrible feeling of emptiness he'd felt since the night Liam disappeared had now gone. He wanted to phone his parents to put their minds at rest, but he knew Vaughn and Mark Talbert were still out there and could be watching, and perhaps listening. He'd call Meryl from a public phone booth and get her to pass a message on to them.

Breeanna was another problem. A problem he didn't want to think about, but every movement she made, every time she spoke, his body reacted, reminding him how much he wanted her. If it had been simply a physical reaction he could have dealt with it, but she was affecting him in ways that other women never had. He wanted to be with her, not just in bed, but in everything. He wanted to share things with her, things that he'd never allowed anyone else to get close enough to even guess at. And most of all he wanted to love her.

But he never wanted to be *that* vulnerable.

A discreet knock sounded at the door, but before they could answer it, the door opened. A young female constable came into the room. She stood awkwardly, fiddling with her belt as though she didn't know what to do with her hands.

Breeanna walked over to her, dread building up with each step. Before she reached the constable, the young woman blurted out, 'There's been a shooting. Your uncle,' her eyes met Breeanna's, then looked away, 'I'm afraid he's dead.'

'Who shot him?' Breeanna heard herself ask even as she tried to deal with the shock. Her mind seemed to be reacting on a different level. Rogan's arm went around her shoulders and she welcomed his warmth against her suddenly cold body.

'We don't know. We've cordoned off the area and we're searching for clues. I've been told to stay here with you until Detective Sergeant Bruin says it's safe for you to leave. Then I have to escort you both to the station so you can make your statements.'

Rogan led Breeanna to a chair and the officer took up duty at the door.

'Why didn't I try to talk to James years ago?' Breeanna almost whispered the words. 'I knew there was something wrong, I think I've always known. Perhaps if I'd been able to help him, none of this would have happened. I have the gift; I should have known. I should have done something.'

Her guilt and sorrow washed through Rogan like a tide, and he hunkered down and grasped her hands. 'You said James always resented you, Breeanna. You couldn't have helped him, because he wouldn't have let you. You might have a gift, but you can't work miracles.' Her hands were cold within his, and he wanted to fold her into him and take away her pain.

'Oh, how am I going to tell Paige? She adores James. She's closer to him than she's ever been to our father.'

'Paige?'

They both turned to the bed as Liam called out. His eyes

were open, and his face had lost a little of its whiteness. 'Where's Paige?' he asked, his voice rasping. Rogan stood and took a glass of water from the bedside table and held it to his brother's lips. As Liam sipped slowly, Rogan told him that they would get Paige there as soon as they could.

'I'd better phone Paige and tell her that we're coming to see her as soon as we can. I want to tell her about James myself, not have her see it on television or have the police tell her.' Breeanna picked up the cordless phone and moved away.

Rogan smiled as he felt Liam's anticipation of seeing the woman he loved, then he heard Breeanna gasp. Her fingers were rigid and white on the handset, and the colour had drained from her face.

'Oh, no.' Her voice was thin with anguish. 'Not Paige . . . Surely not . . .' She turned horrified eyes to Rogan. 'I'll be there as soon as I can.'

CHAPTER TWENTY-SIX

As they descended into the foyer, the anxiety emanating from the people grouped there hit Breeanna forcefully. Then she noticed that a police officer was standing in front of the door, preventing anyone from leaving. With Rogan at her side, she hurried over and told the constable that Sergeant Bruin had said they could leave. The officer opened the door and let them through.

Ed Bruin stood in the front gateway. Breeanna walked towards him, then stopped and stared at the covered body on the roadway, and the forensic officers calmly undertaking their grisly work. Her heart lurched, and she averted her gaze.

'I've arranged for one of our cars to escort you,' Ed told them. 'But be careful. Whoever did this is still out there.'

As Rogan followed the police car away from the hospital, Mark Talbert left the crowd of bystanders he'd come back and joined, and sprinted to his car.

*

The police escort guaranteed them a swift trip to Sandringham Hospital. They found Allan Walters pacing the floor of the waiting area of the emergency room, his lab coat flapping around his legs, the blood on its front stark against the whiteness.

'Breeanna! Thank God you're here! Who told you?'

'I phoned the Institute. One of the techs told me Paige was here. What happened?'

'I was at lunch with a couple of the other fellows when we heard what we thought was a car back-firing or maybe an explosion. Then we realised the sound might have come from the other end of the building or perhaps the office, so we started to run back.' He brushed his hair aside as it flopped onto his glasses. 'We heard a gunshot and saw a man stepping over a woman's body lying in the doorway that leads into the corridor. He turned and shot at us, then ran up the corridor.'

'Did you recognise him?' Rogan asked.

'No. Never saw him before.' Allan's feet moved restlessly as though he wanted to start pacing again. 'We tried to help the woman, but she was dead. Then we ran up the corridor – carefully, mind you, the bastard had a gun. But we were worried that he might have hurt Paige. Anyway, she wasn't in the office and the man had gone, so one of the others called the police and an ambulance and I went back to the lab wing. I heard this . . . this whimpering . . . coming from the bio-hazard room. I swiped the lock but I couldn't push the door open. That's when I realised someone was pushing back against the door and using the inner door for leverage.'

Breeanna tensed with each word Allan spoke. Paige was a gentle soul, and she must have been traumatised by what had happened.

'I managed to open the door a little,' Allan continued, 'and kept telling whoever was there that I was trying to help. I finally got in and found Paige lying there, absolutely rigid, with blood in her mouth and bits of flesh in her teeth.' He shook his head. 'I picked her up and took her into the first-aid room and washed her mouth. She wasn't injured so I realised she must have bitten whoever was after her.'

A shudder ran through Breeanna as she visualised the desperation and terror Paige must have felt. 'Who was the dead woman?'

'The police found her purse,' Allan said. 'Her name was Carly Otten.'

Rogan swore, and Allan looked at him in surprise, as though he'd only just realised that he had come with Breeanna.

'Excuse me.' A nurse appeared behind Allan. 'The police are going to interview Miss Montgomery now and the doctor thought it might be better for someone she knows to be with her when they do.'

'I'm her sister,' Breeanna stepped forwards.

The nurse nodded. 'Please come with me. We've put her in a nearby room.'

Throughout the interview Paige kept asking Breeanna to get her some water to wash her mouth out.

'The blood. I can taste his blood.' Her eyes were wide, her movements erratic, her voice jerky, and Breeanna knew that underlying the trauma of what Paige had endured was her knowledge and horror of how many diseases were blood-borne. After a while Breeanna asked the police detectives to give Paige a few minutes break, and she went out and asked Rogan to find a cafe or a confectionary-dispensing machine and buy a chocolate bar. At least that might help take the taste from Paige's mouth.

When Rogan entered the small room some minutes later, Paige jumped when she saw him.

'I'm Rogan,' he assured her, suspecting his now dark hair had confused her. 'Liam's safe. He's asking for you.'

'He's alive? He's really alive?' Paige started to cry. Deep, heart-rending sobs that shook her body. Breeanna held her, soothing her the way a mother would, and after a while Paige grew calm, cleaned her face with tissues, and spoke in a more normal voice. 'When I asked Allan about Carly he said she was dead, but she was still alive after that man shot her the first time. Allan said she'd been shot in the head as well. That's when I decided that Liam must be dead too. He'd been missing so long, and if that horrible man had him . . .'

'Miss Montgomery,' the senior police detective interrupted, 'at the Institute you gave us a description of the killer,' the officer read out what Paige had previously told them, 'can you tell us anything else that could help us identify him?'

'It's Vaughn,' Breeanna said, looking at Rogan for confirmation.

'Certainly sounds like it,' he agreed, and wondered if they would ever be free of the man.

Several hours later Breeanna and Rogan had looked through hundreds of photos of criminals who matched theirs and Paige's description of Vaughn, and they'd done the same for Mark Talbert.

The police had also contacted the Defence Department after Rogan told them about Mark Talbert's ID card but, as Rogan had suspected, they had no record of him.

Although Breeanna explained that Carly's death and the

kidnapping of Liam were linked by the professor's notebook, the police considered them separate cases with separate perpetrators. They did, however, see the sense in allowing Paige to stay in the hospital room with Liam as she would then be protected by Liam's police guard.

After Rogan and Breeanna made their statements about James confessing to his involvement with Frank Delano and Darren Kennett, and Liam's kidnapping, they were allowed to leave. Ed Bruin walked with them to their rental car.

'I didn't want to tell you this in front of your brother,' he said to Rogan, 'because I wasn't sure how sick he was, but Janey Dearmoth died last night.'

Before Rogan could ask any questions, Ed explained how he had discovered Janey and why he had decided to follow Frank and Darren. 'Look,' he continued, 'I was told to drop my investigation into your brother's disappearance, and that order came from high up. If this Vaughn person was behind it, you're dealing with someone who has a lot of power. I'm just warning you to be careful.'

'What about police protection for Breeanna?' Rogan asked. 'Until Vaughn is caught she's still in danger.'

'I'm sorry, but there's nothing I can do. You have my mobile number; call if you need help.'

'Are you hungry?' Rogan asked as he parked at the Chifley. 'It's late, but the restaurant still seemed to be open.'

'I wouldn't have thought I would be hungry after what's happened today,' Breeanna replied, 'but I am.' She got out of the car and breathed in the cold night air. She felt as though all the horror had happened to someone else and she was simply a bystander. It was hard to believe James was dead, but overriding everything was her relief that Paige, and Liam, were alive.

In the time she'd spent at Carnarvon Gorge, Breeanna had wondered if she'd done the right thing in running and not going straight to the police, but at the time all her instincts had told her to flee. After what Sergeant Bruin had just told them, she realised that by going to the police she would have delivered herself straight into Vaughn's hands. So where was he now? He was hardly likely to give up. Not after murdering Carly, and who knows what he would have done to Paige if she hadn't slammed the bio-hazard room door shut when he'd yanked his hand back. Breeanna shivered, and pulled the wig more snugly against her head. Rogan had insisted that she wear it, and she knew he had constantly checked to see if they were being followed as they drove back to the hotel.

The elegant yet cosy atmosphere of the restaurant implied security, but Breeanna was aware that was only an illusion. Until Vaughn and Mark Talbert were apprehended, nothing would make her feel safe. As they ate, she became aware of the frustration gnawing at Rogan. Finally she asked what was bothering him.

He speared a piece of chicken with his fork. 'You need police protection.'

'Why?'

'It's obvious Vaughn is still after you,' he replied, 'and I don't like being unarmed. After what he did today with Carly and Paige, I don't see him being very gentle if he gets hold of you.'

'Ah,' she drew out the word. 'You really didn't want to hand that Glock over to the police, so why did you? And why did you say you shot Darren before I could tell Bruin that I did?'

'You'd told me that your friend didn't have a licence for the Phoenix and I didn't want her, or you, to get into trouble.'

'But you could be in trouble for not handing in the Glock after you took it off Mark.'

'That's different.'

She leaned back in the cushioned cane chair. 'How is it different?'

'I don't live here,' he shrugged, blue eyes intense. 'You do. It's going to be hard enough for you coping with what James did without having a firearms offence against you.'

'When the police check the Glock they'll find it hasn't been fired. And the bullet James took from Darren's arm won't match any of the other guns.'

'I pocketed the bullet before the cops arrived.' He chewed another mouthful, then said, 'Once you have the professor's notebook back and Vaughn and Mark are caught, I'll tell the cops I had the Phoenix but I threw it away.'

Breeanna wasn't sure whether to be angry or amused. 'But why do that?'

'To protect you.'

Now she didn't know whether to feel flattered or insulted. 'So you think I need protecting?'

Rogan put down his knife and fork and sighed. 'You're probably the most capable woman I know, Breeanna, but I don't want to see you get hurt.'

Breeanna couldn't say another word because she suddenly realised the depth of feeling behind his words. His caring wasn't just that of a man for a woman, any woman, in danger. It was deeper than that. He might be terrified of becoming too involved with her, but he was just as scared of losing her. She'd never before experienced such conflicting emotions in anyone. The problem was that she was on the verge of falling in love with him. She liked him, she respected him, and there were few men she knew who could match her independence and strength. The fact that he sent her libido off the scale was a plus she couldn't ignore.

Soft background music played songs from decades ago, and she remembered a record of her mother's that her father used to play when he thought he was alone. It mentioned something about irresistible forces and immovable objects, finally declaring that 'something's got to give'. The melody hummed in her brain, but she doubted anything would give between her and Rogan. The loneliness that had been a part of her for as long as she could remember suddenly became more acute.

'Would you like dessert?' Rogan asked.

She shook her head. 'I think I'd like to have a coffee in the room. I need to take this wig off.'

He grinned, and her heart lurched in her chest. He had a zest for life that she was beginning to wonder if she'd lost, and it drew her like a magnet.

'After tomorrow you can give it a ceremonial burial. Or cremation.' The grin widened. 'I don't think Meryl wants it back.' He stood up and walked around and held her chair for her.

His parents had done a good job with his manners, she thought. But she wondered who'd caused the emotional scarring to his heart.

Mark had followed Rogan's car into the multi-level hotel car park, then drove out after he'd noted where they'd parked. After observing the reception area through the large glass walls and wondering if he should go in and make inquiries, he saw Breeanna and Rogan go into the restaurant. Once they had begun eating their meals, he had taken the opportunity to stride down to a nearby twenty-four-hour mini-mart and buy a pie and a coffee-flavoured milk. He didn't favour high-fat takeaways but they were quick and filling, and he hadn't eaten since breakfast.

He returned to the Chifley and waited where he could spy on Breeanna without being seen. Her wig, he had to admit, was an effective disguise, and if he hadn't seen her with Paige that morning and remembered her clothing, he wouldn't have considered it could be her.

Obviously they weren't the lingering-over-coffee kind, he thought gratefully as they rose from their table and walked to the restaurant door. Standing around in the cold was a part of his job he wasn't fond of, and it had been a long day. He watched them walk across the covered driveway and into the hotel entrance. He waited a moment, then sauntered up to the main glass door and spied them getting into a lift.

Faking the rapid breathing of a man who'd been running, he pushed open the door and dashed into the reception area. A receptionist smiled as he approached. Before she could speak, he said, 'I just missed some friends of mine, they came in just now – bloke with dark hair and the woman's a blonde?'

'Mr and Mrs Browning?'

'That's them,' Mark puffed. 'We were supposed to meet for dinner but I was delayed. What room are they in?'

The receptionist shook her head apologetically. 'I'm sorry, sir, but we can't give out room numbers. I can let them know you're here, though.' She reached for the phone.

'Don't worry,' Mark smiled and pulled out his mobile phone, 'I'll see if they'd rather make it tomorrow. It is a bit late now.' He moved away, and pretended to make the call while he watched the woman return to her work.

In reality he was assessing how he could use the situation to its best advantage. Both his and Vaughn's cars were fitted with receivers that allowed them to monitor the calls going to and from police cars, and when he'd heard about the shooting at the Montgomery Medical Research Institute, he'd known instinctively that Vaughn was the man the police were seeking.

He'd also guessed that Vaughn had killed James Montgomery, and he wondered if his motive had been to draw Breeanna out of hiding. If it was, it showed that Vaughn was getting reckless. Or desperate. Mark felt a small degree of satisfaction. Desperate was exactly how he wanted Vaughn to be.

Desperate men made mistakes.

Vaughn had bought strong painkillers from the chemist, and found they were making him drowsy. Too drowsy to drive safely. But still his finger was throbbing. He probably needed stitches, but he'd wrapped a proper dressing around and taped it down. He'd told Mark when he'd phoned in that he'd accidentally caught his finger in the car door, and Mark had expressed sympathy but no interest.

Vaughn had gone back to their hotel room and watched the evening news on television. James Montgomery's killing had been covered, but the police had said they could find no apparent motive. The death of Carly Otten had gained little air time, and Vaughn wondered how the police had managed to keep the details from the ever-hungry media. Not that it mattered. The bitch hadn't been conscious when he'd shot her in the head. He'd wanted her to know what he was going to do, and it irked him that he hadn't had the satisfaction. But at least he didn't have to worry that she could tell the police about him.

It was a pity he was going to have to eliminate Mark. He was the most useful assistant he'd ever had.

Tomorrow, Vaughn thought as he poured himself another Scotch from the mini-bar and lit up another cigarette, he would utilise all the resources at his disposal to find Breeanna Montgomery. He'd already gone far beyond his authority, and he knew he couldn't justify killing Carly and James, but now it didn't matter. As soon as his replacement arrived he would lose all chance of getting the professor's notebook. And all chances of staying alive.

Breeanna tossed the wig onto her backpack and flopped down on her bed. If James had been 'unravelling', she knew just how he felt. The sense of unreality that had pervaded her during the day was beginning to fade, and she recognised that she simply hadn't allowed the horror to penetrate. She had stayed strong and capable for weeks, and now the need was almost over, she felt the strain catching up.

'You don't have to come to Kerang tomorrow,' she told Rogan. 'I can go by myself. You have Liam to worry about.'

'And you have Paige.'

'She has Liam to focus on. I'm sure looking after him will be the best thing for her at the moment.'

Rogan set about making coffee. When he handed her a steaming cup, he said, 'I'm going with you.'

His tone brooked no argument, and relief spiralled through her. She wasn't afraid of going on her own, but she wanted to be with him for a little longer. Stupid, she told herself, because although she knew he felt the same way, it wasn't on a permanent basis.

'I should be the one to tell Dad about James,' she muttered.

'You don't know where your father is at the moment,' Rogan reminded her, 'and you can't go to the Institute to search James' desk. For all we know, Vaughn has the place under surveillance. The police will make sure your father's contacted.'

She drank the rest of her coffee in silence. Rogan walked over to the window, cup in hand, and looked through. She studied the well-defined lines of his face, the way the dark dye in his thick hair accentuated the blueness of his eyes, and experienced a need so acute she quivered with the force of it. But her instincts warned her she could not breach whatever it was that stopped him from giving in to his need for her. With a sigh she gathered up her pyjamas and headed for the bathroom.

Rogan wondered if he could take another night of sleeping in the same room as Breeanna and not attempt to make love to her. Attempt was the word, he reminded himself, because he wasn't sure if she would rebuff him or not.

She wasn't like some of the women who came on board his charter boat looking for passionate nights as well as sun-drenched days. Those women wanted sex without commitment, and sometimes, if the attraction was mutual, he was willing.

Breeanna was different. On all levels. Self-contained, independent, serious, but with a wry sense of humour, she was everything he found fascinating. She wasn't beautiful, but the attraction he felt was so powerful that it scared him. Her empathic talent didn't bother him; he'd experienced enough of that with Liam to be comfortable with it. No, that wasn't what worried him.

After she came out of the bathroom, Breeanna sat cross-legged on the bed and brushed her hair until it shone. Then she brushed it some more, the rhythmic strokes somehow helping to rid her scalp of the feel of the wig. It had made her head feel compressed, and she wondered if it was symbolic of how her life had been for some years.

Rogan had watched her for a few moments, then went into the bathroom. She continued to brush for a little longer, then tossed the brush aside. She felt as if little pieces of herself were flaking off, and soon the fearful, anxious child she once was would be revealed. The child who had hidden behind an aloof exterior because she was afraid of exposing what made her different. Her father had said she would be ridiculed, but she wondered if he might have been wiser to tell her to believe in herself.

The bathroom door opened and Rogan walked out, towel slung around his hips, and her gaze followed the hairs trailing down his chest. With the jolt of lust that shot through her, she made up her mind. No matter what the cost, she wanted to make love with him. By the end of tomorrow he would probably be gone from her life, and she'd spent too many years lately being cautious. Even her previous relationships had been with men who didn't disturb the even tempo of her life.

'How's that cut on your back?' he asked, dropping his clothes on a chair.

'Have a look.' She turned her back to him, and when he lifted her pyjama jacket, she undid the buttons.

'It . . .' he cleared his throat, 'it's healing well.'

His breath was soft on her hair, as though he'd been inhaling the scent of her as he spoke. She turned towards him and slipped the jacket from her shoulders. His sharp intake of air matched the flare of desire in his eyes, and she answered his unasked question by lifting her face until she could feel his breath mingle with hers.

For a moment that seemed like an aeon, they looked into each other's eyes. To Breeanna it felt as though Rogan was weighing up the cost of accepting her blatant invitation. She sensed his inner battle, and for a moment she thought he was going to back away, then his lips met hers in a kiss so tender she almost trembled with the joy of it.

To her surprise, his hands sought not her breasts but her face, cradling it gently, his thumbs soothing her cheeks as his lips tasted, savoured, then finally drew away.

Without a word, he flung back the sheets on his bed, took her hand and led her across. He put his hands on her waist and slowly, slowly, eased her pyjama pants down over her hips. His eyes searched hers, querying her commitment to what she offered. In reply, she took the towel from his hips and let it fall to the floor. He closed his eyes for a brief second, and let out a deep breath as though he'd been holding it. Then he gathered her against him, bodies melding, lips meeting. It was more than heat; it was fire: consuming them, burning their skin where they touched one another.

Rogan felt an urgency that was new to him, a need to bond with Breeanna in a way that would unite them more than the joining of bodies. It was frightening, it was exhilarating, but beyond that, it felt so right it was impossible to ignore.

With his last fragment of sense, he pulled away, strode to where he'd left his clothing, and took out his wallet. Foil flashed, and then he was back in Breeanna's arms, giving in to the sweet madness that he realised had been inevitable from the moment he'd first seen her.

CHAPTER TWENTY-SEVEN

Making love, Breeanna thought as she lay in Rogan's arms and listened to the sound of his steady breathing, was a mild description for what she had just experienced.

For the first time in her life, she had totally lost control. She smiled in bemusement at the memory of her cries, her moans, the fierce, wild need that had gripped her and the sensation of intense satisfaction as Rogan had thrust into her. Oh, but he was good, taking her with him to peaks of pleasure she'd never known before, driving her crazy with the way his teeth caught at her nipple while his fingers teased her sensitive flesh.

Her smile curved higher, a replete cat imitation. She'd known a trick or two herself. Tightening muscles as he drew out, then tightening again so he plunged into pure sensation . . . firm, hot, and moist. She'd enjoyed that, seeing his face constrict in pleasure that was almost pain. But in the end they'd both won. She'd heard a climax described as earth-shattering before, but this was the first time she'd ever experienced it. If the hotel had fallen down while it happened, she wouldn't have been surprised.

They'd been in unison all right, she thought, matching each other's passion, giving a new meaning to the word 'lust', but the sheer pleasure had been tempered by their desire to give to the other. And afterwards Rogan had folded himself around her as though he never wanted to let her go. It was a deliberate, tender action that had spoken volumes and brought her perilously close to tears. She told herself she was just emotional after all that had happened, but she knew she was lying. She wanted him to cherish her, to love her. Because in giving him her body, she had also given him her heart.

Mark waited until midnight, then drove to their office. He picked up two tracking devices and a portable monitor, and returned to the Chifley, stopping at a public phone booth on the way.

Vaughn tossed feverishly on his motel bed. His finger was a throbbing mass of pain that had woken him from crazed dreams and fearful panic. He sat upright, swayed, stopped himself from toppling backwards, and hauled himself to his feet. He staggered out into the main room where Mark sprawled, dozing, in the two-seater lounge.

Vaughn kicked at Mark's leg, and jerked back as he sprang up, drawing his gun in one fluid movement. For an instant Vaughn thought he saw murderous steel in Mark's eyes, then he blinked, and it was gone. It was so unlike the quiet, acquiescent assistant he was used to that Vaughn assured himself it had simply been a trick of the muted light.

'I need you to put another dressing on this finger,' he said.

Mark's eyes narrowed as he looked at Vaughn's face, but he said nothing. He walked over to the small table where Vaughn had left the dressings, then went into the bathroom and returned with a pair of nail scissors. A few snips, and he eased the old dressing off Vaughn's finger. The flesh around the gaping wound was swollen, and redness had spread to the next knuckle.

'That's infected,' Mark said. 'You should see a doctor.'

'We don't have time.' Vaughn went over to the mini-bar and took out a small bottle of vodka. 'Pour that over it.'

'That only works in cowboy movies.' Mark's face was expressionless. It matched his voice. 'These days we use antibiotics.'

'Smartarse,' Vaughn spat, and stalked into the bathroom.

The sharp hiss of pain that accompanied the tinkle of liquid brought a smile to Mark's eyes, but it had gone by the time Vaughn returned, cradling his hand in a white towel. He thrust his finger at Mark, clenched his teeth as Mark taped the dressing around it, then walked, stiff-backed, into the bedroom.

Good, Mark allowed the smile back, and even let it touch his lips as the bedroom door slammed, *he's getting rattled*.

He hadn't told Vaughn yet about locating Breeanna. It was a dangerous move, but he needed to get Vaughn to the edge.

He only hoped that when Vaughn toppled off that edge, he didn't take them all with him.

Breeanna woke to the feel of Rogan's hand on her stomach. He was still curved around her, still sleeping, his skin a delicious sensation against hers.

For a fleeting moment she wished he'd forgotten to use protection last night, so that his hand, which now felt so proprietorial, might one day rest on their unborn child. The thought surprised her. She'd never felt in the least maternal before. For a few more minutes she lay there, luxuriating in the closeness, the pleasure of such intimate contact without the need to assess the emotional impact of what had passed between them.

Because something definitely had occurred when they'd made love, something that went beyond the physical act. She sought to describe it, her rational mind trying to give a concrete classification to something she'd felt purely in her soul. As a child she'd been so open to feelings, both hers and other people's, accepting without seeking explanation, but as she'd matured, she'd searched for scientific rationalisations. In the past twelve months, though, she'd come to believe in the synergy of body, mind and spirit. It was the only reason she could see why some patients survived cancers that should have killed them, and others died from more treatable types.

She ran her hand across Rogan's thigh, feeling the tough hairs spring back against the smooth skin and hard muscle. He stirred, his hand sliding down and cupping her own soft curls. Like a match to a flame, the need flared in her again, and she pushed back against him, and felt him harden. The urge to turn in his arms and open herself to him was strong. In her travels she had taken risks, but they were calculated risks, and in spite of the almost overwhelming desire she now felt, she knew she couldn't make love without protection.

'Rogan?'

He nuzzled the back of her neck and sent delightful shivers down her spine. 'Mmm?' he murmured, keeping up the slow rhythm his hand had begun.

'Do you have another condom?' The words were hard to articulate; her mind seemed to be closing down so it wouldn't interfere with her body's pleasure.

'I slipped another one under the pillow last night,' he spoke softly, his breath warm in her ear. 'I thought we might need it.' His lips moved gently down her neck and across her shoulder. 'I didn't know you were going to wear me out.'

A gurgle of laughter welled up in her chest. 'Who wore who out?' she countered, but smiled at the memory. She did turn then, meeting his eyes, half-lidded with awakening passion.

For once she didn't try to reach into his soul, to know his feelings, but just gave herself up to the pleasure of loving him.

For Rogan, the exquisite pleasure as Breeanna welcomed him into her was confirmation of the rightness he'd experienced in making love with her last night. If this was love then it was the most wonderful thing he'd ever felt, and his barriers began to crumble. It wasn't just the physical, the soft velvet of her breast under his hand, the sweetness of her lips, the fire that consumed him as he lost himself in her heat. It was more than that. It was needing and having those needs met; it was connecting on a level he'd never allowed himself to expose before. And when she took him with her to the peak, he felt his fear shattering inside until all the fragments finally dissolved into blissful peace.

Vaughn cursed as he picked up his toast. His head was pounding this morning, his finger was still extremely painful, and the dressing seemed to catch on everything. Lucky it wasn't his right hand, he thought, but once this was over and he was safe in another country, the bitch would pay. He would have enough money to arrange for all his enemies to suffer.

Mark emerged from the bathroom, showered, shaved and in clean casual clothes, but his face showed the weariness of his lack of sleep. He poured himself a coffee and began to eat the steak and eggs he'd ordered. Vaughn was sure he'd heard Mark leave their motel room much earlier in the morning, but so far Mark had made no reference to his absence. Sharing a motel room with a subordinate wasn't usual procedure, but Vaughn's superior had insisted on it this time, saying that he wanted Vaughn to keep an eye on Mark to assess if he had the skills and experience to be allowed to handle cases on his own. Vaughn had protested, but agreed to the compromise of a suite with separate rooms.

A glance at his watch told Mark it was nearly seven o'clock. He watched the ill-tempered scowl on Vaughn's face. His dislike of the man was growing, but he hid it well. Hiding his feelings had become second nature to him, but this case was becoming precarious and he was tempted to do something, anything, to get Vaughn to show his hand.

When Vaughn began to outline how he proposed to flush out Breeanna, Mark knew he would have to play his ace. 'There's no need to do that,' he said, and took a long drink of his coffee. 'I went for a drive this morning and saw Breeanna and Rogan leaving the Montgomery hospital.'

Vaughn's eyes gleamed with elation, then he cursed Mark for not telling him sooner.

'It's all right,' Mark placated, 'I followed them to the Chifley Hotel, checked with reception and found they're booked in as a married couple under the name of Browning.

I didn't think it would be wise to follow them through the hotel so I grabbed a tracker from the office and attached it to their car. If I'd told you straightaway,' he deliberately grumbled, 'it would be another twenty-four hours before I had a shower and a decent breakfast.'

The fury on Vaughn's face was worth the lack of sleep, Mark decided. 'I brought the monitor up,' he indicated the laptop-sized case tucked next to his small suitcase. 'So we can follow them and grab Breeanna when there are no spectators about.'

'For *your* sake,' Vaughn ground out, 'I hope they haven't given us the slip. Now, phone up the Chifley and see if they've checked out yet.'

'Why?' Mark asked.

'Because,' the words were spaced out as though spoken to a retarded child, 'we are going to pay them a little visit.' He pushed his chair back from the table. 'And put on your suit. This time we'll get it right.'

Before they left to go down to breakfast, Breeanna phoned Liam's room at the hospital and spoke to Paige. She was relieved to hear her sister's voice was back to normal. Looking after Liam had apparently eased the trauma of the previous day. Breeanna thought she had had some easing of her own, and smiled at Rogan as she handed the phone to him so he could talk to Liam.

She wasn't naïve enough to think that a relationship with Rogan would be easy, but he'd been so relaxed this morning that she wondered whether his reluctance to be involved with her had been linked to his anxiety over Liam. Or perhaps, she chided herself, it was something else entirely.

Pain filled her when she thought of James. His death would grieve her father, but his betrayal of trust and willingness to risk the lives of Paige and herself would be equally distressing.

Although the spectre of Vaughn and Mark Talbert loomed before them, Breeanna hoped her and Rogan's altered appearance and identity had thrown the two men off their trail. As an extra precaution, this morning Rogan had phoned the car rental firm and arranged a change of cars.

Vaughn produced his government identification and impressed upon the Chifley Hotel manager that it was a matter of national security that he talk to the couple calling themselves Mr and Mrs Browning. The manager was reluctant to accept Vaughn's demand without verification, but a call to Canberra authenticated his status.

Mark watched the malevolent smile that broke across Vaughn's face as they stepped into the lift. His eyes were fever bright, but focused, and Mark hoped that Breeanna Montgomery did have the professor's notebook. If she didn't, Vaughn would probably kill her.

Breeanna shuddered at the sight of the wig, splayed on the bench like a surfie echidna. She'd learned in her teenage years that short spiky haircuts didn't suit her, and wearing that monstrosity, she thought, had confirmed it. After today, she hoped, she could give it the warm send-off Rogan had suggested. She picked up her hairbrush and tried to disentangle some of the knotted hairs.

Rogan smiled as he watched Breeanna's vigorous strokes.

Loving her was the easiest thing he'd ever done. *Allowing* himself to do so was the hardest. But doubt still lingered, hovering behind the desire to take her into his arms and keep her there forever. He took a step towards her, then turned as he heard a noise at the door.

Before he could move, the door was flung open and Vaughn and Mark Talbert rushed into the room, guns raised.

CHAPTER TWENTY-EIGHT

Breeanna managed to control her reflexive instinct to throw the brush at Vaughn.

Rogan immediately moved in front of her, using his body as a shield.

Vaughn motioned for him to step aside, but Rogan didn't move. Mark stepped forwards and shoved him away, keeping his gun trained on his chest. Then he spreadeagled Rogan over the bed and searched him for weapons.

Breeanna trembled as Vaughn's gun pushed into her left breast.

'We've had this conversation before,' menace lay beneath his silky tones as he brought his face closer to hers, 'but this time I *will* get what I'm after. Now, where is the professor's notebook?'

There was no mistaking his intent, and Breeanna's eyes sought Rogan's as Mark hauled him to his feet. He moved his head in a barely perceptible nod.

'I don't have it on me,' she said. 'But I know where it is.'

The gun pushed harder. 'Tell me.'

'Someone is holding it for the professor, but they're expecting me to pick it up today. They won't give it to anyone else.'

'Who has it?' Vaughn asked.

'Someone whose existence you haven't a clue about.' Thankfully, her steady voice didn't betray her terror, but she yelped in pain as he grabbed her hair and yanked her head back, moving the gun to her throat.

Rogan tensed as though to leap at Vaughn, but she willed him to remain still. The vibes she was getting from Vaughn told her he was desperate and wouldn't hesitate to kill again no matter what the circumstances. 'I can take you there,' she told him, 'but I need your word that when we get the notebook you'll let us go.'

'Good.' Vaughn smiled. 'Then we'll go and get it.' He looked across at Mark and nodded towards Rogan. 'Bring him along.'

'Where's my gun?' Mark demanded of Rogan.

'The cops took it.'

'And the Phoenix?'

Rogan cursed silently. He was hoping Mark might have overlooked that. 'They took that too,' he said.

Vaughn eyed him suspiciously. Then he looked at Breeanna. Without a word he grabbed her shoulder bag and shook the contents onto the bench. When the Phoenix spilled out he threw the bag aside, picked the gun up and put it in his suit pocket.

'Let's move,' he said.

*

Their little procession through the hotel foyer drew covert glances from the manager and reception staff. Vaughn had his gun under Breeanna's jacket, pressed into her side. Mark's gun was holstered, but he knew Rogan wouldn't try to break free from his grasp. Vaughn had made it clear that he wouldn't hesitate to shoot Breeanna if Rogan tried anything.

Although Rogan knew Vaughn needed to keep Breeanna alive, the man had been explicit in his assertion that he wouldn't shoot to kill, but to ensure maximum pain and damage without being fatal. Rogan's temper simmered, and the knot in his guts grew tighter as they reached Vaughn's car.

'McKay drives,' Vaughn ordered Mark. The big man shoved Rogan into the driver's seat, waited until Vaughn and Breeanna got in the back, then walked around to the passenger side. He drew his gun after he'd fastened his seat belt. 'Do whatever he tells you,' he said to Rogan, and the inflection in his voice made Rogan glance at him, but his face was impassive.

Melbourne's weather lived up to its reputation for unpredictability. By the time they'd reached Sunbury, grey clouds had dumped a shower of rain, been chased away by a strong breeze and an hour of sunshine, then rolled back across the sky.

Vaughn's tension had risen with each kilometre. Breeanna could feel it, humming through his body like an overtuned musical instrument. He sat behind Rogan, intermittently watching him in the rear-view mirror. His grip on his gun hadn't eased, and when he asked her how the professor had let her know where to get the notebook, she told him, hoping to lull him into a more relaxed state. Unfortunately, it didn't work. When he found out how far they had to travel, his impatience grew.

His injured finger seemed to be bothering him, and Breeanna couldn't help the curl of satisfaction in her chest. After what he'd done to Carly and Paige, she figured he deserved worse than that.

What was worrying her more was the feeling she was getting from Rogan. Outwardly calm, inside he was seething with frustration and anger, and, she could tell, a terrible fear for her safety. She just hoped that that fear wouldn't tempt him to try anything foolish.

Vaughn kept a close watch on Breeanna. She looked out the window or through the windscreen, rarely at him, her hands on her lap, only the occasional clenching of her fingers betraying her feelings. She might be afraid of him, he thought, but she knew he needed her. Once he had the notebook, though, he wouldn't need anyone. What he did need was a cigarette. His fingers itched with the craving and his nerves stretched tighter. Using his left hand, he took out the packet and shook one up and grasped it between his lips, then used his lighter and returned it to his pocket.

Breeanna coughed as he blew smoke at her face, and he snorted in contempt.

Right now he faced a dilemma. He hadn't anticipated having to drive into the country to get the professor's notebook, and time was running out. His replacement would be arriving in Melbourne soon and would try to communicate with him. If he couldn't make contact, he would call Mark, and if that was unsuccessful, it was probable that an alert would go out and Vaughn's plans for skipping the country would be thwarted.

His gun hand rested on his lap. He lifted his other hand

and glanced at his watch, pulling his lips thin in annoyance. 'Go faster,' he told Rogan.

They were south of Kerang when Rogan saw a police car in the distance. He pushed his foot harder on the accelerator, hoping the highway patrol officer would give chase, but Mark's gun pressed into his side.

'Slow down,' the big man commanded. 'And don't tap the brake,' he continued as he glanced at Rogan's feet.

Rogan fumed. Any other day he would have picked up at least two speeding tickets. Where were the bloody cops when you needed them!

A few minutes later he turned off the highway and drove through the centre of the town. Garden beds filled with late-blooming roses lined some of the wide streets and roundabouts. Under Breeanna's directions, he soon parked in front of a small red-brick house, its colourful garden a testimony to the dedication of the owner.

'We'll go in together.' Vaughn motioned Breeanna with his gun. 'Remember,' he said to Rogan, 'I won't hesitate to shoot her.' He followed Breeanna out of the car, then tapped on Mark's window and waited while it rolled down. 'If McKay gives you any trouble, Mark, just shoot him. We don't need him now.'

Breeanna waited until Vaughn straightened. 'But you do need me,' she told him. 'And if anything happens to Rogan, you won't get any cooperation from me.'

She watched the hatred in his eyes, and wondered just how far she could bluff him. He had slipped his gun into the holster under his suit coat, but she knew he could get it out faster than she could run. And she wasn't going to desert Rogan.

Vaughn pushed open the white picket gate and stood back to allow her to enter. As she passed him, he whispered, 'If you try anything, the professor's friend will be the first one I kill.'

Legs trembling, Breeanna walked up the path and rang the old brass bell that hung next to the front door. Footsteps echoed inside, then the door opened and a small, white-haired man smiled at them.

'Mr Birchsmith?' she asked. At the man's nod, she said, 'I'm Breeanna Montgomery.'

The smile widened, revealing small, slightly yellowed teeth. 'Come in, come in,' he gestured, but Breeanna didn't move. She didn't want Vaughn to go into this man's house. At least here, in the open, with neighbours about, she could hope that Vaughn would not resort to violence.

'We don't have much time,' she excused them, 'so if you could just get the professor's notebook for me, I'd be grateful.'

'Ah, a notebook, is it? I didn't know what it was. I just did like John's note told me and hid it for him. He wrote it would be him or you picking it up.' He chuckled. 'Just like John to get in touch after twelve months of not hearing from him. I swear he gets slacker as he gets older. What was all the secrecy about? John didn't say in his note.'

'Industrial espionage,' Vaughn's tone was terse. 'We had a problem at the Institute and the professor panicked.'

Gary Birchsmith frowned, then asked Breeanna, 'How is he, by the way?'

'He's had a stroke,' she said, 'and he's —'

'We're running out of time,' Vaughn interrupted brusquely. 'Please get the notebook.'

Gary Birchsmith recoiled and looked suspiciously at Vaughn, then raised his eyebrows at Breeanna.

The air seemed to curdle with the animosity flowing from

Vaughn, and Breeanna almost panicked as she saw his hand move into his coat.

'This is Mr Vaughn, one of our researchers, he's helping the professor.' She spoke quickly, drawing Gary Birchsmith's attention back to herself. 'Could you please get the notebook, Mr Birchsmith?'

The old man nodded. 'I'll have to take you to where I hid it. John said not to hide it in the house, so I had a good idea where he wanted me to put it. I'll get my car keys. You can follow me.'

'Just tell us where it is.' Alarm shot through Breeanna. She didn't want this innocent old man in Vaughn's way. 'We'll get it.'

'You'd never find it, my dear. Don't worry, it's a short drive.'

Before she could argue further, the door closed.

Just after they got back into the car, Vaughn's mobile vibrated. He reached awkwardly with his left hand and unhooked it from his belt, gripping his gun in the right.

'I'll have to call you back,' was all he said after listening for a few seconds, and replaced the phone on his belt. Beads of sweat formed on his face, and he shivered in apprehension. The net was closing in now. At least they didn't know where he was, and they obviously hadn't been in touch with Mark. Yet.

An FJ Holden, immaculate fawn paintwork gleaming in the morning sun, reversed out of the driveway. The old man, head only just visible above the steering wheel, waved to them to follow as he backed out onto the road and drove off.

*

Breeanna's muscles bunched with tension. The desperation emanating from Vaughn was so strong that she was almost overwhelmed by it. She tried to shut him out, tried to concentrate on ways to escape, but all her mind could dwell on was the thought that Vaughn wasn't going to let any of them go once he had what he wanted.

'Just where is the old bastard going?' Vaughn growled.

They'd followed the Holden over the Loddon Bridge and north on the Murray Valley Highway, and he was beginning to wonder if this was turning into a wild goose chase. The road curved lazily through the flat, dry land like a snake in the dust, with trees and scrub soon changing to farms and pasture. The horizon seemed to stretch forever, accentuating Vaughn's growing agitation and the feeling that time was running out on him.

After about eight minutes, glimpses of water showed through breaks in scrub and trees to their right. Just as Vaughn was about to order Rogan to overtake the Holden, its right-hand indicator went on, and the vehicle slowed down to negotiate the turn-off to Middle Lake. Rogan followed it along a narrow bitumen road which eventually led to a car parking area. Patches of salt on both sides of the road bore testimony to the many years of water being drained by irrigation.

Vaughn's anxiety escalated as he glanced at his watch. Any minute now his replacement would try to contact Mark. Vaughn knew the procedure. He also knew that Mark would be required to report their location, something that Vaughn couldn't afford to have happen.

The Holden pulled into the empty parking area, and Rogan followed. Vaughn saw Mark shift a little in his seat, then reach into the inner breast pocket of his suit coat. He didn't need to look to know that Mark would pull out his mobile phone. He didn't need to guess what Mark would reveal.

He slipped his gun into his left hand, still keeping it trained on Breeanna. His right hand curled around the Phoenix. The smaller calibre gun would make less noise than his Glock.

As Mark went to put the mobile phone to his ear, Vaughn called his name and raised the Phoenix.

Mark turned his head towards the back seat.

The gunshot resounded in the car's confines as Vaughn pulled the trigger.

CHAPTER TWENTY-NINE

A scream strangled in Breeanna's throat.

Blood poured from the middle of Mark's forehead as he slumped sideways, eyes closing, only his seat belt preventing his body from falling any further. The mobile fell to the floor.

Rogan cursed, and hit the brakes. Adrenaline pumped into his veins, and an icy calm crept over him.

'Park further away,' Vaughn ordered, pushing the Phoenix into the back of Rogan's neck.

The Holden had pulled up, and the driver got out and looked questioningly at them as Rogan slewed to a halt about twenty metres away. Then he started to walk towards them.

'Use two fingers and hand me Mark's gun,' Vaughn told Rogan as he put the Phoenix back in his coat pocket and transferred his gun to his right hand. He grunted in satisfaction as Rogan complied, then placed Mark's gun on the floor near his feet.

'Push the body out of sight, then get out and reassure the old man that nothing's wrong,' Vaughn ordered as he eased back in the seat. 'And remember, I'll kill Breeanna if I have to. I don't need her now that I have the old man.'

Rogan glanced at the blood trickling from Mark's forehead and the pallor of his skin. He unclipped the seat belt and eased the body down so the head rested on the centre console. He got out of the car, closed the door, and walked over to meet Gary Birchsmith. He hoped that Vaughn hadn't heard him take the keys from the ignition and pocket them.

Vaughn looked at Breeanna. 'Get out of the car. Carefully.'

She looked at him, her horror at Mark's shooting still evident on her face. Then her look changed to pure loathing. 'Just remember,' she said softly, 'that I'm the only one who has the ability to determine whether what the professor sent here is his real notebook. For all we know it could be a ploy. The real notebook could be somewhere else.'

'And you just remember,' Vaughn snarled the words, 'that I won't hesitate to kill the old man. If you want him to walk away after he gives us the notebook, don't give me any trouble. I'm going to hide my gun under my coat, but I'll use it if I have to.' Although Vaughn would kill Gary Birchsmith without hesitation, he hoped the threat to the old man's life would stop Breeanna from trying anything foolish. The intelligence he'd gathered on her showed she was likely to consider other people's safety before her own, and he wanted to keep her alive as long as possible. Not only might he need her scientific knowledge, but a female hostage would be a greater bargaining tool than a male, if the need arose.

In spite of the rapid beating of her heart and the sweat on her palms, Breeanna managed not to let Vaughn see she was shaking inside. She sensed his desperation, and knew that he wouldn't hesitate to take advantage of any show of weakness on her part.

Vaughn walked around the car and put his left hand on Breeanna's back at the waist. He felt her involuntary shudder, and a smile curled his lips. 'Just do as I say,' he whispered, 'or I'll kill McKay first, and then the old man.'

Gary Birchsmith hurried over to them as they approached. 'Did you hear a gunshot as we drove in?' His eyebrows pushed together in concern, accentuating the vertical grooves to his nose. 'That young man,' he nodded towards Rogan, 'said it was probably hunters, but Middle Lake is an ibis rookery – a sanctuary, for heaven's sake – who would be stupid enough to shoot here?'

'There are always some people who will do something stupid without thinking of the consequences,' Vaughn said in agreement, but he looked at Rogan as he emphasised the last word.

The paleness of Breeanna's face tore at Rogan. He noted Vaughn's hand under his coat and the other touching Breeanna, and clenched his teeth at the revulsion that swept him. Although he'd wanted to warn Gary Birchsmith about Vaughn, he hadn't been sure how the old man would react. He looked around at the large, empty car park and the surrounding saltbush and native trees. Past them, and closer to the lake, grew thick stands of red gum and other eucalyptus trees, their peeling bark revealing patches of smooth, pale trunk. Clumps of curving stringy grass grew in profusion in their shade.

A walking track led off through the grass and trees, but Gary Birchsmith ignored this. Instead he headed over to the entrance to a much wider track, one that once might have had vehicle access. Native shrubs had been planted on either side of it, and trimmed underneath so that their long, cane-like branches joined at the top to form a tunnel. With the bleakness of the day, only patchy light penetrated the thick foliage, and it reminded Rogan of an animated cartoon of a bewitched forest.

'The bird hide was built a little over twenty years ago,' Gary said, the words spilling over each other as though he was nervous but unsure why he should feel that way. 'John and I used it as a base when he came up to take samples for that bird flu he was researching. We've had some good rains recently, so the lake's reasonably full.' He walked quickly, and Rogan wondered if he was trying to escape the gloominess inside the tunnel or the dread that seeped through them like a mist.

Soon they came to a tall, irregularly shaped building painted green to blend with the natural surroundings. Through the doorway Rogan could see wooden stairs leading up to a viewing area, with several horizontal window openings. To his surprise, Gary bypassed the doorway and walked around the outside of the building, bending to avoid the close-growing shrubs and trees.

When they came out on the other side of the hide, they could see the lake only metres away, its still waters interspersed with dead trees and islands created by reeds and lignum. Cumbungi, a native bulrush, grew more than two metres high at the edge of the shore, forming a barrier that stretched several metres out into the water. The overcast sky reflected grey on the lake's surface, and the calls of wild birds came softly across the stillness.

Pale rocks formed a mound around the base of the bird hide, and Gary picked his way across them to underneath one of the windows. 'Give me a hand,' he said to Rogan, his glance flicking briefly at Vaughn. A nerve twitched at the corner of his mouth, and he began shifting the rocks away from the hide, pulling out the tufts of grass that had sprouted and died in the crevices. Rogan walked around and began to help, but he kept a close watch on Vaughn and the hand he kept inside his coat, holding his gun. He had no hope that Vaughn would let them go once he had what he wanted. Shooting Mark had proved that. But all Rogan wanted was a small window of opportunity, anything that would give him the chance to tackle Vaughn and provide Breeanna with the possibility to get away.

Vaughn's impatience was almost palpable. To Breeanna it felt like an electricity charge sparking and hissing behind her. Her stomach knotted tighter with each rock that Rogan and Gary removed.

'Here it is.' Gary pulled a plastic-wrapped, A4-sized hardcover book from the hole they had created. He picked his way across the pile of rocks and handed it to Breeanna. He hesitated, glanced at Vaughn, then stepped back and waited. Breeanna unfolded the thick, clear bag the book was wrapped in. Before she could take it out, Vaughn stepped up beside her. His left hand touched her back again, as he looked at Gary.

'Thank you, Mr Birchsmith. We'll tell the professor how helpful you've been.' He waited a second as Gary hesitated, then continued. 'I'm sure your wife must be waiting for you.'

'My wife's at bowls.'

Breeanna's nerves were strangling her vocal cords. She wanted to tell the old man to run out of there, get away while he still could, but she just smiled crookedly and hoped. He looked at her uncertainly, then back at Rogan, and gave a small shrug.

'Give John my best,' he said, and walked to the other side of the hide so he wouldn't have to pass by Vaughn.

No-one spoke.

The rocks moved under his boots, and the dry grass crunched.

Just as the old man reached the edge of the hide, Rogan saw Vaughn bring out his gun.

The crack of a gunshot drowned out his yell of warning.

CHAPTER THIRTY

Gary Birchsmith pitched forwards, blood staining the middle of his back. He twitched once, then was still.

Birds screeched in alarm and flew into the sky, their wings flapping in dissonance with the echoes of the shot across the water. Ibises, ducks, egrets, swans, even several pelicans scattered across the lake then settled into the reeds again.

Oblivious to Vaughn now aiming at him, Rogan went over and knelt beside the old man. The staring eyes told their own tale, but he still placed his fingers against the neck and searched for a pulse in the carotid artery. As he did so, he noticed an old-fashioned Holden key ring poking from the side pocket of Gary's jacket. Leaning forwards to disguise the movement, he slipped the keys out and concealed them in his closed hand. After a few seconds he stood up and shook his head at Breeanna. Her eyes were saucered, darker than ever against a skin now alabaster with shock.

His guts twisting, Rogan took a step towards her, but

Vaughn motioned with his gun to stop. Rogan put his hand in his jacket pocket, clenching his fingers around the car keys. They weren't heavy enough to be used as a weapon, even if thrown, but they, and the set from Vaughn's car, were all he had.

'Open the book,' Vaughn commanded, pointing the gun at Breeanna but watching Rogan.

At first Breeanna just stood there, gazing at Gary Birchsmith's body, then, her hands shaking, she took the book from the plastic bag. Written on the front were the professor's name, the project details, book number and dates. She scanned the graphs and charts and symbols and cryptic notes on each page, her interest growing in spite of the feeling of disbelief that had swept her at the old man's murder.

With each page she read, and in spite of her determination not to give anything away to Vaughn, excitement began to thrum in her veins.

Rogan watched Breeanna's face reflect her fervour. Whatever was in the book apparently *could* be worth killing for.

The minutes ticked by as she read. When she got to the last page, her mouth opened in a shocked whisper. 'Oh, my God. This is incredible.'

Vaughn wrenched the book from her hands and thrust the gun at her face. 'Tell me!' he growled. 'Tell me what it says.'

'You know what it says,' she challenged him, tamping down her anger that so many people had died because of this man's greed.

'I know the end result. I want you to tell me how he discovered it.'

It was absurd, Breeanna thought, standing in a bird sanctuary and telling someone who killed without conscience about a scientific discovery that had the potential to change life as they knew it.

'What difference will it make for you to know?' She couldn't keep the incredulity from her voice.

'I intend to sell to the highest bidder,' the glitter in Vaughn's eyes came from greed as much as fever, 'so I need to know exactly *how* what I'm selling came about.'

Breeanna looked at him, and all the revulsion she felt poured out in thick sarcasm. 'I don't think you'd have the intellect to understand.'

Rage heightened the colour in Vaughn's cheeks, and his hand holding the gun shook. Rogan started to run towards him.

Vaughn aimed at Rogan's feet and fired. The bullet ricocheted off a stone and Rogan went still.

'All right!' Breeanna cried, and spread her hands in a placating gesture. 'I'll use layman's language.' She rubbed a trembling hand across her forehead as though contemplating how to begin. 'Cells are growing and dying constantly,' her voice shook, and she drew a deep breath, 'and that's how the body controls growth. Cancer occurs when that growth gets out of control and creates too many of one type of cell.' She turned to look at Rogan as she spoke, as though the importance of what she said would be diminished by telling Vaughn. 'Apoptosis is cell death. It's an important part of growth – just as important as which cells *grow*,' she stressed the word, 'is which cells *die*. By cells dying off, it allows the body to control how many cells are there.'

Vaughn glanced at his watch, but didn't interrupt.

'The growing foetus is a good example. The hand is one mass, with no differentiation between the fingers,' Breeanna explained. 'Cells are programmed to die to create the gap so fingers form. That's the control – without that, there are no fingers, just a lump. That happens throughout the body. That's how arteries, muscles, bones, etc, form.'

'The book. The experiment,' Vaughn yelled at her. 'What does it say?'

Breeanna looked at him as though he were a heavy metal groupie at an opera, then turned her attention back to Rogan. 'The professor had various cell models and cell cultures. He was growing cells to watch them live or die. To do this you have to provide them with warmth and nutrient so they'll grow. These cultures need attention every day. The media in some has to be changed every two days or they will die.'

She took a step forwards, her excitement growing as she explained, oblivious to Vaughn's grunt of disapproval. 'You expect cells to die at a certain rate. But the professor found some cells were living longer than they should. He would have been pretty excited when he discovered this, but after his previous debacle I can understand why he didn't tell anyone. According to his records,' she pointed at the notebook, 'he discovered that he couldn't repeat the process. It was then he realised that he must have made a mistake in the amount of nutrient or warmth he'd given the culture, or perhaps he'd even used the wrong nutrient. Quite a few scientific discoveries are made by serendipity.'

'How long did it take him to work this out?' Rogan asked. He wanted her to keep talking. Every second they stayed alive gave him a chance to get closer to Vaughn, and the closer he got, the better his chances to tackle him.

'Years,' Breeanna replied. 'This book is the last one and shows which formula was finally successful. Then he went on to the next phase, testing the process on animals. He found that mice were living a lot longer. He perfected the dosage, and there were no side effects, no long-term problems. The next phase is to go to human trial.' She couldn't suppress her eagerness. 'Just think, Rogan, we'll be able to slow down the ageing process. Cells will still be dying, but we can slow down the rate of dying; the body still needs control. But people will live longer – much, much longer.'

As if her words had triggered it, she suddenly looked over at Gary Birchsmith's body and wrapped her arms around herself as silent tears coursed down her cheeks.

'Exactly what I'll tell my buyers.' Vaughn shoved her in the back, and she stumbled forwards.

Rogan took her in his arms and held her. He realised that not only was she distressed about Gary Birchsmith's killing, she was finally giving in to her grief over James' death.

'Very touching,' Vaughn sneered, 'but we're not finished yet. Pick up the old man, the two of you, and take him out into the lake.'

Breeanna stared at him as though she hadn't heard him correctly. Rogan pulled her gently with him as he walked over to the body. Under the pretext of giving her a reassuring hug, he pushed the Holden keys into her pants pocket and whispered, 'When we get to the water I'll distract Vaughn, then you run deep into the cumbungi and hide. Whatever happens, don't come out, don't let him get you. Use these keys to the Holden to get away if you get the chance.'

She wanted to protest, but Vaughn snarled at them to hurry.

Vaughn had intended taking Breeanna with him, but reasoned that even as a hostage she could prove a liability. No, he decided, better to get rid of her here, where there was cover for the body. Let them take the old man's corpse into the lake, then shoot them both. The cumbungi would provide an effective concealment.

Rogan picked Gary's body up by the shoulders, while

Breeanna grabbed the legs. They shuffled the few metres to the shoreline. Stepping into the cold, knee-deep water, they pushed against the thick masses of erect cumbungi leaves. Half turning as he waded, Rogan saw that Vaughn had followed them to the shoreline.

Trying not to make it obvious, Rogan manoeuvred so that Breeanna was forced to walk further ahead of him. He knew there was no way Vaughn would let them go, and this was probably the only chance they had to get away. He smiled grimly – the only chance *Breeanna* would have.

The water had reached their thighs and the cumbungi was springing back around them when Rogan glanced back and saw Vaughn raise his gun. He let go of Gary's body and reached into his jeans pocket for the keys he'd taken from Vaughn's car, praying that Breeanna would do as he'd told her.

'You won't get far without these,' he yelled at Vaughn, dangling the keys at shoulder height and edging sideways so he could get in front of Breeanna.

Vaughn's finger stopped its pressure on the trigger as his brain registered what McKay was holding up.

Car keys.

His car keys.

He swore.

The spares were in his briefcase. And the briefcase was back in the motel room.

'Throw them to me.'

'Let's make a deal.'

'I don't do deals. I have the gun.'

'And *I* have nothing to lose. You shoot me and the keys go straight to the bottom.' Rogan shrugged. 'You might find them. But it'll probably take you a while. And the Holden keys fell out of the old man's pocket as we carried him in here. You'll never find those.'

Vaughn suddenly realised that McKay had stepped in front of Breeanna and partly obscured his view of her. Then he saw her move backwards into water up to her waist and pull the cumbungi back together in front of her. Another step or two and she would be completely hidden.

He fired just as McKay threw himself sideways.

The keys fell into the water.

Birds screeched and took flight.

McKay fell, flattening the cumbungi and causing a splash.

Vaughn fired again at where Breeanna should have been, but she had disappeared.

CHAPTER THIRTY-ONE

The coldness on her legs hadn't prepared Breeanna for the shock of immersion. She huddled down, edging slowly through the thick cumbungi, careful not to disturb it too much. She reasoned that if she couldn't see Vaughn, then he couldn't see her.

Birds were still calling out. Some wheeled in alarmed circles above the lake. Another shot sounded, and they flew towards the far side of the water.

Breeanna heard the plop and zing of another bullet entering the lake and froze for a moment. Then she moved a few more metres.

With relief she saw the outer edge of the cumbungi growth was only an arm's length away.

McKay's body floated, face down, semi-supported by the crushed cumbungi.

Vaughn watched, and waited for movement.

He wished he knew if he'd got Breeanna. The tall leaves hadn't rustled after his last shot, but that was no guarantee it had been successful. McKay still didn't move, and Vaughn glanced at his watch. And waited. If McKay was dead, he wouldn't have to worry about him. If he was still alive, he might be useful in luring Breeanna back. He didn't like loose ends, and she would be the only one who knew that he had the professor's notebook, and what it contained. He could afford to be patient a little longer.

Several minutes went by while he stood and watched and listened. Sure now that McKay was dead, he cursed him for taking both sets of keys. Now he had no option but to go in and search for them. He went back and placed the notebook on the rocks, then walked into the water, still clutching his gun.

Breeanna hadn't known she could move with such stealth. But then, she thought, she'd never had so much depending on her ability to create barely a ripple as she hunched down in the water with only her head and shoulders showing, and pushed forwards in a bent-knee action. The cumbungi appeared sparse here and she wasn't going to risk Vaughn spotting her.

She'd heard no voices, and the silence seemed to confirm what she most dreaded: that Rogan was dead. She hoped she was wrong, hoped that, like her, he was silently making his way out of the lake.

Pain drummed through Rogan's side as he lay in the water. Only his diving training had stopped the automatic reaction of lifting his head to gulp in air when he'd realised he'd been shot. The movement would have been an open invitation to Vaughn to shoot him again.

He heard the slight splash as Vaughn entered the lake and walked towards him. He had good lung capacity, the best in his navy diving team, but not enough to go without breathing for much longer.

Ripples sloshed around him and he realised that Vaughn was close. He opened his eyes, but the silt had been disturbed and suspended in the water, limiting visibility. He felt movement close by, then Vaughn's leg appeared, the shoe turning away from him.

It was a risk, but one he had to take. His body felt like it would implode with its craving for oxygen. Cautiously, he turned his head until his mouth cleared the surface, and allowed precious air to sneak into his lungs. He saw that Vaughn now held the gun in his left hand, his taped little finger at a right angle to it, and was groping under the water, obviously searching for the keys. Rogan debated the wisdom of trying to overpower him, but knew that by the time he could reach his feet down to gain traction and jump him, Vaughn would have used his gun. Besides, the longer Vaughn stayed here, the higher were Breeanna's chances of getting away.

Glancing to the shore, he saw the notebook lying on the rocks.

He turned his face into the water again.

Breeanna waited another minute, her heart still beating wildly, before she decided that she had to know what had happened to Rogan. She began to move back through the cumbungi, but further away from where they'd entered the water.

As she got closer to the shore, she hunched over even further, anxious not to be seen. When she reached a point where she could see the open ground in front of the hide, she stopped.

The professor's notebook lay on the rocks, and Vaughn wasn't in sight.

It was impossible, Vaughn thought. If the keys had landed on the crushed-over cumbungi he might have found them, but if they had slipped between the leaves to the lake's bottom he could be searching for days and not find them. He straightened up, stretched his back, and cursed the bones and muscles that were making him feel his age. When he was safely in South America he would willingly be a participant in the human trials for the professor's longer living cells therapy.

A shiver ran through him and he blamed the cold, but his injured finger throbbed, and his head burned so that sweat formed on his forehead. He knew he needed antibiotics, but they wouldn't do him much good if he couldn't flee the country. His lies might convince his superior that the killings were justified, but his failure to get the notebook to his employer would lead to his swift elimination. When he'd agreed to selling himself, he'd accepted the terms. The money had been good, but he wanted more. Now he wanted immortality, and the professor's discovery was the closest chance he would ever have of it.

Frustrated, he kicked out at McKay's body, noting the hole in the back of the jacket. The blood had dispersed in the water, and Vaughn surmised that McKay mustn't have lived long after he'd been shot. He was just about to turn the body over to check when he wondered if McKay had lied about the keys to the old man's FJ Holden. He waded over to Gary Birchsmith's body and began to grasp at the pockets in his clothing.

No keys in the jacket.

No keys in the pants.

Breeanna's boots squelched as she left the water, but she didn't stop to pull them off. As she got closer to the notebook she saw Rogan lying in the water, face down, unmoving. Her heart thudded hard and missed a beat. A scream of protest welled up in her throat but no sound came out.

He couldn't be dead, her heart cried.

But her mind asserted that he must be. Vaughn was near him, searching through Gary Birchsmith's pockets.

Breeanna felt herself crumbling inside. She trembled, then shook with rage.

Almost without being aware of her actions, she crept over to the notebook, picked it up and scurried away.

Vaughn thought he heard a noise and spun around, but there was no-one there.

He turned back to Gary's body, and double-checked the pockets. Cursing, he pushed the body aside. Hot-wiring the old vehicle was his only option now. If he could work out how to do it.

He waded back to the shore, faltering in surprise as he saw the notebook wasn't where he'd left it. He raced forwards, disbelieving, then he saw the trail of water leading around the bird hide.

★

When he heard Vaughn move away, Rogan risked taking another breath.

Vaughn was walking onto the shore. He went up to the rocks, bent over and looked at the ground.

Rogan turned his face back into the water.

When he gambled it might be safe to take another look, he saw that Vaughn had gone. It was only then he realised that the notebook hadn't been on the rocks when Vaughn was walking up to them, and a terrible foreboding gripped him.

Breeanna ran faster than she'd ever run in her life, her wet jacket flapping around her, cold in the shadowy tunnel. By the time she reached the car park her breath was coming in great gasps, and she stopped for a brief second before racing over to Vaughn's car.

Mark's gun! Vaughn had put it on the floor in the back. She wrenched open the door, and grabbed it up. The polymer grip felt foreign in her hand, unlike the delicate instruments she used in her work, the fine scalpels, the slender tweezers.

She closed the door, then froze as she heard a soft moan. It sounded as though it had come from the front seat. She raced around, opened the front passenger door, and stared in astonishment. The bullet wound in Mark Talbert's forehead had risen like a miniature volcano. His eyelids fluttered, but didn't open.

Breeanna's first instincts were to check his vital signs, but she had to get away. If he'd lived this long, it was possible he could live longer, she consoled herself as she ran towards the FJ Holden. She threw the notebook and gun onto the passenger seat as she opened the door, and thrust the key into the ignition.

The Holden jerked forwards as it started, then stalled. Breeanna cursed herself for forgetting to put the car into gear and use the clutch. It had been too many years since she'd driven a manual. And she'd never driven a car with the gear stick on the column before.

She slammed the clutch in, pulled the gear stick into what she felt was neutral, and turned the key. The car purred into life. She pulled the gear stick down and eased out the clutch. The car inched forwards. Reverse, she had to find reverse.

A shot rang out.

The passenger window shattered, spraying glass into the car.

Stuff finding reverse. Breeanna pushed the accelerator down hard and eased off the clutch, spinning the wheels as the car pushed through the saltbush and turned in an arc.

Another shot sounded, then a bang.

The steering wheel flicked in Breeanna's hands as the Holden lurched down on the front passenger side before getting back onto the car park bitumen.

If Vaughn had had enough breath to utter the words in his mind the air would have been blue with the foulness of them.

The Holden's bulky shape made it impossible for him to accurately aim for the driver, so he shot at the tyres. The front tyre blew, but the car kept going.

He took aim at the back tyres, and smiled maliciously as he hit the right rear. The car began to wobble like a drunken duck, but kept going.

Cursing, Vaughn began to run after it.

*

Nausea rose in Rogan's throat as he heard the shots. His side pounded agony through his chest and stomach as he ran to catch up to Vaughn.

He burst through the track opening to see Vaughn running behind the Holden and firing as the car lumbered out of the car park.

Breeanna's wrist hurt from the flick of the steering wheel when the front tyre blew out, but she considered herself lucky to be escaping Vaughn.

It took all her strength to keep the Holden reasonably straight as it shook and tried to pull hard to the left. She was just going to turn onto the road leading back to the highway when she saw a bus coming along the bitumen about a hundred metres away. Although the people in it might help her, there was the definite possibility that Vaughn could get close enough to shoot them so he could use the bus to follow her. Small arms pointed through the windows, and she realised it was a school bus. The thought that children could be put at risk decided her. Enough innocent lives had been lost already.

She pulled on the steering wheel, fighting the car's lack of stability, and turned left, away from the highway.

With relief she saw that Vaughn followed, and she kept the Holden at a pace that allowed him to stay with it, but not catch up. She had to draw him away from the bus.

She wasn't sure how much longer the car would stay on the road. With each metre it pulled harder to the left, and she knew it would be impossible to control if the road turned to dirt. The notebook bounced on the seat, and she made a decision. She would rather destroy the book than see it fall into Vaughn's hands.

★

The approaching bus was a temptation Vaughn almost couldn't resist, but it was coming slowly, and he didn't want to lose sight of the Holden. The tyres were beginning to shred, and Breeanna was obviously having trouble controlling the vehicle. If she abandoned it and fled into the bush, he might not find her. Or the notebook.

He kept running.

The driver of the bus gasped in shock at the sight of a man, completely wet and with blood seeping through his fingers where he held on to his side, running out of the car park.

The man waved him to stop. The driver wound down his window as he braked. A teacher hushed the children's chatter with a few stern words.

'Get out of here!' the man yelled. 'Call the police. A man's been shot. He's in the lake.'

The driver nodded, then reached for his radio microphone as the man turned and ran up the road.

Breeanna looked in the rear-view mirror as she wrestled the car around a curve, and almost jammed on the brakes in shock.

Rogan!

He was alive! And running after Vaughn.

If Vaughn turned around and saw him . . .

A few metres ahead an old wooden bridge traversed a channel. She slowed down. A course of action had occurred to her.

It might be the only way she could save Rogan's life.

CHAPTER THIRTY-TWO

Vaughn felt as though his lungs were on fire. His leg muscles were pinging with the strain, and he was grateful to see the Holden slew to a halt at an angle on a narrow wooden bridge further on.

He ran harder.

The driver's door opened and Breeanna jumped out. Before he realised what she intended, she held the notebook past the bridge railing.

'Shoot and the book goes in the channel,' she shouted.

Vaughn stopped. His gun arm had risen automatically, and he lowered it in surprise. What was the bitch up to?

Her heart beat a staccato pattern and her left arm trembled as Breeanna rested it on the rail. The notebook seemed to grow heavier with each second that Vaughn stood there, staring at her.

It was a stand-off, and she had no idea what to do next. She held Mark's gun by her side, hidden by the Holden's boot, but she wasn't sure if she could fire it accurately. She'd only fired the Phoenix before, and that hadn't been deliberate but a reflexive action when she'd thought Rogan might have been shot. The thought of actually killing someone made her feel sick. She'd devoted her life to healing, not destroying. Vaughn's callous disregard for life was abhorrent to her. He was close enough that she could see his expression, and it left her in no doubt that he would not allow her to live.

'Put the book down and I won't kill you,' Vaughn shouted.

She looked past him to where Rogan ran around the curve towards them. 'Put your gun on the road first,' she called back.

Rogan halted when he realised what was happening.

Whatever Breeanna was trying to accomplish, he couldn't see how she would come out on top. The FJ wasn't capable of going any further. The two burst tyres were now in shreds, and the smell of petrol had accompanied the wet trail he'd seen on the road.

He wasn't close enough to catch what she said, but if she thought Vaughn would comply with her demands, she was mistaken. Rogan knew desperation when he saw it, and Vaughn couldn't afford to give up now.

Quickly, quietly, he stepped into the scrub and trees lining the road on his left. Pain knifed into his side with each breath, and blood dripped across his fingers where he held them against the wound.

Using all the energy he could muster, he began to move stealthily through the scrub.

*

Although she'd threatened it, throwing the book into the channel wasn't something Vaughn thought Breeanna would do. He'd seen her excitement when she'd described the professor's discovery, and had recognised the fervour of a committed professional.

No, it was a bluff, he decided. Something to buy her time while she waited for . . . What? Did she think the people in that bus would come and help her? He turned around. In the distance he glimpsed the bus making its way back to the highway. He frowned. They hadn't had time to see the bodies in the lake, so why were they leaving? Something wasn't right.

He had no more time to waste. Gun by his side, but finger ready on the trigger, he began walking towards the Holden.

'Stay back!' Breeanna's voice was steady, but he detected the thread of indecisiveness.

'We both want that book,' he told her calmly, and took another step towards her.

Breeanna wondered what Rogan was doing. She couldn't see him in the scrub, but she'd bet he was trying to get into a position to tackle Vaughn. The gun felt heavy in her hand, almost as heavy as the notebook that was threatening to slip through her fingers. She tightened her grip.

'We can do a deal,' she called to Vaughn, watching his slow but inexorable movement towards her.

'What sort of a deal?'

'If you throw your gun into the bushes,' she said, thinking quickly, 'I'll put the book in the car. Then I'll walk into the bushes on the opposite side of the road while you come to the car to get the book. That way I stay alive, and you get what you want.'

The sneer on Vaughn's face showed her what he was thinking even before he spoke. 'Why don't I just shoot you now and dive into the channel for the book?'

Breeanna drew in a deep breath, and realised she could smell petrol fumes. She concentrated on Vaughn. 'Because you can't risk the ink running in the water. The professor always used a fountain pen, not a biro. You might not find the book straightaway,' she added. 'You don't know what's on the bottom of the channel.'

The bitch was right, Vaughn conceded, but if he could get close enough it might be possible to retrieve it quickly. He had nothing to lose. He'd walked into the centre of the road now, angling towards her where she was partly concealed by the rear of the Holden.

She wanted the book, that had been obvious, and he was counting on her waiting until she felt she had no choice but to drop the book and try to run from him. Because she *would* run, he didn't doubt that, just as he didn't doubt he would kill her whether he got the book or not.

A few more steps and he was almost on her side of the road.

If she dropped the book, Vaughn would shoot her. Breeanna was convinced of that, and at the moment the book was the only thing keeping her alive. Soon he would reach the bridge. She trembled with the adrenaline surging through her body.

Just as she was going to call out again to Vaughn to stop, she saw Rogan emerge from the bushes, his body tensed to dash across the road and tackle him.

Her stomach plummeted.

Rogan would never reach him before being spotted. Even now, Vaughn was turning his head as though sensing his presence.

She brought up Mark's gun, pointed it at Vaughn, and fired.

The shot went wide, but if Vaughn hadn't been trained to cope with unexpected gunfire he would have pissed himself in surprise. His feet stopped as though they'd been glued to the road.

The bitch had Mark's gun!

Fear snaked down his belly before logic told him that an experienced marksman couldn't have missed at that close range. He'd bet it was the first time she'd fired a handgun.

But it did add another dimension to the scenario. If he got too close he'd provide a target that not even an amateur could miss.

'You'll have to improve on that, you stupid bitch,' he shouted, hoping to rattle her. 'You've seen how accurate I am. Your boyfriend is bleeding his guts out into the lake because he thought he could beat a professional. You don't have a chance.'

He grunted in satisfaction as she flinched at his words.

As soon as Rogan saw Breeanna's shot miss, he slipped back into the bushes. He'd known he'd had an infinitesimal chance of running up to Vaughn and overpowering him, but he'd been willing to try rather than see him get to Breeanna.

Now the odds were different. Now he knew Breeanna had a gun. If he could reach her before Vaughn did, he would easily show Vaughn what a professional could do.

Checking that Vaughn hadn't begun to move again, he hurried quietly through the scrub and slipped into the channel where Vaughn couldn't see him. Agony ripping through him with each stroke, he swam underwater and surfaced beneath the bridge.

Normally a swim like that wouldn't drain him at all, but now his head spun with the exertion, and he clung on to the side of the channel, fighting off pain and nausea.

Vaughn glanced up as dark clouds rolled across the already dull sky. He was running out of time, and without the keys to his car he had no transport. Luckily they were close to the highway: he could flag down a vehicle. But without the notebook there would be little point in fleeing the country to eke out a pauper's existence in some godforsaken South American backwater.

He contemplated agreeing to her demand to toss his gun into the bushes. He still had the Phoenix in his pocket; perhaps she'd forgotten about that.

'All right,' he called out. 'I'll throw my gun away if you throw yours in the channel and put the book in the car.'

He took a small step forwards.

'Breeanna!' Rogan whispered as loudly as he dared. 'If you can hear me, stomp your foot.'

She was almost directly above him, but he wasn't sure if she would hear him through the timber planks. He waited a few seconds, then called again, a little louder, but hopefully not so that Vaughn could hear. Immediately, a soft thump echoed onto the water.

'I'm going to crawl onto the bridge,' he whispered again, 'and get the gun from you. Just keep Vaughn talking.'

Rogan pulled himself quietly out of the water under the bridge and paused, catching his breath. He'd need a few seconds to reach Breeanna, and hopefully take her gun and shoot Vaughn before he realised what had happened.

Rogan wouldn't make it, Breeanna realised. Vaughn would probably see him the moment he climbed out of the channel. She had to distract Vaughn to give Rogan a better chance.

'I'll throw my gun away,' she countered, holding it up so Vaughn could see it, 'but I'm keeping the book over the water. When you toss your gun away, I'll put the book on the bridge.'

She saw him smile as he ventured closer. Holding the book steady, she turned sideways and flung the gun behind her. It hit the edge of the bridge where it met the road again, and went off.

Breeanna recoiled in shock, nearly dropping the book.

Vaughn raced forwards, panic flaring as he saw the book slip down in her hand.

Hauling himself onto the bridge, Rogan rolled to where he'd heard the gun land.

Breeanna dropped down, dragging the book with her.

Just as Rogan grabbed hold of the gun, Vaughn saw him. Shock cost Vaughn a fraction of a second, and he pulled the trigger as Rogan's bullet tore into his body.

The force knocked Vaughn back against the rail, his gun spinning from his grasp into the channel below. Then he toppled forwards onto the bridge.

The blood on his shirt told him he'd been gut shot, and he knew he should be in agony, but there was no pain. It surprised him. He tried to get up, but his legs wouldn't move, and he realised his spine had been damaged.

Shock and despair swiftly turned to rage. He looked up to see Breeanna hurrying over to where Rogan lay, unmoving, and hatred ate into him. The smell of petrol was strong, and he could hear it trickling out from the Holden's bullet-ruptured tank onto the timber. The thought of vengeance was bitter-sweet. A peculiar feeling of disconnection swept over him, and he smiled. His doctor had warned him that smoking would kill him. The smile disappeared into a snort. He might be dying, but he would take them with him.

Slowly, he reached into his suit pocket for his cigarette lighter. The material was still soaked from where he'd leaned over into the lake, searching for the keys, and desperation gripped him. He flicked the wet lighter with his thumb, again and again, but no spark appeared.

His nerves started to spasm, and the lighter fell from his fingers. A terrible weakness swept him, leaving his mind trying to cling to something . . . something important.

The professor's notebook.

It lay on the bridge in front of him. He wasn't sure he could reach it, let alone pick it up, but Vaughn's effort was rewarded as his fingers wrapped around the hard cover.

In the distance, like the wail of wounded animals, sirens sounded.

Vaughn shuddered with the effort of lifting the notebook over the bottom beam of the bridge.

He died before it hit the water.

CHAPTER THIRTY-THREE

As soon as he'd seen Vaughn collapse onto the bridge, blood flooding the front of his shirt, Rogan made an effort to rise, but pain had wrenched through his body and he'd passed out. Breeanna told him later that a white sedan had pulled up at the bridge before the police car, and three men – *suits* she'd called them – had stepped out, instructed her she wasn't to say anything to the police, that it was a federal matter, and they'd deal with it. It was only then she'd seen the notebook was missing. One of the *suits* had immediately worked out what had happened, and gone into the channel after it. Then the police and ambulance had arrived, and Rogan and Mark had been taken to Kerang Hospital.

Rogan had woken in the ambulance, frantic with worry when he realised Breeanna wasn't there, but the paramedic had assured him she was safe. Mark Talbert lay on the other stretcher, unconscious. One of the *suits* had been in the ambulance as well, and he had assured Rogan he was there in a protective capacity, but Rogan wasn't sure just who or what he was protecting.

It was only when he saw the bullet hole in the back of his jacket when they took it off at the hospital that Rogan realised how lucky he'd been. The jacket must have twisted around when he'd flung himself in front of Breeanna to protect her from Vaughn's bullet, and that had made the exit hole appear to be in the middle of his back. No wonder Vaughn had been so sure he had died.

Late that afternoon Rogan woke to the sound of a tray being placed onto the mobile table beside his bed.

A young woman smiled at him, then said, 'I've got a meal for your friend, too,' and walked out of the room. In a moment she returned and put another tray next to the first. She seemed about to say something else, but hurried from the room.

Rogan looked over to where Breeanna lay, fully clothed, on another bed. She was on her side, facing him, frowning in her sleep and her hand moving restlessly as though she were searching for something. His heart beat faster at the sight, and he remembered how her hands had moved so assuredly that morning, savouring his body with the same joy that he found in her. For a moment he allowed the wonderful searing sensation of love to sweep through him, then fear returned with a rush, squeezing his heart until he almost couldn't breathe.

'Your clothes are dry.'

Rogan looked back to the doorway where the voice had come from. He hadn't seen the man before, but he guessed he was one of the *suits* Breeanna had mentioned when she'd come in earlier.

'After you eat,' the man said, 'get dressed and we'll drive you back to Melbourne.'

'Did the doctor say —' Breeanna's sleepy query was cut short as the man told her that Rogan was cleared to leave. Then he put Rogan's clothes on the bed and walked from the room.

Twenty minutes later, the *suit* came and ushered them into another room further along the hallway. He closed the door behind him and stayed outside.

Mark Talbert was lying in bed, his head and shoulders supported by several pillows. A dressing covered the wound in his forehead, and the skin under his eyes was dark from the trauma.

'Glad to see you're still alive,' he said. 'I'm sorry I didn't stop Vaughn before he tried to kill you.'

'Just who *are* you?' Rogan demanded.

A wry smile twisted Mark's lips, then turned into a grimace.

Rogan almost flinched in sympathy. Mark would have been given painkillers, but he'd still have one hell of a headache. Apparently the bullet had deflected off bone and bounced around in Mark's sinus cavities. He was lucky to be alive. If the Phoenix had been a larger-calibre gun, things would have been different.

'I've been working undercover for the past eighteen months,' Mark said, 'to try to find out the identity of Vaughn's employer. Vaughn was a key agent for a secret intelligence service that answers only to the prime minister, but he was also in the pay of someone who has infiltrators in similar agencies throughout the world. For years his superior in our intelligence service had noticed anomalies in some of the cases Vaughn handled, and he discreetly checked them out. He also liaised with overseas intelligence agencies, and though they weren't too forthcoming, he was able to ascertain that they, too, had had similar problems.'

Mark paused and closed his eyes for a brief moment. 'When Vaughn said he'd received intelligence that Breeanna's uncle was working on something that could be a problem for national security, I checked and found out he was acting on his own initiative and had lied to get clearance to investigate. It was the first chance we'd had to catch him out and trace his employer.'

'If all this is so secret,' Rogan asked, 'why are you telling us?'

Mark sighed. 'I figure I owe you an explanation. I'm not quite the heartless bastard you might think I am. Besides, if you say anything outside this room the government will deny everything I've told you. Vaughn's dead, and so we've lost the only link we've had.'

'Do you have any idea who Vaughn was working for?' Rogan's curiosity was piqued.

Mark almost started to shake his head, but stopped the slight movement. 'No. We don't know if it was one man or an organisation, or even a consortium. One man could do it if he was wealthy enough. Everyone thinks that the world's wealthiest men are listed on databases and written up every year in *Forbes* magazine, but we know of some who are never mentioned because they keep their identity secret. Billionaires like Bill Gates are visible, but others are not, and they don't want to be. Their money doesn't always come from legitimate sources. We think they use people like Vaughn to get information they can use to increase their wealth or power.'

'It was hard for you,' Breeanna said, 'going along with Vaughn when your heart wasn't in it.'

He flashed her a startled glance, as though she'd read his thoughts, and Rogan did feel sympathy for him this time. Breeanna's talent could be unsettling.

'How did the other agents know where you'd taken us?' she asked.

'A tracking device on Vaughn's car. I'd managed to pull some strings and get him put under more pressure, and I wasn't sure how he'd react. A fatal mistake. I should have seen it coming. He'd already killed your uncle and Carly.'

'A lot of people have suffered,' Breeanna said, her dark eyes fixed on his face. 'And you haven't come out of this unscathed.'

Mark stared at her as though her words had had a different meaning from their surface value, and as Rogan looked at the expression on her face, he knew they had.

'When will your men give me the professor's notebook?' she asked.

'Our experts will try to preserve what they can of the book,' Mark replied, 'but from what I've been told, the ink has run extensively, so there may not be much they can save. But it will be returned as soon as they've established that the professor's experiment isn't of concern to the government.'

Rogan thought of the social and economic consequences of a population living twice as long as it currently did, and doubted the book would ever be returned.

In the time it took for one of the intelligence agents to drive them to Melbourne, Breeanna could feel Rogan withdrawing from her. She tried to tell herself he was simply physically and emotionally exhausted, but she knew it went deeper than that. She felt the turmoil of his emotions, and knew she was losing him.

The agent explained to the Chifley manager that a mistake had occurred and Breeanna and Rogan were law-abiding citizens. A few minutes later they walked into their room. The first thing Breeanna saw was the wig, spiky blonde hair still tangled, lying on the bench. She picked it up with finger and thumb, and looked at Rogan.

'Sorry,' she said wryly, 'I don't have the energy for a cremation.'

A tiny flicker of amusement touched Rogan's mouth, but not his eyes. The tension that had been building in the car now felt brittle, as though one wrong word from either of them would topple the sense of relief and security that had begun to return since Vaughn's death.

All Rogan wanted to do was lie on the bed and sleep for several days, but he knew he had to talk to Breeanna first. He owed her that.

'It won't work between us.' Shit! That wasn't the way he'd planned to tell her: too brutal, even if it was true. He could have kicked himself, especially when he saw the colour drain from her face. Her mouth tightened as though she wasn't game to allow herself to speak.

'We're too different,' he tried to explain. 'I watched your face when you were reading the notebook, Breeanna, and when you were explaining what the professor had discovered.' He half turned away, and rubbed at the back of his neck. 'James said you're brilliant at science, and it's obvious he was right. You belong at the Institute. You have so much to offer, to accomplish. We come from different worlds. We lead different lives. I couldn't live down here, it would destroy me.'

'Liam lives here,' she said, grasping at anything to dissuade him, even though she knew he was right.

'I'm not Liam.' His voice was gentle, but it cut through her heart like a knife. No, he wasn't Liam. But she loved him. And she didn't want to lose him. So she fought with all the weapons at her disposal.

'All along you've been afraid to love me, Rogan, and you're still afraid. It's not just us being different, is it?'

Rogan walked over and sat on one of the chairs. The anaesthetic was wearing off, and his side was hurting like hell. He wanted to lie on the bed but he wasn't strong enough to do so and not beg Breeanna to lie with him. She deserved an explanation, even if the telling of it would expose his innermost fears. 'When I joined the navy,' he explained, 'I teamed up with another bloke and we became good friends. I was best man at his wedding. We ended up on a patrol boat together, operating out of Cairns. I was Ex O and ship's diver, and Tezza was coxswain.'

Breeanna watched as he closed his eyes, as though what he had to say would be easier if he couldn't see her.

'Patrol boats go out for two to three weeks at a time, which is hard on the families on shore who have to be on their own. Tezza's wife was clever, talented and ambitious. They loved each other, but it wasn't enough. She wanted him to leave the navy and go to Sydney so she could further her career. He loved her, but it was tearing him apart because he didn't want to leave the navy. It was all he knew and he loved it. On the last day of our shore leave his wife told him she was leaving him. She'd found someone else, someone with the same ambitions. Tezza was devastated. He promised he'd leave the navy but she said it was too late.'

Rogan stopped talking. He'd never told anyone what had

happened, and time hadn't dimmed the memory. He opened his eyes, and saw Breeanna looking at him, a world of pain in her eyes. A terrible agony shot through his chest, and he knew it had nothing to do with his wound. He looked at her hands where they now twisted around the wig. Slender but strong, and very capable. He focused on them.

'We'd been at sea nearly two weeks,' he continued, 'and I was really worried. Tezza's depression had deepened, even though he'd applied for compassionate leave so he could try to talk his wife around. The boat's engine broke down but we were able to limp into a port in Papua New Guinea. The navy sent a new engine up, but we had to use a civilian crane to put it in. Tezza was dogman, directing the crane driver. I was on the flying bridge, observing and doing my normal pre-nav duties. Tezza was the only one in a position to see that the wire sling was fraying. He would have known it was about to give way. He signalled the crane driver to swing the engine away from where several crew members were standing, and towards himself, but instead of jumping out of the way when the wire snapped,' Rogan's voice caught as he remembered, 'he stood there and . . . was crushed by the falling engine.'

Breeanna waited while Rogan's eyes re-focused on her face. He leaned forwards in the chair, almost pleading for her understanding.

'I yelled to him, Breeanna, before the engine fell. He could have jumped out of the way, but he didn't. He'd decided to die. He looked at me as the engine fell, and I saw it in his eyes. They buried him as a hero, but I knew he'd chosen not to live. A letter had come from his wife when the engine arrived. She'd written that she was pregnant to her lover and was filing for divorce.'

'So you think people can't compromise.' Breeanna's voice

was soft, almost sorrowful, as though she'd believed in him and he'd disappointed her. He had, he knew, but he'd disappointed himself as well.

'Love doesn't always conquer all,' he murmured. 'Some differences are too great.'

Breeanna wasn't certain if she was too tired to plead with him or just sure that he couldn't be dissuaded. She knew that in the morning she'd be angry at him, but now she just wanted to go home and cry. She picked up her shoulder bag from where Vaughn had flung it, and scooped the contents off the bench and back into it. Feeling as though her body was hollow, she walked to the door.

'You're right, Rogan,' she said as she opened it. 'I can't work miracles.'

Rogan watched the door close slowly behind her. His instinct was to run after her and beg her to stay, but his fear kept him immobile. Better to lose her now, he thought, than in several years time when the agony would be worse. But as he sat there, he wondered if any hurt could be greater than what he was already feeling.

Four days later, Breeanna observed the small crowd of mourners at the cemetery disperse. She watched as Rogan walked across to the small, blonde-haired girl who had thrown roses on her mother's coffin. He leaned over and spoke to her, and the child's face lit up as he talked.

Breeanna knew he was telling Carly's daughter that her mother was brave, that she'd given her life to save another person, and that she had loved her very, very much. In a small way, he would gain for Carly what she hadn't been able to accomplish in life. Her daughter's respect.

Pain filled Breeanna as she walked away. Janey Dearmoth's funeral had been held the previous day, and then, like today, she had watched from a distance, feeling Rogan's grief as he and Liam had stood, Paige at Liam's side, as the coffin was lowered into the ground.

She knew Rogan was leaving Melbourne that afternoon. And there was nothing she could do or say that would change his mind.

CHAPTER THIRTY-FOUR

The sweet, fresh smell of rain came to Rogan as he chained another cow into the milking bay and roped its leg. Then he sat down to clean the cow's teats, and the warm odour of hide and milk filled his nostrils. He looked out to where the last two cows stood patiently, aware of their place in the pecking order. Misty rain sprinkled them, and gleaming droplets rolled down to sparkle on their thick eyelashes.

His parents had been gone two days now, and as soon as they returned from their holiday, Liam and Paige were flying up to see them. Liam was recovering well, and considering going back to practising law so Paige wouldn't have to worry about him staying in what she thought was a dangerous profession.

Happy though he would be to see his brother, Rogan wondered if he could talk to Paige without asking for news of Breeanna. Even saying her name to himself was almost as painful as the memories of holding her in his arms and loving her. The thought of her body moulded against his, her eyes warm and hazy with passion, made him harden, but the ache in his heart worsened.

Because he *did* love her. More than he'd thought possible. And he was beginning to realise he'd made a mistake. Especially last night, when his mother had phoned up to make sure things were running smoothly in their absence, and she'd remarked how much the Gold Coast had changed since her time there as a cabaret dancer before she'd married. Rogan couldn't imagine a greater change than from the night lights of the Coast to the early mornings and tranquillity of a dairy farm. But his mother had made the transition, and his parents were still happily married. Perhaps he *could* move to Melbourne. Divers were needed everywhere.

His spirits lifted as the thought hummed in his mind, easing the monotony of milking. Meryl had given him a hand yesterday, but she was working today, and it took longer on his own.

He'd just let the last cow through into the holding yard and turned the milking machine off when he heard her car pull up at the shed. The rattling from the exhaust reminded him that he'd promised to fix it for her. A door slammed and the car drove away. Puzzled, he walked to the door. And stopped in surprise.

Breeanna stood on the track, backpack over one shoulder, dark hair curling and sparkling with the gentle rain, tension in every line of her body as she pushed one hand into her jeans pocket.

'Got a glass of fresh milk for a weary traveller?' she asked. She hesitated, obviously unsure if she was welcome, then she must have felt the wild surge of joy that raced through him. She walked into his embrace.

Their lips met, greedily seeking, reassuring, their tongues savouring the taste of each other. Rogan's breathing was just as ragged as Breeanna's when they drew apart a little. 'Why . . . How . . .' The questions wouldn't form, and all he could feel was the wonder of having her back.

'Liam phoned me this morning,' she breathed. 'He said you were finally coming to your senses.' A hopeful smile lit her face up even more. 'Was he right?'

Rogan grinned. 'Guess a man can dive anywhere there's water.'

'There's a research institute in Brisbane that's one of the best in the country,' she told him. 'I phoned them before I flew out. Just in case they were interested. They want to interview me.'

'Has Mark Talbert sent back the notebook yet?'

She shook her head. 'They would have a lot of trouble cleaning it up. It must have opened in the water and landed in heavy silt, it was such a mess. I've written down everything I could remember that I read in it, but it might take years to replicate the experiment, and it might never be successful.' She sighed. 'If only the professor hadn't destroyed his computer.'

'What about your father? How will he feel if you leave the Institute?'

'He understands. He'd give up everything if it would bring my mother back.' Sadness welled in her warm eyes. 'He still loves her, you know. He's never found anyone else he could love as much. My poor stepmother – she couldn't compete with a ghost.'

Rogan nodded in understanding. He knew he could never love anyone else the way he loved Breeanna.

'But Paige and Liam are planning to give him lots of grandchildren, so that will help fill his life,' she smiled.

'We could work at that, too,' Rogan murmured. 'And there's a view I want you to see.' He grinned. 'In daylight, this time.'

EPILOGUE

A ten-year-old boy raced his bicycle into a suburban Melbourne front yard and dropped it on the lawn. He knocked on the front door, and grinned broadly as it was opened by his best friend.

'Look at what I got!' He reached into his shorts pocket and drew out a silver rectangular object, smaller than a cigarette lighter, and with a see-through plastic cap on one end.

His friend's face screwed up in puzzlement. 'What is it?'

'A computer pen drive. Better than floppies and this one's got lots more memory than a CD.'

'Wow!' the boy exclaimed as they hurried into his bedroom. 'Where'd you get it?'

'Geoffrey found it in the gutter a few weeks ago. I swapped him my cricket bat for it.'

'Anything on it?' his friend asked as he booted up his computer.

'Nah. Geoffrey said there was something when he found

it, but he didn't have the program to open it so he deleted it. Now his computer's busted and he can't use the pen drive.'

The boy grinned. 'Just think of all the games we can put on it.'

Also published by Pan Macmillan: